Into the Light

the Light

CHOSEN PATHS BOOK 1

L.B. SIMMONS

D1457090

SPENCER
HILL
PRESS

Please visit www.lbsimmons.com

First Edition: April 2014
L.B. Simmons

Into the Light: a novel / by L.B. Simmons—1st ed.
ISBN: 978-1-63392-097-2
Library of Congress Cataloging-in-Publication Data available upon request

Summary: When Aubrey Miller begins her education at Titan University, she is no longer the beautiful, blonde-haired, blue-eyed girl of her youth. In fact, she is no longer even Aubrey Miller. Now with jet-black hair, multiple sets of eccentric contact lenses, and several facial piercings, she has veiled herself in complete darkness as a form of protection for herself and others.

As she enters her first year of college, her goal is simple: earn a degree with the least amount of social interaction possible. What she never anticipates is the formation of very unlikely relationships with two people who will change her life in ways she never believed possible: Quinn Matthews, the overly cheerful pageant queen, and Kaeleb McMadden, a childhood friend who never really let her go.

Spanning the course of four years, this is the story of a young woman's plight and her journey to finally reemerge, finding strength within unbreakable bonds as she delivers herself from her own manufactured darkness and safely back . . . Into the Light.

Published in the United States by Spencer Hill Press.
This is a Spencer Hill Press Contemporary Romance.
Spencer Hill Contemporary is an imprint of Spencer Hill Press.
For more information on our titles, visit www.spencerhillpress.com

Distributed by Midpoint Trade Books
www.midpointtrade.com

Cover design by: Hang Le
Interior layout by: Scribe Inc.

Printed in the United States of America

Chosen Paths Series

Prologue ✳

"Um, hi.

"My name is Aubrey Miller, or Raven Miller, depending on what part of my life I'm referencing, and this is my story.

"I'm not going to bore you with every single detail, not yet anyway. All you need to know at this point is that my life had been a dark, endless abyss of death. It followed me around like I was some sort of knockoff, subpar Grim Reaper. My overwhelming guilt in each death reigned over my life; many of those days consisted of just trying to keep my head above my consuming grief.

"But that is neither here nor there. What *is* relevant for you to understand is that this is my story—my fight to emerge from underneath the shroud of death that I was fearfully hiding behind for so many years. And it happened over the course of four years, my college years.

"Those years, while for most are defined by constant partying and keg stands, with an occasional random hookup—more than occasional for some people—for me were just pitiful reminders of my lack of social skills and personal grace. In the beginning. By the end, I had acquired lifelong friends who helped guide me through some of the darkest parts of my life. In them I found the strength to lay to rest the person who walked onto campus that very first day, the one cloaked in death and darkness, and become the person speaking to you today.

"I am here to finally share my story.

"A story of discovering not only myself but the meaning of true friendship and unconditional love. A story of some of the most challenging, yet most beautiful and awe-inspiring years of my life, in hopes that you will take something away from my journey.

"After all, when life gives you lemons, aren't you supposed to make lemonade or some shit like that?

"Wait. What? I can't say that?

"Oops. Sorry about that, folks.

"Anyway, back to why we're here.

"Drumroll, please.

"So without further ado, here is my journey from darkness into the light . . . the story of my resurrection."

Freshman Year

Chapter 1 ✳
First Day Jitters

"The blue . . ."

Glancing over, I see lips moving but hear nothing else so I gently tug the earbuds out of my ears. After pausing Hole on my iPod, I look at my legal guardian as she concentrates on the road in front of her.

"What?"

Linda breaks her stare from the seemingly endless highway to look in my direction. "I *said* the blue looks good on you." Removing her hand from the steering wheel, she reaches to touch the lower layers of my hair barely brushing the top of my arm, and holds a section between her fingers before lifting it up in front of my eyes. The electric-blue tips of my blackened hair bend fiercely toward my face as the breeze from the air conditioning blows against it. My mouth tilts downward, then I remove her hand from my hair and place it back on the steering wheel.

Safety first, Linda. *Always.*

As I recline back into my seat, she adds, "The cat eyes kind of freak me out, though."

"Good," I respond. "That's what I was going for when I bought the contacts." I snatch up the layer of the hair she has just released, inspecting the blue. "Anyway, I thought *Blue Goth Punk Emo #B000* would be a nice choice for today, seeing as I'll be meeting new people. I wouldn't want to make a bad first impression," I say, sarcasm coating the last words.

Linda snickers to herself, her blonde hair falling across her shoulders as she dips her head in laughter. She's so not looking at the road right now.

"Eyes on the road, please." Releasing my hair, I watch until she focuses on the gray pavement. Once satisfied that we're not going to drift into oncoming traffic, my head finds the back of the seat and soon the sound of humming tires almost lulls me to sleep. "God," I moan and stretch my arms, attempting to release the pressure of my aching back muscles. "How much longer?" Even shifting in my seat does nothing to alleviate the throbbing.

"Not much. Half an hour, maybe," she responds, her green eyes *once again* breaking away from the highway to meet mine. "Seriously, the cat eyes are creeping me out. They make *my* eyes water." Right on cue, moisture brims her dark lashes.

Pointing at the windshield, my blackened eyebrow lifts, and I narrow my stare. "Then stop looking at them and focus on driving, please. I would like to get there in one piece, limbs intact, preferably alive if you don't mind. Living and breathing is kind of crucial to attend college."

Turning away, she inhales deeply, then releases a long sigh. "You're so morbid."

No return remark is necessary. That's like saying water is wet. Morbid and I go hand in hand.

Flipping down the visor, I glance at my reflection, noting my latest physical manifestation. Deep black covers the top of an entire base layer of electric blue, concealing my naturally light-blonde hair. The contacts in my eyes are completely white, with the exception of the black pointed ellipses right in the middle. A sixteen-gauge circular barbell crosses through the septum in my nose, the newest addition to my piercings.

I run my tongue across the back of the tiny skull-shaped stud currently residing in my left dimple piercing, a mirror image of the one on the right, while my fingertips graze over the twelve-gauge mini curved barbell in my eyebrow on the same side. The sight of the skulls serves as a constant reminder of the permanent loss of my once beaming smile, its grave marked with silver.

After pinning my hair to the nape of my neck, I glance briefly at the industrial piercing at the top of my left ear and then at the seven silver closure rings that line the side of the right.

I look like a freak.

Sometimes I wonder if I overdid the attempt to deter anyone and everyone from ever getting near me.

Well, if the piercings don't work, the cat eyes should definitely get my point across.

Sigh.

After releasing my hair, my other hand extends one finger, touching the surface of the contact before moving it aside to reveal a bright, sky-blue iris staring back at me. The color suited me at one time. Happy and alive, sunny.

No longer though.

Death becomes me.

I release the contact, and after it slides back into place, I bend over, feeling for the backpack beneath my feet. After zipping open the front pocket, I blindly finger through the items encased inside: eye drops (wearing contacts day in and day out tends to dry out my eyes, *go figure*), a tiny notebook (which contains the ramblings of my journal), a full can of mace (forced upon me before leaving by Linda earlier this morning), and finally I find what I'm looking for, nestled in the corner. Extracting the pot of pigment-based cream eye shadow and a round tube of lip stain from the pocket, I lay them in my lap and scoot back into my seat, centering my face in the mirror.

Inhaling deeply, I relax my face and begin to apply the stain to my full lips, the hue of red so deep it's a smidge shy of appearing black as it settles, creating a sharp contrast against my pallid skin. As the color sets, I place the tube back in my lap, then rub the side of my pinky finger along my bottom lip where the coloring has bled beyond its edges. Once my lips are taken care of, I unscrew the cream pot and dip my forefinger inside, the tip now coated in what looks like black paste. After smearing it over both eyelids, I follow it up with another application underneath my eyes.

The familiarity of the ritual—the cloaking of my face, if you will—settles my nervous heartbeat. I don't do so well around . . . *people*, so needless to say, my first day of college is going to be interesting.

After throwing the contents back into my backpack, I recline into my seat. As the wheels of the car continue their soothing roll, I chance a glimpse at the driver, whose eyes are thankfully concentrating on the road.

Linda Walker.

She is the epitome of beauty.

I watch the short sleeves on her cream-colored wrap dress dance along the skin of her upper arm as the cool air circulates inside the car and notice the leather of her black belt is expertly coordinated with her heels.

But it's not only her tailored outfit, or her thick, long, blonde hair, or her magnificent green eyes, or even her *almost* contagious smile. Her beauty is internal, derived from the enviable amount of ferocity with which she chooses to live her life. I would never tell her, of course, but sometimes I find myself envious of her valor. It's something I know I will never be able to possess. Hell, simply processing it doesn't seem possible.

She took me in at the tender age of eight as a lost and frightened, blue-eyed, blonde-haired little girl and will be leaving me at Titan University as a terrified, cat-eyed, black-and-emo-punk-blue-haired woman. She must wonder where she went wrong, but I've tried several times to explain to her that you can't break something that's so clearly already broken.

With the loss of my parents—first my mother and then my father shortly after—I was handed over to her since, as my mother's best friend, she had been dutifully ordained as my godmother when I was born. She has since retained full custody, due to the fact that I have no other living relatives. *Those* deaths I thankfully did not play a part in. Although, both of my mother's parents passed away while I was in utero, so maybe I did.

Yeah, I probably did.

Anyway, after the death of my parents, I was shuttled her way via CPS, four hours from the tiny town of Wilmer and the home I grew up in to her residence in Canton. I don't remember much around that time. I was pretty much a zombie for the next year or so, trying unsuccessfully to integrate myself into a new, much larger school and make new lifelong friends.

Right.

Saying I had a hard time adjusting would be a massive understatement. I had just lost my family and left the only *real* friend I ever had back in Wilmer, so the transition was not an easy one to say the least.

Yet the more difficult it became, the harder Linda tried.

One day she decided to bring home a parakeet, thinking having a pet as *one* friend would help me move on and find some sort of joy again. It died the next day when it face-planted into the sliding glass door in the living room.

Undeterred, she brought home a kitten the next week. It was run over by our neighbors the next Thursday.

I don't *even* want to go into the puppy she attempted to bring home for my twelfth birthday. That one still breaks my heart. Who knew six-week-old puppies weren't allowed copious amounts of chocolate cake?

"Why are you staring at me?" Linda's voice disrupts my thoughts. I realize I've been gawking at her for the past couple minutes, lost in my memories. Looking forward, I fold my hands together and lay them on top of my olive-green Dickies while extending my legs until my Doc Martens hit the bottom of the glove compartment.

After releasing a weighted breath, I respond, "Walter."

"Walter? Was that the bird or the kitten?"

"Neither, it was the puppy."

Linda's gasp doesn't go unnoticed, just unmentioned.

"It wasn't your fault, honey. How were you supposed to know that too much chocolate can poison a dog?"

Puppy, Linda.

And why the hell she refuses to give in and call me by the name I prefer I have no idea. Trying to dissolve the conversation about poor Walter before it starts, I correct her.

"Raven. My name is *Raven*. Please use it."

She huffs forcefully before speaking, the same response I get every time we broach this subject. And I couldn't agree more with her gesture. I'm tired of having this same conversation with her. We've been having it since I was twelve, when my new naming convention was prompted by the loss of Walter.

Sigh.

Like I said, I took his death pretty hard.

"No, I will most certainly *not*. I refuse to reinforce your ridiculous theory that you are some winged bringer of death to all who come across your path." She inhales deeply, then once again exhales her breath. "I'm so tired of having this conversation with you."

Likewise, Linda.

Rolling my eyes, I lean my forehead against the window, watching the terrain slowly evolve from trees and open ranges to tall, gray buildings offset with stoplights at every corner. Shortly after entering the city, we turn onto campus and are immediately greeted by a huge academic building with a square limestone sign placed just at the edge of the grass-laced clearing.

Welcome to Titan University

Gooo Titans.

A mental fist pump in the air ensues before I take a deep calming breath. My heart begins to pound, the knowledge of required social gatherings just on the horizon sending it into overdrive.

Barely able to squeeze our way through the congested roadways, we follow the green arrows pointing us in the direction of my dorm, practically running over *three* unsuspecting pedestrians paying absolutely *no* attention to the cars around them as they walk with their noses melded with the campus maps in their hands.

Three.

Jesus.

After nearly taking out two more possible victims, Linda finally parks the car right in front of Harris Hall. My arms are tingling, the result of being forced ramrod straight for the past five minutes; muscles are flexed to full capacity as my nails dig into both the door handle and the center console separating us. Slowly, I turn in her direction. Mouth wide open and with eyes the size of saucers, I watch her carefully run the palms of her hands over her blonde hair before she returns my aghast stare.

Hair important.

Pedestrians not so much, I guess.

I watch in fear while several people nonchalantly carry luggage, boxes, microwaves, and minifridges as they file into the main hall. Seemingly mindless activities for them while they chat and laugh upon their entrance. My mind is, however, continuously pounded with the same recurring thought.

So many accidents waiting to happen.

I sigh to myself in resignation before opening the car door.

Well, I guess it's official.

Ready or not, Titan University . . . here I come.

Chapter 2 ✳

New Roommates

"HOLE. LEE. SHIT."

Three separate words make up the only response I'm capable of speaking, observing my dorm room for the very first time.

Linda huffs behind me, and the sound of her fishing through her purse is all I can hear as I take in the sight. There are no words.

Well, actually, there are three very choice words.

Just before I take another step, Linda's heels click against the floor and a pint-sized glass jar mysteriously appears right above my shoulder. I don't even have to turn my head to know what it is.

"Quarter in the swear jar, please."

Sigh.

Reaching into my pocket—which happens to always be overflowing with "swear quarters"—I dutifully deposit one into the half-full jar, pushing it through the "swear slot" in the top. Not bad, considering she just emptied it yesterday.

I have no idea what she does with the money, but she could have a Swiss bank account receiving the earnings from the priceless gems that tend to fall from my mouth.

Just as the quarter lands on top of the mountain of silver, my eyes rake over the left side of the room. It looks like someone threw up cotton candy, drained an entire bottle of Pepto-Bismol into their stomach, then threw up again.

Pink.

It's everywhere.

Pink poster of a ballerina, pink knickknacks lining the shelving built into the walls, pink scepter with matching tiara lined in clear crystals along its edges, and—wait.

Hold up.

Is that a pink boa?

Fuck. Me.

Without even registering that the expletive was internal, I reach into my baggy Dickies to grab another quarter. Before I can retrieve it, Linda's palm lands on my shoulder blade, and she presses forward gently, trying to force me into the room. My feet, however, are in total sync with my brain and refuse to step any farther into this atrocity. As I remain rooted to the floor, my hand makes its way out of my pocket and crosses my body until my fingers find my forearm, which suddenly has become unbearably itchy. Is it possible to be allergic to a color?

Pink teddy bear.

Pink comforter with darker-pink crowns donning its surface.

Pink. Pink. Pink.

Every single time my eyes fall on something new, my brain is assaulted.

After shaking my head, I finally manage to force myself into the room just as the bathroom door swings open and my eyes land on the person responsible for this mess. Long, straight blonde hair gathered into a high ponytail, exuberant light-green eyes, and the widest, brightest smile you've ever seen make up the person suddenly standing right in front of my blank face. In fact, if I had an "exact opposite mirror" and stood in front of it, I'm pretty sure . . . no, I'm *100 percent sure* this person would be my reflection.

I glance down at her attire, relieved when I see her wearing a *blue* button-up poplin, layered over a pair of *white* flare jeans that almost entirely cover her bare feet. My reprieve is short-lived though, because each one of her toes is painted . . . *yep*, you guessed it.

Her megawatt grin doesn't dim in the slightest as she extends her arm in my direction, hand held out for a friendly handshake. "Hi," she states, bouncing on the tips of her toes, "I'm Quinn. Quinn Matthews."

Watching her ponytail swing side to side as she excitedly springs up and down, I find myself wanting to offer her a Valium.

Quinn.

Surprisingly, a pretty cool name.

As I take in her striking appearance . . . well, as much as I can because it's really hard to focus with her bounding off the floor with an obvious case of "inability to stand still," I'm taken aback. I would have thought her to be named something more regal, due to her beauty and most likely the whole scepter/tiara combo I spied earlier.

Like Alexandria.

Or Diana.

Perhaps even Princess Fi-Fi, ruler of Unicorn Land, where rainbows reign and all things are pink and sparkly.

That one makes me smile inwardly in spite of my usual morose demeanor.

Before I have a chance to respond, Linda nudges my shoulder with hers, and I break my gaze from Quinn's blurry face to the hand in front of me, waiting patiently for me to reciprocate. The thought of touching someone makes me break out in a cold sweat.

I tighten my grip and sweep my fingers over my palm to lessen the clammy condensation forming before finally managing to shake her hand. "Raven. Raven Miller," I respond curtly.

Linda expels a harsh sigh at the same time I release my grasp on Quinn's hand. Turning my head, my lips purse, wordlessly requesting Linda to keep her mouth shut about my name. She mirrors my expression, then ups the ante by crossing her arms over her chest and cocking her hip. The repeated taps of her shoe against the white linoleum floor fill the air, breaching the silence between us.

But thankfully, she says nothing.

My eyes find the back of my head, ending our silent argument. This form of communication is pretty much the norm for us.

When I redirect my gaze back at Quinn, she offers yet another beaming smile. After a brief moment of taking in my appearance, she merely states, "Raven. It suits you. I like it."

You have absolutely *no* idea, Fi-Fi.

She happily pivots away from me on the balls of her feet, and I watch her skip off into a pink oblivion.

Throwing Linda an I-told-you-so look, I head to the bare bed on my side of the room and drop my backpack on the floor. I'm shocked by the lack of horrified expression that I expected to receive from my new roomie. It's as though she doesn't notice the freak factor standing in front of her. I'm going to have to step up my creepiness or I might just end up liking this girl, and that could be very dangerous.

For both of us.

After a quick introduction between Linda and Fi-Fi, we go back to the car to gather my belongings, leaving Fi-Fi alone to pink-puke more while I'm gone. While I grab my luggage, Linda collects all my priceless music posters: Garbage, Hole, Paramore, Poe—some of my all-time favorite female-led bands—and shuts the passenger door with a swing of her hip.

"Don't bend those," I remark, luggage in hand. I turn to survey the normal first-day-of-college chaos and observe it as it unfolds, and as I watch the usual feelings of gloom and apprehension begin to coat the inside of my chest.

Sometimes there's an overwhelming sadness that manages to seep into my heart whenever I'm reminded that I will never be like any of the people in front of me. I'll never giggle with my peers, walk arm in arm with my best friend or hand in hand with the love of my life, or even allow a contented smile to cross my face. Yet I watch in awe as all these moments play out right in front of my eyes.

The simplicity of living astounds me.

But it's the terror of death that devours me.

Breathing deeply, I blink away the fire in my eyes and swallow the torturous knot in my throat. I can't afford those luxuries. I won't allow it. Too many lives have fallen victim, lost due to my mere existence. No. Normality or simplicity will never penetrate my walls.

Following Linda up the cement path, forlorn grief sets in that my time with her is drawing to an end. After the death of my parents, she took me in, no questions asked. Her love for me is unfathomable, considering I managed to keep her at arm's length while she raised me.

She loves me. I know this.

There's no other explanation for her putting up with my shit for the last ten years.

Purposely withdrawing from the world, hoping to never be found, successfully evading every single therapy session and grief counselor she attempted to force upon me, masking my true appearance in an effort to not only keep others safely away from me but also mark my own death . . . she has taken my oddities all in stride. Not without mind-numbing lectures mind you, but I think she still holds on to the hope that this lost little girl will one day be found.

However, while I will forever remain captive to my darkness, I know she will still be there loving me as much as I will permit. After a few seconds of that comforting knowledge, I watch her smiling at several passersby and quickly extinguish the warmth that sparks inside my chest, forcing it deeply into one of the many compartments in my heart before slamming the steel door shut behind it.

Entering Harris Hall, I fortify my walls with a healthy reapplication of mourning and anger, hoping to God that this sudden release of emotion is purely the tragic side effect of the uncertainty that comes with being in a new place, surrounded by loads of new people, and not the ultimate weakening of my defenses. Yet as I head to my room, I also have to consider the waning could be due to the recent battering of my brain by a certain unnamed color covering the entire left side of my room. A color that may or may not prove to be my kryptonite, or at the very least, the source of a newfound allergy.

Or maybe it's just the person behind it.

Because as I watch my new roommate bounding barefoot over every square inch of the room, I'm repeatedly struck by her nearly contagious level of excitement and laughter.

And as each bounce pummels my fortitude, I find myself squashing the very unlikely desire to smile for the first time in a very, very long time.

Chapter 3 ✳

Memories

"Can't. Breathe."

I struggle for an influx of air to my lungs, but with Linda's Herculean arms wrapped around me, I'm unable to catch my breath. When the hell did she get so strong?

"I just don't want to let you go yet," she whispers lightly, her cheek resting snug against my shoulder as she follows up with a sniffle. Hesitantly, I lift my arms to envelop her in a halfhearted embrace while giving her an awkward pat on the back.

"I'm not letting go until you give me a real hug, damn it."

I begin to joke about the swear jar, but she follows her request with an even tighter death grip—*who knew it was possible?*—and I have no choice but to relent. Easing my hold, I reluctantly embrace her, allowing myself to nuzzle ever so slightly into her neck and inhale the floral perfume that's just . . . Linda.

For roughly three seconds, I hold on and allow her fragrance to transport me to a once familiar place, one saturated with the essence of light and warmth—a complete contrast from the bitter darkness I find myself constantly wading through these days. My eyes prick with tears, and I release her before my hardened shell dissolves.

Stepping away, Linda inhales deeply and wipes her eyes with her fingers before she reaches into her purse to—I kid you not—pull out the swear jar and sets it on the table between Fi-Fi's bed and mine. Looking up at me, she holds a semiserious expression as she states, "Be good."

I open my mouth to reply with my usual witty retort, but she stops me short. "You're a good girl, honey. You have a lot of love to give to those around you, if you would just break free from whatever unnecessary chains you have bound around that heart of yours." She sighs and takes my hand into hers. "You've convinced yourself you're merely protecting those around you from whatever you *think* will happen, but the only thing you're accomplishing is the guarantee of leading a very lonely and miserable existence." With a sad smile, she places her hand on my shoulder, squeezing it gently. "Life is full of so much that you refuse to let yourself experience. The blanketing comfort of love, the fulfillment of contagious laughter, the peace of finding true joy, the butterflies of uncontainable excitement . . . these are all things that make up *life*. They should never be taken for granted. You of all people should understand that, sweetheart."

I sigh forcefully before making my long-awaited clever response.

"I'll be sure to add those to my Christmas wish list, Linda."

The vigor of hope previously present in her eyes quickly diminishes, and I immediately wish I could take back my spiteful words. Shooting my mouth off is a defense mechanism that I haven't learned how to control. Hence the swear jar. Good thing there's not a hateful spew jar. That one would rake in an ungodly amount of money.

Linda releases my shoulder, and her somber expression makes me wish I was capable of simply reaching out, to bring her close and never let her go. But I don't. I watch her draw in a deep breath before she turns away, quickly saying her good-byes to Fi-Fi and heading toward the door. As soon as her fingertips skim the handle, my body seizes with regret.

"Linda . . ."

My own muffled voice is barely recognizable as I breathe her name. It's coated with a painful mixture of heartbreak, sorrow, and shame. I hate the person I've become. I'm trapped in this pathetic existence, watching the only person who cares about me walk out of this room, knowing she'll never know how I truly feel about her. Regardless of how much I ache to take the vulnerable steps toward her, I remain where I stay.

Linda stills upon hearing my voice, then swiftly turns and closes the gap between us in three long strides, wrapping me in her arms once again as tears build along the base of my lashes. Looping my arms under hers, my fingers clutch the back of her dress and I crush my cheek against her shoulder, squeezing her with a strength I never thought I was capable of. Silently, I offer my apology, and with one light stroke of my hair, I know she accepts.

The sound of the bathroom door closing breaks the still of the moment and we release each other from our embrace. Bringing her hand to my face, Linda wipes the one traitorous tear that managed to escape, then dips her head to meet my eyes.

"See you in a couple of months?" she asks, swiping her own cheek.

Unable to speak and, therefore, at a loss for sarcasm, I simply nod my response. She offers me a genuine smile full of relief, and after another reassuring squeeze, Linda disappears through the doorway, leaving me on my own and sealing me in with Princess Fi-Fi.

Quinn. Her name is Quinn.

I lock that tidbit of information securely into my memory bank before heading to my bed. Something tells me that her nickname, while I find it extremely entertaining, wouldn't yield the same positive response from my new roomie.

Sighing, I collect my emotions and begin to sift through the items strewn on my bed. I hear the click of the bathroom door opening as Quinn makes a reappearance with a bashful look in her eyes.

"Sorry for disappearing," she states with her slow approach. "It just seemed like you two were sharing a moment. I didn't want to intrude." She shrugs her shoulders and casts her glance down to my bed where her eyes land on my Poe *Hello* poster.

"Oh, I love Poe! I saw her in concert recently with Tegan and Sara. She is AMAZING!" she squeals. Clapping her hands together excitedly, her ponytail swings back and forth while she resumes bouncing off the floor. After a few small jumps, she launches herself onto my bed and begins rummaging through the remainder of my wall art.

I just stand there, not really sure what to do.

Segregating myself from the populace has left me unable to deal with some random person who has deemed it acceptable to lie on my bed and touch my possessions after only the mere exchange of our names. I watch her for a minute or so, listening to her *oohs* and *aahs*, waiting patiently for her to kindly get *off* my bed, but when thirty more seconds tick by, I see this really isn't an option at the moment. She's lost in my excellent taste in music.

It happens.

Bending down, I unzip the front pocket on my backpack and pull out the heavy-duty double-sided tape, mentally selecting the locations for poster placement, when Quinn finally decides to come up for air. She rolls onto her side and assesses me before speaking.

"So Raven, what's up with the kitty eyes?" she inquires.

Shifting my weight, I stall a bit before answering. "Um, I guess you could say I'm different. Why? Does that bother you?" My tone is clipped, suddenly saddened that my initial perception of this girl may have been totally off-base.

She throws her head back in laughter and after a couple of unnecessary hiccups, she brings her green eyes back to mine. "No, it doesn't bother me in the least. I think it's kinda cool that you are who you are, with no worries about what people think."

Her eyebrows draw together and her mouth curves toward the floor as she continues. "I learned a long time ago to never judge a book by its cover. It seems what people try to represent on the outside very rarely mirrors their inside. Beautiful people tend to be ugly, ugly people tend to be beautiful, storms tend to brew below a person's cool, calm exterior, and tremendously happy people tend to be overcompensating for their own grief. Nothing is ever really what it seems."

She takes in my appearance. "Except with you, I think your representation is probably pretty accurate. And I think that's brave."

I almost, *almost*, laugh in her face. Like, deep from within the pit of my stomach, very unattractive, heinous laughter because I know I'm anything but brave. The whole appearance that she's so freaking fond of is the *result* of fear.

The irony is not lost on me.

I keep my blank expression as I shrug my shoulders. "You seem pretty happy," I remark.

Her eyes still locked onto mine, she simply responds, "Exactly."

The seconds pass between us as I try to figure out the exact meaning of that statement, when there's a sudden knock at the door. A wide grin spreads across her face, and her eyes light up with unadulterated glee. "YAY! Our first official visitor."

Quinn bounces herself off the bed to answer the door, and I take the opportunity to regain control of my private realm as I step onto the bare mattress, dispensing a piece of tape while grabbing my favorite poster. A deep, masculine voice comes from the doorway. I keep my attention solely on the task at hand, not wanting to intrude in case it's her boyfriend. Using the adhesive, I tack a piece to each of the top corners and adhere the left side of the poster to the wall at the head of my bed, making sure my back is turned to Quinn and her male visitor.

Just as I extend my arm to attach the other side, Quinn calls, "Raven! You *have* to meet my boarding buddy!"

Great.

Boarding buddy.

The whole reason I skipped freshman orientation. Who needs to be paired up with some random person just to find your way around campus?

I can do that shit alone, as I intend to.

I abort my avoidance mission, turning my head barely over my shoulder, but as soon as I see the person to whom she's referring, I lose the hold on my poster. The scraping sound it makes swinging back and forth along the wall hardly registers due to my dumbfounded state of shock. Blood quickly drains from my face, and my legs feel as though they've been dragged through cement before reattaching to my body.

I pray these reactions comprise the typical response when you see the *one* person in your life that you never, ever, expected to see again. Otherwise, I'm sure I'm having a heart attack and will be struck dead where I stand within approximately two and a half seconds.

But with one more look into those familiar hazel-brown eyes, with a tinge of green so undeniably familiar, my possibly failing heart is revitalized as a jarring shock spurs throughout my entire body, immediately transporting me to my past.

You see, when I was a little girl, I spent a lot of time alone—Linda worked nights as a nurse, so I became a victim of a lot of television, and most wasn't child friendly. One night, I was fully immersed in a crime show marathon where they were explaining how some trauma victims store their memories by way of compartmentalization. I then created and defined my compartments, sealing away certain memories where no one, not even me, could access some of them. It's a very intricate system. For example:

LEVEL 1 MEMORY BIN: Very easily accessible. Like an open door, memories flow in and out, allowing my day-to-day function. Items that would fall into this category would be things such as exam schedules, dental appointments, and the name of my new roommate, Quinn.

LEVEL 2 MEMORY BIN: A little more difficult to gain entry than level 1. More like a closed door, where it takes some actual effort to recall these memories. Examples include the time Linda fell down the stairs and broke her collarbone, when I accidentally washed her favorite cashmere sweater in hot water and dried it on high heat, the unfortunate time she attempted to make chicken pot pie, and the death of all the animals Linda brought home. Not necessarily the most terrifying of my memories, but definitely not the best.

LEVEL 3 MEMORY BIN: These remain safely behind a locked door, for which only I have the key, and are mostly a lump sum of some pretty painful memories from my past. Some happy, some sad, but all memories that are guaranteed to bring heartbreak over and over again. So they remain locked safely in level 3.

LEVEL 4 MEMORY BIN: Steel door, passcode, and retinal scan required for entry. Some of the most painful of my recollections. The death of my mother, the death of my sister, and the pain associated with both will forever stay hidden in this place.

LEVEL 5 MEMORY BIN: Top secret military clearance required. Titanium encases a steel vault buried approximately thirty feet underground. It's booby-trapped with C-4 and other deadly explosives that will be detonated if anyone comes within ten feet. Only one memory resides here, never to be freed again.

Like I said, I had a lot of time on my hands.

But now, as I eye the person in front of me cautiously, it becomes painfully obvious that my Level 3 memory bin has been compromised.

Either that or somehow I unknowingly relinquished a key to the one and only . . . Kaeleb Kristopher McMadden.

Chapter 4

Necessary Expletives

The confined memory escapes slowly, almost hesitantly, before finally freeing itself, rushing my mind so quickly I wince in response. The pain it will yield is inevitable, and I'm defenseless against it as it begins to replay in my mind:

"I don't want to go, Kaeleb. I'm scared." I wipe the tears from my cheeks as I search desperately for some sort of comfort from his shining eyes. But there's nothing that can help me now. Cold darkness suffocates me as I'm pulled under and barely breathing. I'm dying. Just like my family.

"Bree," he responds, quickly removing the moisture from his face. "You have to go. You—"

"I know. I have no one here." I sigh. "They're all . . . gone."

Kaeleb nods slightly before pulling me into his arms. Only eight years old, same age as me, yet his hold feels so strong, so secure. I know he doesn't want to let me go, and when the pretty lady with rose perfume comes to break us apart, our need to grasp each other becomes more desperate. She calls for help, and as they try to tear us apart, tears continue to roll down our cheeks, knowing this will be our last moment together. We hold on to each other as tightly as we can but are eventually broken apart, our fingers the last to let go.

"I love you, Kaeleb," I whisper to myself as they gently guide me into the back seat of an unfamiliar car. Before they close me in, I scream as loudly as I can, "You're my best friend!"

His eyes meet mine when they shut the door between us. Determination fills his eyes as he walks to the car, and just when they start the engine, he places his palm flat on the window with his fingers spread as far as they will go. Slamming my hand against the cool glass, I do the same, knowing this will be the last time I will ever be in the presence of my friend. My best friend.

As we drive away, I watch out the back window as he runs down the street as long as his legs can carry him. They eventually lock underneath him and his knees hit the ground, unable to keep up any longer.

I throw my hand against the back window as the car turns the corner and continue to watch until I lose sight of him. Not until he's gone do I allow myself to fall into the darkness. I no longer fight for the need to breathe as I let go. I just step out of myself and watch the pretty, blonde-haired, blue-eyed little girl slowly dying as she sinks, spiraling lower and lower until finally disappearing into the bottomless pit that swallows her.

"Raven? Hell-ooo!" Quinn's voice filters slowly through the searing pain of my memory, bringing me back into the present where I'm still standing on my bed and the damn poster is still swinging behind me. But now, instead of the sound barely registering, it's grating against my eardrums like nails on a chalkboard.

Quinn and Kaeleb have made their way to the corner of my bed during my brief mental vacation. They're so close, I fight the urge to step back in order to put some distance between us. The corners of Kaeleb's mouth twitch slightly when my hand finally slams against the poster.

His eyes break away from my stunned gaze to address Quinn. "So this is your roommate? *Raven?*" he asks, before once again turning his attention back to me.

My eyes wander his appearance, the little boy I once knew no longer present in his features. His youthful, rounded face has molded into high cheekbones, highlighting a strong, well-defined jaw lined with a day's worth of stubble. The same hazel, greenish-brown eyes are there, but instead of love and acceptance, I find them full of curiosity and apprehension. The reddish tint I used to love in his brown hair is no longer noticeable due to a *ridiculous* amount of hair gel coating it, expertly styled so that it all comes forward forming an off-center peak right in the front. And his body is *definitely* not that of the eight-year-old boy I remember. His white undershirt pulls tight across an insanely sculpted chest, barely hidden underneath a gray lightweight hoodie.

As we stand eye to eye, I take comfort in the fact that at least we're still the same height.

Except, I'm still standing on the bed, so actually, that's not true.

After seconds of stupefied, open-mouthed gawking, I manage to take a step and jump off, thankful for Quinn and Kaeleb's backward movement out of my personal space. Once I hit the ground, I shyly glance back up at the boy-turned-man that now towers over me. His eyes narrow as he cocks his head, and for the first time since seeing him, I remember that his isn't the only changed appearance. Although, mine is much more drastic. So drastic that, as he stares, I realize he doesn't recognize me. And while my initial reaction is sadness that he'll never know it's *me*, that *I'm* standing here in front of him, relief eventually floods me and drowns out the sorrow.

"As Quinn stated, I'm Raven," I respond abruptly in the direction of Kaeleb, giving only my first name, worried that the mention of Miller will give me away. Kind of a moot point I guess, since my student ID is right by the swear jar on the table behind me.

Quinn gives a look of appreciation. "Isn't she cool?" she states, looking back up to Kaeleb for his approval.

The left side of his mouth jerks up before he replies, "She's definitely *something*."

I roll my eyes and release a breath. *Whatever.* I know I'm a freak. I accept it wholeheartedly. But hearing him say it out loud feels as if he just stabbed me in the heart with a dull spoon, taking the liberty of twisting it approximately three times before removing it. It hurts.

"You're my best friend!"

In an attempt to clear my thoughts, I reach for my luggage and open it, hoping they grasp that I'm really not up for conversation or damning conclusions. Not from *him* anyway.

Instead, they remain and the awkwardness of the moment flusters me. "If you don't mind . . ." I trail off, pulling mounds of black clothing out of my suitcase and throwing them onto the bed.

In other words, leave me the fuck alone.

Just like Pavlov's dog, my conditioned response lures me to the swear jar where I insert a quarter without question. Apparently, my freak mode is in full effect today. *Perfect.* Not at all embarrassing.

Pulling the rest of the quarters out of my front pocket, I set them on top of my ID just to the side of the jar, running my finger gently along its lid before turning to face the questioning expressions of Quinn and Kaeleb.

Quinn scrunches up her nose and giggles before inquiring, "What *is* that thing anyway?"

"It's my swear jar," I respond, completely straight-faced. "It's Linda's way of discouraging my unfortunate addiction to 'vulgar language and unnecessary obscenities' as she calls them. But sometimes it's necessary to throw in the word *fuck* or *shit* to really get your point across, you know?" I let out a weary sigh. I think I just met my obligatory conversation quota for the next two years with that one statement.

Quinn, on the other hand, belts out a laugh. "Fuck yeah, I do."

Abandoning Kaeleb at his post next to my bed, she skips her way over to her desk before pulling open the drawer, grabbing a handful of change, then whirling back around to head in my direction. She passes right by me and approaches the table, depositing a quarter before adding the others to my already established collection next to the jar.

When she turns, a sly grin slowly spreads across her face. "Well, *now* it's the 'beer fund' jar. Feel free to express vulgarity and obscenity anytime you feel the need. This way we can kill two birds with one stone, freedom of expression and the acquisition of alcohol."

"Nice," Kaeleb pipes in, still holding the fort down in my personal space behind me. "Can I get in on this?"

"Sure," Quinn squeaks, once again bouncing on her feet while clapping.

I twist to observe Kaeleb, whose mouth spreads into an absolutely gorgeous, wide grin displaying his perfectly white, straight teeth—much to my detriment. Casting his eyes down to me, he adds with that stupid smile still on his face, "You're shittin' me with those eyes, right?"

Asshole proceeds to reach into his pocket and examines the change in his palm until he finds a quarter, leaning in and reaching around my waist to deposit it into the jar while I do the same. Our hands brush lightly, and surprised by our close proximity, I step back into the safety of my no-one-allowed-past-this-point zone. My knees hit the bed behind me as his body once again crosses in front of mine; the breeze wafts the familiar scent of fresh-cut grass and clean laundry between us. More Level 3 memories threaten to escape as I inhale deeply, rushing forward in anticipation of their release. But before they can breach my mind, I slam the door and lock it once again, hoping Kaeleb's access was just a one-time occurrence.

His hazel orbs fill with silent laughter at my response, but his broad smile lessens into a crooked grin as he assesses me. I regain mental capability and yank my mind from the heightened security of the memory bins, and my eyes tighten into thin slits. "You're shittin' me with that question, right?"

Quickly leaning forward, I throw one more quarter into the jar and take three large steps to ensure more distance, forming a triangle between the three of us. Quinn to my right, watching our exchange with way too much interest, and Kaeleb on my left, his expression void of the previous humor, yet not unkind. Almost as though the terseness of my comment piqued his curiosity.

We all remain locked in our places, and seconds awkwardly turn into minutes, no one sure where to take the conversation next.

Sadly, I tend to have that effect on these types of situations.

After a long while, Quinn is the first to break the silence. "Well, this is fucking awkward." (deposits quarter)

Kaeleb chuckles and responds with, "It sure as shit is." (deposits quarter)

Quinn follows that up with, "What the fuck are we going to do about it?" (deposits quarter)

To which Kaeleb answers, "Hell if I know." (deposits quarter and mouths "That counts")

Quinn laughs and states, "Hell yeah, it does." (deposits quarter)

They both stop their expletive-charged dialogue to stare at me, obviously expecting me to be a willing participant in this sad excuse for a conversation. My eyes first find Quinn's, full of hope, and then Kaeleb's, urging me to say something.

My eyes flick back and forth between the two a couple times before I manage to do the impossible.

A barely there smile plays lightly on my lips and a hint of laughter lodges its way through my mouth as I finally conclude the discussion.

"Fine. You win." Reaching toward the table, I add, "Fuck the beer fund and break open the jar. Let's get the hell out of here to go get some fucking dinner." (deposits three quarters and then empties jar)

And with that one obscenity-filled statement, we stride out of the dorm room together, forging unlikely friendships—some old, some new—that will forever change the course of our lives.

See. I told you, Linda.

Sometimes expletives are just . . . necessary.

Chapter 5 ✳

Issues

"So," Kaeleb begins, wiping the grease from his extra-large fries onto the paper napkin in front of him, "you need a boarding buddy."

Freaking traitor Quinn left me stranded when she went to refill her water and has yet to return. My eyes rake over the tables until they land on her, laughing with two extremely skinny, yet equally boisterous blondes across the cafeteria.

Damn it. I was depending on her to make conversation.

Sigh.

"Is that a statement or a question?" I ask, avoiding his gaze while feigning interest in the unappetizing slab of meat on my plate.

"General observation only." Kaeleb offers nothing else, so I force myself to make eye contact.

He chuckles under his breath, throwing the napkin on top of his empty plate and relaxing back into his chair. "You're not very fond of conversation, or people for that matter, are you?"

"No, not really," I remark, stabbing the mystery meat before once again meeting his curious stare.

The corners of his mouth slip downward and he tilts his head slightly. "Why is that?"

Mayday! Mayday! Man Down!

QUINN!

Trying to calm my anxiety level, I inhale deeply before answering.

"I don't know," I lie. "I don't really see why that's any of your concern."

My eyes break from his, raking over a group of girls flocked just behind his chair, giggling while eyeing him. Their faces are all smiles as they nod and speak to one another, most likely discussing their strategic plan of attack. And then, right on cue, they disengage their stares and each set of eyes land right on me. Their smiles fall and their expressions turn from pure delight to absolute disgust. In response, I tighten my gaze and lean forward, causing them to quickly clear their faces of revulsion and disperse every which way. Satisfied with their reaction, I lean back, laughing to myself as they all run into each other, clearly not having planned an effective escape route.

Dumbasses.

Shaking my head, I bring my attention back to Kaeleb, who's clearly amused by my silent threat.

"Don't you have something to do?" I inquire. "Like go talk to someone who actually would like to reciprocate?"

His lips jerk upward as he attempts to fight yet another annoying smile . . . and loses. "Yes, I guess I could do that. But I'm talking to you, which is like pulling teeth. I find it fascinating, so if you don't mind, I think I'll just stay put for now. I'm always up for a good challenge." He tilts his head. "So I'll ask again . . . what drives this lack of fondness for conversation and people?"

Tightening my gaze at his audacious tone, my hold on the fork hardens as I lean forward, attempting the most ferocious glare I can muster. With the cat eyes, I'm pretty sure I look downright terrifying right now.

"You really want to know?" I mock his stupid head cock and raise my brow.

Okay, maybe not so terrifying because he counters with some kind of sexy smirk that probably melts the panties off normal girls. With me, it only manages to get my panties in a wad.

"I wouldn't have asked if I didn't," he counters.

The look in his eyes tells me he won't be giving up anytime soon, and the fact that he seems so blasé about it further peeves me off.

Fuck it. He asked for it. It's his funeral.

"People die around me."

The panty-sweltering grin disappears along with the coloring in his face as his head jerks back.

"What? What do you mean? Like, you kill them?" He narrows his stare, assessing me before seeming to draw his own conclusion.

Humor settles into his features as he leans over and lowers his voice, whispering, "Do you *shank* people, Raven?"

I refuse to smile, but a tiny breath of laughter bubbles through my nose. "No, I don't kill people. Or *shank* them, idiot."

I release a long breath, the all too familiar morbidity of the conversation suddenly draining my energy. As much as I would like to pretend I'm like every other normal girl traipsing through the cafeteria at the moment, I'm not. I never will be.

I clear my throat and finish my statement with ample warning. "They just tend to meet an untimely death, and if you knew what was good for you, you would cease this random line of questioning, or there's a likely chance you could drop dead tomorrow."

His breath stalls, and I feel victorious and very self-satisfied with the delivery of my message. That is until he draws a huge breath of air into his lungs and then proceeds to laugh in my face.

Right. In. My. Face.

And he *continues* laughing. So loud that he begins to draw very unwelcome attention to our table. Questioning stares are all I see as he slams his hand down repeatedly, bending over, hiccupping as though I just told the most hilarious joke he's ever heard.

Literally sinking into my seat, my face heats with embarrassment, and I have no choice but to watch his overtly conspicuous reaction, until he rises and leans back against his chair, wiping the tears from his eyes with his recline.

"Phew," he draws out breathlessly. "It's just so funny. I'm sorry."

He's totally not sorry.

"*What's* so funny?" I inquire, rising and cupping my free hand across my forehead, throwing my hair forward in an attempt to just disappear from the humiliation that *is* this moment.

Slicing my fork through the mystery meat, I vow to chew and swallow as quickly as possible so that we can just get the hell out of here. Just before it hits my lips, Kaeleb leans forward and points at my plate, stalling my attempt to eat when he says, "That."

I glance up at him from underneath my hand only to see that same craptastic smile crossing his face again. "What? My plate?" I ask, lowering the fork.

"No. Not the plate. It's just . . ." He chuckles under his breath, but finally manages to compose himself. "It's the fact that you're so worried about triggering the *untimely* death of everyone you meet. So much so that you don't speak to others, rarely make eye contact, and try to make yourself look like a freak. Yet you eat . . . *meat*. And it doesn't seem to bother you. At all."

He unsuccessfully tries to hide his amusement. "I can't help but laugh. The irony of it all kills me." His eyes latch onto mine as he adds, "Pun intended."

Our stares remain locked, and I watch his lips twitch as he clenches his jaw in an effort to keep a straight face. Glaring, I push the plate as far away from me as I can and not so subtly reach to grab the lone apple from where traitor Quinn is *supposed* to be sitting. I say absolutely nothing as I take a bite and begin to chew, suddenly missing the mystery meat. There's no denying I will be starving later, but it's the price I'll have to pay, because here and now I take my oath and pledge my allegiance to vegetarianism, trying to push the new-found guilt of every single hamburger I've ever eaten out of my mind.

A breeze blows by and I catch the scent of sunshine and rainbows as Quinn decides to grace us with her presence for dinner. She lands forcefully in her seat, the excitement rolling off her in waves. Her eyes fall to the table and then to the apple in my hand. Smiling, she shrugs her shoulders, "I ate something over there with Candace and Sabrina. You can have it."

Glancing to where the emaciated bobblehead twins stand, I find myself met with two very disapproving and unattractive grimaces. I sneer back, partly because I already dislike them immensely, but mostly out of some instinctive need to protect Quinn. They remind me of two grotesque demons, hungry and ready to feed on her love of life and genuine kindness.

I really need to stop watching so many exorcism documentaries.

Or maybe I'm just experiencing meat withdrawals already because all I can think about as I watch them is hunger and eating.

Regardless, I don't like them.

Forcing my stare back to Quinn, I gesture at the empty space on the table. "You couldn't have eaten much, considering they have like one piece of celery on their plates, and you only had an apple, which I took. Sorry about that."

Guilt flashes in her eyes before she timidly shakes her head. "I ate before we came anyway. I'm not really hungry." A fabricated smile magically appears as she adds, "I just wanted to hang with you and my boarding buddy."

Just as I'm about to challenge her, because I know for a fact I didn't see her eat anything before we left together, Kaeleb interjects, "Speaking of boarding buddies . . . where's yours, Raven?"

I roll my eyes so hard it hurts. I have no idea why he's focusing on me so much. This freak getup is supposed to frighten people, not invite inquiry. Unfortunately, it seems to be having the opposite effect with him.

"I don't have one," I remark. "I skipped orientation."

"So you need one then?" For once, his face is devoid of any sarcasm or laughter. Sincerity laces his expression as he leans forward, clasping his hands together in front of him.

I, however, have sarcasm coursing through my veins instead of blood. "Um, not really. I own a map and possess a brain. I can figure it out on my own."

Not even remotely fazed, Kaeleb reaches his hand across the table. "Let me see your schedule."

"What? No." My face scrunches, and I shake my head.

"Yes, do it, Raven! We can all tour the campus together and plan out our schedules tomorrow," Quinn screeches from beside me. Leaning far away, I stick my finger in my ear, wiggling back and forth a bit to try to lessen the pain of my now bleeding eardrum, while giving her a hesitant, wide-eyed stare.

Kaeleb, of course, just laughs.

Quinn's face falls a bit with disappointment, forcing an incomprehensible emotion into my cold, dead heart known by others as *caring*. Dislodging my finger from my ear, I hold my palm up to her face before responding, "Okay. But please . . . *don't* scream." She nods and claps, but makes no sound.

Scooping the handle of my backpack, I fling it onto my lap and open the second pocket to produce my schedule before handing it over to Kaeleb. I can *feel* Quinn eagerly bouncing up and down next to me, and I swear she's about to explode with her attempt to contain her excitement. Without the release of a scream, I'm actually afraid she might.

Kaeleb casually peruses the paper and I'm a bit surprised when his eyes widen a fraction once he's finished. It's slight, probably not even noticeable to most, but I saw it. He hands the paper back to me and I immediately turn it in my hands to read over it again.

Peering back at him over the top of the paper, I ask, "What's with the face?"

The corners of his mouth dip slightly. "What face?"

"You made a face." The heels of my hands hit the table when I lower the schedule completely to get a better view of him while he stares blankly at me.

The standoff lasts a couple of seconds before he relents. "The Elements of Trust course threw me a bit, I guess. I wasn't planning on knowing anyone in there."

Surprised, my head jerks back. "You're in that class? With me?"

He cups his jaw, running his fingers back and forth along his stubble as he stares at the table. Once he lifts his head, our eyes meet and he grins.

"Yet another irony." He releases a lighthearted laugh. "A trust-based course in which you're forced to depend on random peers to ensure your safety while attempting death-defying, extremely dangerous activities."

Clearing his face, Kaeleb leans across the table and his eyes fill with defiance. He drops his voice to a low whisper. "I guess, in essence, one could say I will have to trust you with my life. Interesting turn of events, don't you think?"

Cue annoyingly perfect smile.

After his point is made, he stands quickly, the seat screeching across the floor, then steps away from the table, leaving me alone with Quinn and the realization that Linda absolutely screwed me when she made me sign up for the stupid course.

And although I'm rendered speechless, I make sure to mentally document twenty IOUs to the swear jar as I silently curse her in my head.

Chapter 6 ✳

Unbreakable Ties

The curses against Linda are mounting today, my fifth time attending the Elements of Trust class.

The classes started off harmless enough. Eye contact exercises, proximity awareness, trust leans as a group, but today . . . today is no simple task for me.

Rappelling.

Are you kidding me?

And with Kaeleb as my anchor?

Dr. Palmer has lost his fucking mind.

Oh, Dr. Martin Palmer. Plump and bearded Palmer. He seems to be genuinely caring as he guides me through the various activities. His kind blue eyes are always watching my interactions with the students, and it almost seems as though he's monitoring me for some reason. Maybe I'm paranoid, but it feels as if he shows more interest in me than the others.

Or maybe it's my freakish appearance that he's drawn to.

Or the neon-yellow contacts I've been sporting this past week.

Who knows? For whatever reason, it doesn't really seem to bother me.

But today, I'm seriously questioning his sanity.

"Come on, Raven. Open your eyes. You need to *see* your progress," Palmer shouts from about five-hundred feet below. Okay, not really. I don't know how high I am because my eyes are sealed shut, and my breathing is panicked as I hesitantly lower myself down the wall.

"Yeah, Raven," Kaeleb yells. "I'm sure you can see the mountains from up there."

I rappel a little farther, my voice shaky. "Shut up, Kaeleb."

His laughter bellows below me. "Just wait until we do the Leap of Faith."

My body shivers at the thought of standing on a fucking telephone pole and jumping off with nothing more than a cable and the people holding onto it to provide me safety. I can't believe I let Linda talk me into this shit.

"Am I almost done?" I ask, sliding the rope between my hands and pushing off. I think I just flew down about ten feet.

My Docs land hard, sending me spinning, and I don't stop until my body bounces off the wall. All with my eyes still closed.

"Not even close. I'm surprised you can even breathe with how thin the air is up there." Kaeleb's mocking tone furthers my aggravation.

After taking a deep breath—thankfully, the air is *just* fine—I push off again, unsteady with jerky movements. "Shut. Up."

And just when I think Kaeleb can't possibly irritate me further . . . "That harness is giving me a great view of your ass by the way. Your cargos are usually way too baggy."

A loud gasp escapes me, and I quickly let go of the rope to cover said ass, the release catapulting me farther down the wall until I'm practically upside down, all the while subjected to heinous cackling from below. At least Kaeleb somehow managed to stop my freefall during his fit of laughter.

"Kaeleb, enough," Palmer reprimands. "Raven, you're going to have to open your eyes and right your body. You can do this."

With his encouragement, I try to grab whatever shred of dignity I still have and pull myself upright with the help of the rope. Once I'm set, I lean back and rest my weight in the harness, trying to catch my breath.

My legs brace against the wall as I allow my torso to gingerly recline and my eyes to open slowly. The view isn't of mountains, but I can see the tops of the trees and the people walking through the courtyard area aren't nearly as small as I imagined they would be.

I breathe in deeply.

I can do this.

Kaeleb manages to stop his theatrics long enough for me to get my bearings, then I give the rope a little slack and kick my feet off the wall. My hands are shaking, but I keep a firm grip as I sail downward a bit and then land firmly. I repeat these motions until I'm about ten feet off the ground.

Blood is rushing through my veins, adrenaline is coursing through me, and for about five seconds I feel like I can do anything.

Until Kaeleb completely drops his very important anchor role, releasing the rope and throwing me into another freefall. An unexpected squeal escapes as I plummet the remainder of the way down, only to land in his arms with an *oomph*.

My arms fly around his neck, stirring his scent all around me. I find myself inhaling deeper than probably appropriate. And when my lungs can take no more air, I enjoy its soothing effect until I remember that I'm pissed.

He could have killed me.

And now I'm going to kill him.

"Kaeleb, you asshole," I yell, jumping out of his hold and planting my feet on the ground. I haul back and shove him as hard as I can. "You could have dropped me."

His shoulders shake with his silent chuckles. "No way. I'm six three. That was like a two-foot drop."

Palmer watches our interaction with interest. I swear I spot the tiniest look of amusement flash across his features before he states, "Something tells me Kaeleb would never drop you, Raven." He directs his eyes in Kaeleb's direction, all amusement lost and replaced with caution. "That being said, your actions were not at all conducive for this exercise." Palmer looks back to me before adding, "I hope that your maturity level is greater than that of Mr. McMadden's, seeing as it's his turn next. We need to maintain a serious environment for the others who actually hope to gain something from this class." His voice is as stern as his glare.

What? Now *I'm* in trouble?

Sneering at Kaeleb, I respond, "Yes, sir." Palmer gives a brisk nod before marching onto the next pairing of people.

"You're an ass," I snip at him, yanking the harness off and stepping out of it.

"I never said I wasn't." He kicks the nylon contraption off the ground with his foot, then easily catches it midair. "I'm sorry, but that shit was too funny to pass up."

My eyes narrow. "And what if you'd dropped me?"

His arrogance lessens and his expression softens. "I wouldn't have dropped you." He maintains eye contact with me and his stare is so full of sincerity, I'm forced to break it.

My cheeks warm and I cast my glance to the ground, kicking the grass with my Docs.

"Well, at least you didn't grope my ass," I concede, looking up.

His lips form a crooked smile, and he chuckles under his breath. "Who said I didn't?"

"I would've felt it," I counter.

He shakes his head, his eyes filling with humor. "I have ninja hands." He steps into the harness and pulls it up, securing it before adding, "And *you* have a nice ass."

I gasp, but before I can say anything he steps into my personal space—the very space he *knows* I hate anyone to breach as evidenced during our proximity awareness exercises—and eyes my gaping mouth.

"There was no way I was letting you go." He pauses, then pins me with an earnest stare. "Our bonds were secured."

My eyebrows pinch together in confusion with the intensity of his statement, but then his mouth relaxes into an easy grin as he holds the rope in front of my face and adds, "These ties can't be broken."

Kaeleb gives me a wink and turns on his heel, heading toward the stairs along the side of the wall. Before taking the first step, he twists back around and shouts, "Try to focus on keeping me *alive* and not the magnificence of *my* ass."

I flip him the bird and another loud cackle fills the air as he makes his way to the top of the wall. Once he's securely harnessed in, he flies backward with abandon and rappels masterfully down the side, with absolutely no help from me.

And it's a good thing.

Because Mr. McMadden does, in fact, have a magnificent derrière.

Not that I was looking.

Chapter 7

Evading Questions

Over the next month, Quinn and Kaeleb make it their personal mission to try to break through my painfully obvious attempts at obscurity. It's been nonstop. Kaeleb's questioning especially.

Sigh.

Kaeleb.

Much to my relief, after several more inquiry-filled classes in trust education, he's still very much alive, but honestly, some days I really want to kill him—metaphorically speaking, of course.

It's usually when we perform the trust fall exercise, which we're forced to do during every single class. Not once has he performed this exercise without making an asinine comment—normally referencing some random way he could die if I drop him—prior to falling backward into my arms.

So recently, as a form of payback for the rappelling incident as well as other stupid comments he makes during class, it has become habit to catch him but then promptly let his body fall to the ground from the safe two-foot height. This often results in very inappropriate laughter—his aloud and mine inwardly—as well as an extremely disapproving glare from Dr. Palmer.

No matter how hard he lands, it doesn't seem to deter his sarcastic remarks about death or his probing questions about my personal life. Quinn's resolve never falters either, and between the both of them, I'm losing my mind. Partly because their tenacity won't let me just *be*. But mostly, it stems from the constant confusion warring in my mind when subjected to their repeated attempts. Because the fact of the matter is, I actually *want* to answer them, to let down my manufactured walls, and allow them into my highly dysfunctional, warped mind.

And that scares me shitless.

So instead of offering actual answers, I give them only monosyllabic and/or elusive responses, often in the form of a returned question. For example, Successful Evasion Number One with Quinn Matthews, one month ago between Quinn and me:

Quinn (as we eat ramen noodles in our room): "Do you guys know each other?"

Me: "Who?"

Q: "You and Kaeleb?"

Me: (full facial flush accompanied by throat clearing) "Who?"

Q: "Kaeleb. You guys just seem really comfortable. Well, not comfortable, but familiar. With your banter and how you seem to get under each other's skin. It just seems like you know each other."

Me: "Huh. Weird. How was class?"

Successful Evasion Number Two, approximately three weeks ago, brought to you by Kaeleb McMadden on our way to class:

Kaeleb: "So, *Raven*, what's your story?"

Me: "Um, story?"

K: "Yes, *Raven*. Please shed some light on the enigma that is you."

Me: (sighs inwardly) "Why do you keep saying my name like that?"

K: "What? Like *Raven*?"

Me: "Yes. Like *Raven*."

K: (shrugs shoulders) "I don't know. I guess I just find it an interesting choice for a name. Obvious symbolism and all. It's almost as though it was prophetic in nature."

Me: (narrows glare and smirks) "Can you please stop saying it that way? It's getting on my nerves. *You* are getting on my nerves."

K: (chuckles lightly under breath) "As you wish . . . *Raven*."

Me: (internal blood-curdling scream as I increase my pace and distance)

(loud cackling from fifteen feet behind me)

Successful Evasion Number Three, about a week ago, tag-team, and quite possibly the worst, attempt by Quinn Matthews and Kaeleb McMadden in our dorm room:

Kaeleb: "Seriously, *Raven*, I have to ask what's up with the contacts?"

Quinn: "Yeah, I mean, I like the purple today, but why do you always wear them?"

(both stare expectantly)

K: (clasps hands together and points at Quinn) "Dude, she should get some zombie ones. Those would be so fucking cool." (deposits quarter into the jar)

Q: "O-M-G, yes! Or those ones that are completely black with no iris."

K: "Like I said, zombie."

Q: "No, totally black ones would be like a demon or something. Zombie ones would be like, you know, gray and cloudy looking. Like my grandpa's." (glances back at me) "He has cataracts."

K: "Are you sure?" (pulls out phone)

Q: "Yes, it's really creepy. It makes my eyes water when I look at him."

K: (laughs) "Kinda like when I look at *Raven's* cat eyes."

Me: (sighs and picks up backpack to head to the library) "You guys really need to get a life."

And for the finale, a compilation of questions dodged over the last four weeks (I'll let you guess who said what):

"What color is your hair naturally?"

"What are your parents' names? What do they do?"

"Do you ever do anything but scowl?"

"Do you have any pets?" (sigh . . . Walter.)

"Do you have a boyfriend?"

"Have you ever had a boyfriend?"

"Are you a virgin?"

"Do you have any siblings?"

"What are your hobbies?"

"Who is Linda to you?"

"Where did you go to high school?"

"Did you play sports?"

"Do you own anything other than baggy pants, concert T-shirts, and Docs?"

"So no tight-ass minidresses?"

And this has been the hell I have had to endure since school started.

So needless to say, when waking up this morning to *"Raven, seriously, what color is your hair? I'm dying to know."* I have no choice but to finally cave under the pressure. I guess Quinn has decided to change tactics and hit me up before my brain has a chance to fire any neurological activity, leaving me defenseless against her line of questioning.

Slowly dragging the pillow shielding my face from the dreaded light of morning, my eyes fall directly on Quinn as she exits the bathroom with my black hair dye in her hands, the golden flecks in her green eyes lit with curiosity, hope, and determination.

A small growl escapes my lips and I throw the pillow onto the floor. I can tell she's trying to contain her excitement at the possibility of breaking me but failing miserably. After placing my beloved hair products on my desk, she sits on the edge of my bed, and I find myself shocked that, for the first time since school started, I don't have to fight the urge to scoot away from her. I do sit up and stretch, stalling.

My hands fall to my lap, and I release a defeated sigh before answering. "Okay, here's the deal. I will give you *five* questions that I promise to answer honestly. That being said, do you really want to waste the first one on the true color of my hair?"

Quinn considers my question for a while before bringing her legs onto my bed and curling them underneath her as though getting ready for a really enthralling story. All she's missing is the popcorn.

Scrunching her mouth to the side, she deliberates for a lengthy amount of time before landing on her all-important first question. "Your parents. What are they like?"

A breath lodges in my throat and my heart stammers for a brief second before it begins thudding against my ribcage. I can feel blood draining from my already ashen face as I speak. "They died when I was younger." And for some reason, I dimwittedly throw in the answer to what could have possibly been another question. "Linda is my legal guardian. She has been since I was eight years old."

Stupid.

Stupid, stupid, stupid.

Quinn's expression falls to the floor. She breathes in deeply and nods slightly before proceeding. "Siblings?"

"I had a sister once. She also died," I respond with a forced lack of emotion. Tears threaten my eyes, but I swallow them back along with the pain. Quinn's tears, however, slide gracefully from her eyes and trail slowly down her cheeks. I mentally shake my head. This is exactly why I don't talk about the past. I don't know why I offered to answer these God-awful questions. I blame the early morning assault, but unfortunately, my brain is fully functional now, and there's no escaping the crippling heartache that comes with the answers.

Breathing deeply through my nose, I quickly compose myself while Quinn continues to watch my reaction warily. After wiping the moisture from her face, she places her hand on top of my leg, enveloped within the warmth of my black-and-gray-striped comforter. "I'm so sorry. I can't even begin to imagine."

"That's life, I guess," I answer with a shoulder shrug. "Unfortunately, for the people around me, life tends to come with extraordinarily short expiration dates. Like milk."

Completely ignoring my attempt at deflection, Quinn dips her head in my direction. "So . . . the hair, the contacts, the piercings . . . they are to keep people away from you?"

I nod my answer. Her mouth once again angles downward as she takes in my mind-blowing revelation.

"That's three. Two more to go. Unless you're done, which is completely fine by me." She hesitantly shakes her head, curiosity clearly outweighing her sorrow for my sucky-ass life. Leaning forward, she snakes my student ID off my bedside table. After glancing at it, she flashes it in front of my face. I can literally see the light bulb click as it rests in its imaginary space above her head.

"Is your name really Raven?" Lowering the laminated square a tad, she peers at me over the top of it.

My lower lip is sucked between my teeth as I nibble, debating my answer. Honesty in this case is completely subjective. As much as I want to disclose the true answer, I don't. I can't. Acknowledging my birth name would rip open a gaping hole in my fortress, linking my past with my present. *Raven*, for me, is a name that provides me with a comforting sense of autonomy, relinquished from the horror of actually having to face my past. To come to terms with it. Speaking about the death of my family, I'm still able to keep that connection severed. But the acknowledgment of my birth name, in my own twisted mind, would be an act of resurrecting the girl I buried right along with them. And that's never going to happen. I *am* Raven. The little girl no longer exists.

"Yes," I state calmly. Quinn's eyes narrow further, forming crinkles around the sides, as she holds her stare on my vacant face. After a few seconds, she seems to accept my answer and relaxes. Drumming her fingers on my leg, she glances up at the ceiling. "Last one. Better make it good, huh?"

I remain still, patiently awaiting her question while reinforcing my walls that have bowed and weakened since the beginning of this inquisition. Just as I have them fortified, she drags her stare away from the fluorescent lights overhead to meet mine.

A slight smile crosses her lips as she removes her hand from my leg and stands, taking a small step back before speaking. "Wanna go get some breakfast?"

A relieved breath makes its way out of my mouth, and damn if a smile doesn't break across my face too.

With that one stupid question, my defenses are pierced, and an unfamiliar warmth slowly begins to seep inside and spread throughout, her infiltration sparking to life the tiniest little "Quinn Matthews" section in my heart.

For a split second, I allow myself to enjoy the foreign feeling before nodding my head and hauling my ass out of bed to join my new friend for breakfast, selfishly blinded and oblivious to the danger I may have put her in.

Chapter 8 ✳

Surprises

Breakfast was a success. In fact, it was so successful that it quickly became a staple for our morning routine. We've actually added some other occupants to our shaded table in the courtyard area outside the cafeteria since this started. One welcome, the others not so much. Kaeleb, of course, was welcome. Candace and Sabrina, a.k.a. The Annoying Emaciated Bobblehead Twins, along with some seriously stupid 'roided-out tagalongs, Josh and Luke, were definitely *not* welcome. Not by me anyway. Kaeleb didn't seem to enjoy their presence too much either, but poor Quinn has seemingly fallen head over heels in love with Mr. Beef-and-Brawn-with-no-Brain—Josh for short—since she first met him a couple weeks ago.

While eating my Froot Loops, I notice the dopey, love-struck grin plastered on Quinn's face as she listens to his highly intellectual account of some "sick"—his word not mine, obviously—keg party he attended Friday night. Sabrina and Candace look equally enthralled. My gaze darts to Kaeleb, and I choke down my laughter at his expression. Grimacing as though he bit down on a lemon wedge, his face is puckered with a look of absolute distaste. A strip of bacon falls from his fingers onto his plate as he tears his eyes away, throwing me a questioning sideways *What the fuck?* glance. My left eyebrow rises along with my shoulders as I answer him with my own look of uncertainty.

"Quinn, seriously, you aren't going to eat *all* of that, are you?"

I quickly disengage from Kaeleb's stare, *my* face now pinched in disgust, to eye the outspoken, hollow-cheeked bitch sitting across from me. Sabrina's eyeballs practically bulge from their sockets as they glare at Quinn's plate that—I kid you not—contains a meager piece of unbuttered toast with a small helping of fruit salad. I guess that's a lot when you compare it to the two lonely coffee cups in front of both Sabrina and Candace.

Mmm . . . the breakfast of champions and anorexics everywhere.

Quinn's face falls. She sheepishly looks back at Josh, who seems unaffected by Sabrina's statement and makes no attempt to shield her from the scathing comment. Her cheeks brighten with embarrassment as she hesitantly pushes her plate in Kaeleb's direction.

"I got this for Kaeleb. I ate earlier in the room."

Completely stunned, I watch Quinn practically fold into herself in an effort to disappear after her blatant lie. She didn't eat a goddamn thing. I know this for a fact. Why isn't she sticking up for herself?

My stomach tightens and churns and my heart rate increases, instigating raging anger, which spreads across my face like wildfire. I open my mouth, fully expecting to spew venom all over this undernourished wench, but as the words are about to fly off my tongue, Kaeleb's menacing voice stops me cold.

"You're kidding me, right?" he scoffs, shoving Quinn's plate back across the table before his eyes return to Sabrina, darkened with brute ferocity. "You look like a starved carcass, Sabrina. It's not only unattractive; it's ironically unappetizing. You really should eat something for the sake of everyone at this table."

Heat rolls off him, warming the entire left side of my body. "You're a bitch," he adds matter-of-factly, but his anger unmistakably fills the air around us. Sabrina and Candace simultaneously gasp in response while Josh and Luke blankly stare. Big surprise.

My eyes find Quinn next, who's clamping her jaw shut. I guess it flew wide open along with mine.

Sabrina quickly recovers, responding with, "Whatever, Kaeleb. Your opinion doesn't mean shit to me." She gestures to Quinn. "Hey, I'm just trying to do Quinn a favor. We all know she's in the pageant circuit, and from where I'm sitting, the top of her jeans is the only thing getting crowned." Her blue eyes slide in Quinn's direction. "Watch that muffin top. That's all I'm sayin'."

Candace snorts and Quinn's face crumples in anguish and embarrassment, her light-green eyes glistening as she bolts from the bench with her backpack. Tripping over her own feet, she tries to make a somewhat graceful exit and whimpers, her hand swiping the tears from her cheek before heading in the direction of the dorm. Kaeleb's body tenses to rise, but I place my hand on his leg, keeping him still as I stand.

My palms find their way to the cool cement of the tabletop, and my fingers stretch as I lean over, positioning my face a mere inch away from Sabrina's. I shoot a quick glance at Kaeleb over my shoulder, and based on the throbbing vein on his forehead, he's using every single bit of restraint within his possession not to jump across the table and strangle this skank. Giving a subtle shake of my head, I wordlessly let him know that this retribution will be within *my* jurisdiction.

I casually turn my attention back to Sabrina and lean in closer. Her coffee breath hits me in the face as her breathing picks up with my threatening stance. "It looks like Quinn isn't the only one sporting a crown." Grabbing my cereal bowl, I swiftly raise it above her head, making the most of the fear flitting across her face before quickly turning it upside down, dumping the contents right on top of her perfectly coiffed blonde hair. "Watch your fucking mouth. That's all *I'm* sayin'."

As soon as the cold milk hits the top of her head, she lets out a grating shriek. Milk and Froot Loops ricochet off Sabrina's shoulder, spraying onto Candace's face and hair until I finally drop the empty bowl back onto the table. Kaeleb stands quickly, throws his heavy forearm across my upper body, and forces me backward, but not before I get my final vengeance. With all the strength I can muster, I press against his imprisoning limb and break free. My body flies forward and my right arm swings across the table, sending Styrofoam coffee cups flying into the laps of the already shaken victims. Sabrina and Candace bound from their seats, wildly swiping at their laps while Josh and Luke remain completely still, blank faces still on display as they watch the girls screeching and jumping.

Unfortunately, that's the last thing I'm able to see before I'm somehow whisked onto Kaeleb's shoulder. His left arm curls around my waist while his right immobilizes my shins, most likely a protective measure against the Docs covering my feet. I'm forced to watch Kaeleb's own boots step over the bench as he turns us away from the chaos, but eventually I raise my neck so I can fully appreciate the glorious commotion playing out in front of me. Sabrina's head jerks up with our retreat, her eyes shooting daggers in my direction. "You fucking goth *freak*," she screams, projecting pure hatred with her words. "You will pay for this, bitch."

My response? Full-on laughter that ultimately morphs into an *eat shit* grin. I add the extension of my middle finger as my upper body jostles against Kaeleb's back, his strides increasing in both strength and speed. My eyes remain latched onto hers until I'm carried around the side of the cafeteria, and she can no longer be seen.

As soon as we round the corner, Kaeleb gently places me back onto my feet, and by the gleaming look in his eyes and the wide, toothy smile he's giving me, I'd say he approves of my inappropriate behavior. I find it impossible not to mimic his expression, not only because of his obvious delight, but because staring back at me is a face much resembling the eight-year-old boy that I loved so deeply. The same boy who dared me into jumping homemade bike ramps and was forced into attending many a tea party.

Yes, I said tea party. Don't judge.

In this one and only moment, I allow the playful, childhood memories of us to flow without trying to contain them, the familiar recollections washing over me and warming my insides. Damn, that boy must have a skeleton key to my memory bins.

"That was fucking EPIC," he shouts, then breaks into laughter. "She's going to be digging Froot Loops out of her hair for months. And her face? Priceless! Candace's too."

A small chuckle passes between my lips as I tuck a strand of black hair behind my ear. "Sorry about that," I respond. "But in my defense, she deserved it."

"Hell yeah, she did." Kaeleb hands me my backpack and eyes me curiously, our laughter soon falling into an awkward silence. I avert my stare, scanning over a passerby exiting the cafeteria. Slowly, he leans into me and raises his hand toward my face, grazing the side of my chin with the tip of his finger.

Now usually, I would have taken a step back out of his reach, protectively placing distance between us. So color me surprised when I remain standing in place, allowing the heat from his touch to penetrate my skin. Our breaths mingle together as we lock eyes, the mood tangibly shifting from its previous lightheartedness. He takes a small step forward and closely surveys my reaction.

Instinctively, I lift my hand when his drops away, his eyes still glued to my chin. "What?" I ask, rubbing the area he just touched. Just as my finger skims along the small indentation, I know. I know exactly what he's looking at.

"How did you get that scar?" His voice is gentle, almost timid as he redirects his eyes to mine.

Blood warms my face. "This? Uhh . . ." I stall and then lie, "tripped last year, hit my chin on the corner of a fireplace. Why?"

I plaster my face with contrived innocence, my mind trying to skirt the memory of how I *actually* busted my chin wide open. The fact is, I remember it quite well. We were six. He was trying to teach me how to skate and I slipped, falling approximately one point two seconds after my wheels hit the pavement. Haven't touched a pair since.

Eyes narrowing, he holds my stare before stepping back. "Wow. Looks like it hurt. I had a friend who fell on her chin like that once and it was pretty nasty. Blood everywhere." A mischievous smile crosses his face. "Yeah, she pretty much ate the curb. Skating accident. She was freaking out, crying and stuff. I had to carry her back to my house because she couldn't skate back, obviously."

At that, my blackened brows rise toward the sky. He totally *did not* carry me back—we were *six*—and I sure as hell didn't freak out or cry. He chuckles under his breath and shakes his head. "Man, I miss her."

A breath catches in my throat as it constricts with his sentiment. Although I want to say, "I miss you too," what passes through my lips is, "Quinn."

His head jerks back in surprise. "Not Quinn. Her name was—"

"No," I cut him off, throwing my thumb over my shoulder, "I mean, I should probably go talk to Quinn. You know, make sure she's okay."

Nodding slightly, Kaeleb's expression saddens. "Yeah, probably. Don't you have class though?"

"Yeah, but so does she. I have a feeling we'll be skipping today."

"Near-assault and truancy all in one day." He tsks. "You're just full of surprises, aren't you, *Raven*."

He has *no* idea.

After giving Kaeleb a lengthy look, I hoist my backpack onto my shoulder and pivot on my heel, heading toward the dorms to console Quinn and escape the slew of emotions I've experienced today.

Emotions that are seemingly impossible to avoid, yet surprisingly welcome.

Chapter 9

Layers

"You okay?" Shutting the door behind me, I cautiously set my backpack on the floor of our now darkened room. Quinn is sprawled out on her bed, her face hidden in her pillow as her muffled cries escape into the down feathers. Not really experienced with how to handle sobbing people, or people in general for that matter, I sit quietly on the edge of her bed, giving her plenty of room to cry. I remain there for a very long time, silently hoping my presence is comforting for her and not freaking her out.

Eventually, her shoulders stop trembling and she rolls over, hooking her arm over her eyes. Tears still stream along the sides of her face, but she seems more composed.

"I'm just . . . so embarrassed, Raven," she whimpers softly. "I hate her. I really do. She said all of that shit in front of Josh because she knows . . . she knows I like him, and obviously, so does *she*."

"Sabrina's a fucking asshole, Quinn. Seriously, don't waste your tears on her." Anger once again resurfaces, but I manage to keep it safely inside my chest. Glancing at the swear jar sitting on the table between our beds, I thank God we've retired it. That thing was bleeding us dry. It now serves as a reminder of our first day together, when friendships were formed with Quinn, Kaeleb, and me. The pile of change remains though—for laundry, of course.

"I know. It's just she knows everything about me, and she loves to push my buttons to hurt me. And I can't get rid of her."

"Why the hell not?" I inquire. I'm so over that bitch. And I have a feeling we won't be sharing any warm and fuzzies . . . ever.

"Because . . ." Quinn pauses to wipe her eyes, finally moving out from behind the safety of her arm. "Because she's in the same pageants as me. We've been doing them since we were kids. I've been forced to put up with her shit for years by my mother. It's never been an option to stand up for myself because it would knock her clear off that precious country club social ladder she's been climbing for years."

My right dimple sinks into my face as my lips purse, considering her statement, bringing back Sabrina's words about the pageant circuit. I guess that explains the tiara/scepter combo.

So my new friend is an actual, bona fide pageant queen. Lovely.

As I eye her face cautiously, it becomes apparent how much I actually *don't* know about her. I guess this friendship thing is supposed to be a two-way street, and I've been traveling down one-way Raven Ave.

I really suck at this stuff.

That being said, I did just crown the new reigning Froot Loop Queen, so that counts for something, right?

"Well . . . I kinda took care of that for you."

Quinn's eyes almost fly out of their sockets before she snaps straight up in bed, catapulting her body inches from mine and scaring the shit out of me. "WHAT?"

I spy a subtle grin on her lips before she quickly voids it and clears her throat. "What did you do?" she whispers, eyes still wide.

Once my heart rate settles—thanks for that, Quinn, as if I haven't had enough adrenaline-fueled moments today—I wave my hand dismissively. "It was nothing, really. I just addressed the crowning comment . . . bypouringmycerealonherhead." My words are quick in hopes that they fly right through her brain, not giving them ample time to sink in. Unfortunately, it's a sad and futile effort.

"WHAT?" she screams, eyeballs bulging further than I thought possible.

I raise my guilty eyes to meet hers. Her mouth is wide open, and her skin is a bit ashen, but at least her eyes are still intact.

Phew.

Slowly, I reach over, press her jaw closed with my fingers, and lean back, shrugging my shoulders. "It wasn't *that* big of a deal."

Quinn peers at me from underneath her lashes, her shocked expression falling into a smirk that definitely rivals Linda's when she knows I'm full of shit. I just lift my shoulders in innocence.

"Anyway," I dismiss, "this isn't about her. I want to talk about you."

And now we're back to being shocked.

"You . . . you want to talk about *me*?"

My face relaxes as I give her my best attempt at a comforting smile. "Yes. I do. If we're going to be friends, I should know things about you, right?" I motion back and forth between us and add, "Isn't that how this works?" The question sounds rhetorical, but unfortunately, it's not.

Quinn answers with a nod of her head. "What do you want to know?"

"Hmm . . ." I drawl. "I guess I'm trying to understand this lack of eating issue we've got going on here. I mean, you *have* to eat, Quinn. You run every day like you're training for a marathon, and some days you eat nothing more than an apple. That can't be good for your body." It's true. An apple a day may keep the doctor away, but tack five miles onto that with nothing else to eat and I'm pretty sure it negates the whole idea.

The resulting look on Quinn's face is an equal mixture of guilt and sadness. The pain in her features is blatantly evident as her expression falls with her tears. No words are spoken between us until she's ready.

"I'm just so . . . *tired*, Raven. So, so tired. Tired of Sabrina picking at everything I do. Tired of letting her do it. But most of all, I'm tired of thinking."

Her eyes fill with unshed tears as she speaks. "My mind runs nonstop, all day long. *I shouldn't have eaten that. If I eat this, then I can't eat this. These jeans are tighter than they used to be. I'm getting a pouch on my stomach. I can definitely pinch more than I could yesterday.* I just can't take it anymore," she finally shouts, bolting off the bed.

Quinn strides over to our shared table, fists the pile of change in the palm of her hand, and screws open the lid of the retired swear jar, throwing every last bit of our money inside. Well, with the exception of the lone quarter that just hit the floor. I listen to it roll, not really sure why she's dumping change into the jar because we don't use it anymore.

Maybe it's a metaphorical statement she feels she needs to make.

She slams the jar back down onto the table and turns to me, her eyes blazing with anger and frustration. "I AM SO FUCKING EXHAUSTED!" Her head falls into her hands, and her shoulders tremble with her sobs.

Tears pool on my lower lashes and my chin begins to quiver, her torment slicing my heart wide open as I watch her break right in front of my eyes. I step toward her, the sight temporarily obliterating my need for self-preservation. I feel every ounce of her hopelessness as I travel the short distance, not stopping until I'm standing in front of her. Awkwardly my arms rise, the hesitation causing them to bob up and down. I take a deep breath, calming my anxiety, and circle them around her tiny body. Uncertainty still pounds within my ears, but I tighten my grip on her, hoping like hell this is what I'm supposed to do when comforting a friend.

Quinn stills immediately, her cries ceasing briefly before she wraps her arms around my waist and buries her head into my shoulder, letting her pain flow. The moisture from her tears drains onto the neckband of my favorite Pink Floyd T-shirt as I hold onto my friend, trying to absorb her despair. She's too good, too pure, to have to hold this much anguish in her heart. I already have plenty; what's a little more on top of it if it helps her?

My arms continue to envelop her until her sobs soften into light whimpers. Once I feel she's finally found the release she's needed, I lessen my hold, careful not to let go until she's ready. Slowly she unwraps her arms and takes a step back, self-consciously tucking a strand of her blonde hair behind her ear before clearing the moisture from her face. Sucking in a breath, she finally brings her eyes to mine.

"I'm sorry," she says on a ragged breath. "It's just . . . I've been holding in a lot. I didn't mean to explode like that in front of you."

I give her a small but genuine smile. "It's fine, Quinn. Really."

An unfamiliar ache spreads throughout my chest, because as I speak those words of comfort to my friend, I'm forced to acknowledge the longing buried somewhere deep within my soul that wants to yell and scream and tear the room apart for all the loss I've endured.

That I've caused.

Quinn praises my strength, the ability to look and act like a freak without the fear of judgment rendered, but in truth, she's the only one in this room with true courage. Mine is merely a facade.

My throat narrows, making it increasingly difficult to swallow. I break eye contact, catching a flash of silver on the floor. Bending down, I pinch the quarter between my fingers, then hand it to Quinn. With a subtle grin I drop it into her palm. "This one's mine. You don't get the monopoly on breakdowns around here." A sheepish smile appears before she turns and places the quarter in its rightful place next to the jar.

Twisting back in my direction, she gives my arm a slight squeeze. "Thank you, Raven. I feel like I can breathe for the first time in a long time." After releasing me, she steps back and jerks her chin toward the bathroom. "I'm going to take a quick shower before our next class."

I watch her walk away and then sit on the edge of my bed to take in a much-needed breath, suddenly exhausted.

Before the bathroom door shuts, it whips back open and Quinn's head pops out from behind it. "And you are going to tell me the full, unedited version of what happened with Sabrina after I left as soon as I step out of this shower." She smiles widely, and once again begins to close the door, but not before jutting her hand out. "Oh, can you get my brush? It's somewhere around my desk, I think."

"Sure," I respond, getting off the bed.

I see no brush on the desk. I open her top drawer, still no brush, but when I fling open the second drawer an envelope slides across the slick bottom, hitting the side wall, the impact spilling out the contents.

A gasp passes through my throat at what is strewn out right in front of me. Tears once again prick my eyes as I stare open-mouthed at a picture of a girl—her haunting, desolate expression glaring at me. *Quinn.* A much younger version, and about one hundred pounds heavier, but it's definitely her. I'm transfixed. The vacant expression in her eyes is nothing like the cheerful look I've come to know. My fingers tremble as I reach into the drawer and slowly fan out the pile of photos to see what's underneath. What I find chills me to the core.

Every single picture has been defaced. In some, gaping holes show where the eyes are supposed to be, leaving nothing but jagged edges.

In others, the face has been scratched beyond recognition—dull, angry white marks embedded deeply into the glossy finish. Words like pig, repulsive, heifer, disgusting, and ugly are carved into the paper, her revulsion permanently engraved across her body. *Muffin top* catches my eye. With Sabrina's words fresh in my mind, a jolt courses through my veins. I sift through a few more, horrified at the inscriptions of hatred and loathing.

As I reach the bottom of the pile and read the etching displayed on the last picture, a single tear falls, flowing freely down my face.

I want to die.

"Raven! Brush?" The bathroom door creaks open, and I quickly shove everything back into the envelope before softly closing the drawer. Just as I turn and take a small step, the tip of my shoe sends the brush sliding across the floor until it hits Quinn's bare foot. Her eyes flit quickly over the desk before landing on the brush. She slowly and deliberately bends her terrycloth-covered body to retrieve it, before rising and meeting my gaze.

"Found it," I offer meekly, worried that if I say anything more my guilt will be obvious.

Quinn's eyes narrow, her expression curious. "I see that. Find anything else?"

"Nope," I reply. The words can't get off my tongue fast enough.

The seconds tick by until finally Quinn's face begins to soften and she offers me a smile. "Okay. Well, I'm gonna take a quick shower and then we can head to class."

I manage a small nod before she spins around, shutting the door behind her. Robotically, I walk to my bed and as I fall backward, I look to the ceiling. My mind is reeling.

I know I should say something, talk to her, but as Quinn's mutilated pictures flip repeatedly in my mind, one after another, I'm painfully reminded that she seems to have just as many protective layers as I do. Layers that can't be forcefully ripped away in haste; the damage would be irreparable.

I want to die.

Staring upward, I say a silent prayer that I'm doing the right thing . . . Because I know better than anyone how consuming the desire to die can be.

Chapter 10

Secrets

"Quinn okay?" Kaeleb asks, heaving his backpack on his shoulder as we head to our Elements of Trust class. "I haven't seen you guys at breakfast lately."

"She's okay. Quiet. She did make up with Sabrina though." Kaeleb's irritated expression reflects my own inner dissatisfaction.

"I know," I concede. "I think it's easier for her right now to forgive and forget. Evidently there are some deep-rooted ties that she doesn't want to mess with . . . family stuff, you know?" I explain, not that I really understand it.

A harsh grunt next to me tells me he feels the same way.

"I'll try to get her to come to breakfast tomorrow," I add.

Kaeleb nods before grinning back at me. "Have you seen Sabrina or Candace? You know, since . . ."

I smirk, still extremely self-satisfied with my cereal vengeance. "No, but I'm sure I will, unfortunately."

"Sign me up for that shit."

I chuckle under my breath as we continue walking, cutting across the lawn, the fresh-cut grass clinging to my Docs. A bitter gust of wind and the reddish hue of the leaves remind me fall is ending, and it will be winter soon. Even with the sun shining, it's getting chilly. An involuntary shiver rakes over my entire body, and Kaeleb throws me a sideways glance. I really should have grabbed my jacket. This old worn-out concert tee isn't cutting it.

Kaeleb stops and shrugs his backpack and leather bomber jacket onto the ground, leaving him in a gray hoodie that reads JUST HIT IT above the infamous Nike swoosh. After regrettably reading his delusion of grandeur, another smirk crosses my face. "Get a lot of dates wearing that, do ya?"

"I get a lot of dates no matter what I'm wearing." His lips twitch as he attempts to maintain a serious expression. He's become quite the ladies' man since school started. It's no surprise. Kaeleb oozes *sexy* from every pore in his body.

Not that I pay attention.

"Right. Highly regarded, self-respecting women, no doubt," I respond, the barbell of my black eyebrow lifting in annoyance.

His face breaks into smug laughter. "Hey, it's college. I'm not trying to be a saint."

"Well, you're definitely on your way to dating hell. I'm waiting for you to get that one, clingy, cries-when-you-don't-call, psycho-stalker girl. Sign *me* up for *that* shit."

With yet another laugh, he reaches down and grips the leather jacket, stepping closer and extending his arm, graciously offering it to me to wear. I feel the residual heat from his body as I take it from him.

"Oh, for me?" I yell with mock excitement, "OMG! Kaeleb McMadden just gave me his jacket." I make sure to fan my face for dramatic effect, watching a group of girls pass, their jaws dragging the ground. Rolling my eyes, I fight the urge to give them the finger, which seems to be my favorite form of communication with anyone who isn't Quinn or Kaeleb these days. Well, Quinn anyway.

A crooked smile forms as he watches my fierce monologue, not a hint of embarrassment in his expression. "Did you just make a joke, *Raven?*"

Cue middle finger.

Another chuckle passes as I slip on the brown leather. "I thought you weren't trying to be a saint. I would say offering your jacket is pretty . . . saintly." He grins and shrugs as I slowly inhale his scent, threatening the defenses of my Level 3 security. The smell of grass and his fresh laundry produces a familiar fragrance that just *is* Kaeleb. It's almost enough to overwhelm the lock on my bin, but I have mentally added a dead bolt. His access has luckily been denied.

After exhaling a breath of relief, I give him the tiniest of smiles, situating myself in his jacket and sliding my backpack over both shoulders as Kaeleb does the same. "I *can* be funny, you know."

"I *know* you're funny," he replies, his eyes finding the ground in front of us as we begin to walk.

"You don't *know* anything about me," I snap, possibly a little too defensively.

"Don't I?" He stops his long strides, and therefore, so do I. We're never going to make it to class at this rate.

I turn to tell him this, but as soon as our stares lock, the words escape me, his fierce eyes stealing my breath. They're narrowed, as if he's trying to strip me of my blackened veil. As though he's searching my darkness.

"No, you don't," I reply quickly.

Fear works its way into my throat as he continues to scan me closely, tilting his head. "Hmm . . . interesting." He lifts his hand to skim the scarred area alongside my chin. "I would say I know you better than you think I do."

My brain jolts to life, sending out an emergency distress signal that more Level 3 memories, possibly even Level 4, may be breached. This is not good.

I ignore the way his touch riles my skin and turn, offering him nothing more as I continue on to class. His backpack shuffles from behind me, but thankfully, he makes no attempt to catch up.

Traveling separately, we finally arrive, barely making it to class on time. Once we're accounted for, we make our way out to the field where most of our exercises are performed. As the class begins to congregate, I strategically place as many people between us as I can. I refuse to look at Kaeleb, but his presence continues to suffocate me no matter how far away I stand.

"All righty, kids! We're going to buddy up today." A series of groans follows as Dr. Palmer begins calling out names in groups of two. His pudgy finger taps on his clipboard with each pair.

My heart rate triples, increasing the pressure in my chest. I *always* get paired up with Kaeleb. Every. Single. Time.

"McMadden and Miller."

Sigh.

I turn and weave my way through my brilliant protection plan.

Damn my last name. I should have taken Linda's.

Squeezing by the final person between us, my eyes stay focused on Kaeleb's boots. Strands of black highlighted with plum whip across my face as the breeze picks up and chills me to the bone. Threading my fingers through my hair, I gather it, tuck the heap behind my collar, then wrap Kaeleb's jacket tightly around me, hoping to harness some of the fading warmth.

"You okay? You look more pale than usual."

Squinting, I lift my head and shield my eyes with my hands, locking gazes with Kaeleb.

"I'm fine, just cold."

I'm also extremely short of breath and might be experiencing a mild heart attack, but I leave that unsaid.

"Okay guys, time to start." A hush blankets the students as Dr. Palmer chucks his clipboard to the ground. "Today is going to be less physical and more of an emotional exercise."

Shit.

"I need you and your partner to sit on the ground in front of one another."

Swallowing, I attempt to calm my erratic breathing, facing Kaeleb and meeting his eyes before slowly descending to the ground. His face remains expressionless as he moves to sit cross-legged on the grass in front of me, scooting closer until our knees are touching.

"Now please take each other's hands. This is a time of trust and connecting with one another."

Fuck. Me.

My eyes close on their own as I timidly reach forward. Every nerve ending tingles when the heat from his hand surges over mine, igniting a spark that spreads throughout my body. It rushes along my arms, leaving behind goose bumps as it passes, causing hairs to stand on end. Kaeleb's hand slides into mine, palm against palm, and his fingers curl themselves, gripping me securely.

"I like to call this the Bubble Exercise. As you hold on to your partner, imagine a bubble containing only the two of you, just you and your partner, safely inside. Nothing can escape into the environment around you. This is your haven to speak freely. There is no judgment inside the bubble, only the release of something about yourself that you want to express. A secret of sorts. You decide who goes first. It is up to you what you choose to reveal to the other."

I clutch Kaeleb's hands like a vise, my eyes shooting open only to find the face directly in front of me giving away nothing—completely emotionless, staring back at me. Palmer claps his hands together, and his voice sends my heart into my throat with his next command.

"Go."

It's then that I pick up on Kaeleb's slight hesitation. His Adam's apple bobs as he swallows before clearing his throat. "Right. Well, I might as well go first since you look like you're about to pass out."

My torso is hunched over my legs, which are crossed in front of me, feet tucked under my thighs. My chest rises and falls as panic streaks through my body at the thought of being forced to reveal even one of my closely kept secrets. Lord knows I have plenty of them.

Still holding on to my hands, he leans forward and doesn't stop until his nose is centimeters away from mine.

"I've got one that covers both of us," he remarks. His eyes glide over my face, stopping when they land on the one mark I wish he'd never seen.

Tightening his grip, he moves forward until his heated cheek is flush with mine and his warm breaths tickle the shell of my ear. I hold my breath; my heart ricochets off the back of my ribcage and I listen as he whispers softly, "I know *your* secret, which in turn has been *my* secret . . . *Bree*."

I jerk back instantly, the pounding in my ears now excruciating. *Bree.*

My fingers involuntarily shoot straight out, releasing me from his hold.

It's too much.

Cold replaces warmth as the blood drains from my face, blackening my vision.

I can't breathe.

Upon the name passing from his lips, my past and present collide, an explosion so fierce it blows the steel door wide open. For the first time in ten years, a Level 4 memory escapes its confines, leaving me spinning out of control as it steals my consciousness.

Chapter 11 ✳

Recollections

"Bwee! Bwee!" My four-year-old baby sister Adley yells from across the house. "I'm cold!"

Even though I'm only two years older than she is, I can do a lot of things she can't. So as I step to the bathroom door, I already know what she wants. Peeking my head inside, I watch her for a couple of minutes, her chubby body floppin' around the bathtub like a fish when it's out of water. Golden ringlets just like mine stick to her face; she giggles when she sees me and pulls them away from her eyes. She really hates that.

I can't help but smile at her. I love her so much.

"Bwee, can you turn on the hot watah? It's cold," she asks. Her light-blue eyes beg, causing crinkles to form on her forehead. I glance over my shoulder to look for Mommy, but I don't see her anywhere.

"Sure," I answer and shrug my shoulders.

The tile on the floor is cold on my feet as I walk to the bathtub and turn the "H" knob until the water flows. We practiced writing "H" last week in school. I'm really good at that one.

Holding my fingers under the water, I shoo her back with my other hand. Once it's run a little, I turn the knob until the flow stops. Hot drops fall, and I watch them closely until there are no more, making sure she doesn't burn herself.

Adley stands up, turns, and places her bare behind on the back edge of the tub, her eyes filled with excitement as she leans back and lets herself go. Water splashes over the side and onto the floor as she flies down her homemade slide.

"Adley, you know what Mommy said. Don't do that or you're gonna hit your head on the bottom." She just giggles and turns over and over in the water, her toys floating as they ride the waves all around her.

She's gonna get in trouble . . . again. But Mommy and Daddy won't stay mad. She usually just does something really cute and then they laugh, forgetting why they were mad at her in the first place. She's so lucky.

Shaking my head, I leave the bathroom and her giggles behind. Mommy is in the living room on the phone, so I go to my room to play. This is the only time I don't have to share my toys with her, and I plan on using every minute.

I pull out my favorite Barbie, the one I hid from Adley last week. Just as I take off her shiny pink dress, I hear Mommy scream. I've heard her scream before when she sees a spider or when she trips over one of our toys, but this . . . this is a different kind of scream.

Dropping the doll to the floor, I hop up and yank my door open, running down the hall as fast as my feet can go. The sound of Mommy and Daddy yelling stops my legs from moving as I pass by the bathroom, and my feet slide across the wood floor, almost coming out from underneath me as I skid to a stop.

The door is barely cracked, so I press my face against the side and look through the opening. I watch Mommy running around the bathroom while Daddy pushes on Adley's chest. He pinches her nose and then blows into her mouth, but nothing happens. Her cheeks puff out, and I can't help but think how much it reminds me of one of those fish that blow up like a balloon.

Blood is on the floor under her head, the red so bright against the white tiles I can't stop staring. Suddenly the door flies open wide, scaring me, and Mommy hits my shoulder as she runs out, but she doesn't say anything. She's crying as she runs to the phone on the couch. After she grabs it, I listen to her screaming and the fear in her voice gives me goose bumps.

"She hit her head . . . Water . . . Not breathing . . ."

I'm so scared. So scared, but I have to help. I'm a big girl. She needs me.

The fog in the air makes it hard to breathe, but I step into the bathroom anyway. My feet slowly make their way to Adley, her naked body jiggling around while Daddy keeps pushing on her chest and blowing air into her mouth. Mommy's voice is still loud in the background, but I can't really focus on anything other than Adley's pretty pink toenails I just painted last night.

Daddy stops and looks at me over his shoulder. His face is red and wet with his tears as he says, "My baby's gone . . . my baby's gone."

He no longer pushes on her chest, but scoops her into his arms and pulls her tightly against him as he cries and screams. Adley's arms hang down, and her hands drag across the tile as Daddy rocks her back and forth, brushing his fingers through her hair like he always does. After one time through, his fingers are coated in blood.

My baby's gone.

My legs lose their strength, and I fall to my knees as Daddy keeps crying and Mommy continues yelling in the living room.

I can't breathe.

After a while, all the noise disappears. I don't hear anything else as my eyes lock onto Adley's, whose chin is resting on Daddy's shoulder, her head moving back and forth with him as he rocks.

Her blue eyes aren't alive and happy anymore.

They're dead.

She's dead.

Daddy stops. He looks through the door and then lets Adley's body go, placing his hand flat on her chest when he lays her on the floor. Her blonde hair is streaked with red and her lips are blue.

My throat is tight as I watch Daddy cover her with a towel before he goes, leaving me alone with her. I try to stand, but I can't, so I just crawl across the floor to my sister, my hands sliding on the wet tiles as I pull my heavy legs behind me.

Using my shaking fingers, I remove the wet pieces of hair from her face. She really hates that.

Once the hair is gone, I can see her eyes, and I finally let myself cry. I cry as I lean over and kiss her forehead. I cry as I kiss her on the cheek. I cry as I give her the last hug I will ever give her. I cry as I pick up her tiny hand, bringing it to my mouth before holding it in mine. I cry as I lay my head on her quiet chest. I cry as I focus on her chubby toes. I cry as I curl my arm around her waist and squeeze her as tightly as I can.

"I'm so sorry, Adley," I whisper through my tears. "I'm so sorry I didn't share my toys with you. I'm so sorry I didn't play with you more. I'm so sorry I always called you a baby. I'm so sorry for telling Mommy that you were the one that drew on the wall."

The words get stuck in my throat, but I swallow and keep on talking just in case she can hear me. I need her to hear me. "I'm so, so sorry I didn't tell you how much I love you every single day. Because I do. I love you so much."

The lump in my throat swells so big it feels like I swallowed a rock, but I keep speaking even though it hurts. I have to.

"But most of all, I'm sorry I didn't watch you in the bathtub. I'm sorry I turned the water on and made it too deep. I'm sorry I didn't make you stop sliding like Mommy said." I hug her tighter. "If it weren't for me, you'd still be here."

My body shakes against hers as I continue to cry.

"I'm so sorry. I'm so sorry . . ."

I hold her and whisper to her until Mommy and Daddy rush into the bathroom with a bunch of people following them. Before I know it, I'm yanked off my sister and into my daddy's arms. I watch as the men do the same thing that Daddy was doing earlier, but I know it won't work.

Adley is gone.

And it's all my fault.

My body shoots up and I gasp for air, surrounded by darkness. I clutch my chest, trying to inflate my lungs, but it feels as though a four-hundred-pound gorilla has been camped there for about a year.

"Aubrey?" The sound of a deep voice reverberates in my mind, barely filtering through the dimness that drowns it.

I can't breathe.

My body quakes everywhere as the loss of my sister still lingers. Ice has replaced the blood in my veins. I'm so cold.

"Aubrey. I'm here." The voice is stronger now. I can hear it more clearly.

Bwee! Bwee!

"Adley!" An unrecognizable shrill fills the air with my screams. "Adley, I'm so sorry!" The pain in my chest tightens with the memory of her lying on the floor, lifeless. With my eyes closed tightly, I cover them and cry, knowing I'm trapped somewhere between the past and the present. My head shakes back and forth as I try to clear my mind and find my way. It's so dark here.

A blanket encompasses my body before two strong hands grip my shoulders, pulling me into even stronger arms. "Shh . . . shh . . . I'm here, sweetheart," the voice coos. "You've got to breathe, babe, or you're going to pass out again."

Eyes still cemented shut, I inhale and a soothing scent washes over me, instantly replacing the bitter coldness with the warmth of familiarity.

Kaeleb.

Through the blanket, I fist his stupid hoodie and pull him as close to me as I can. His hand's warmth sifts through my hair as I hold on to him tightly, breathing him in, until the pressure finally releases. And just like with Quinn, another tiny fracture splits open and the warmth that surrounds me seeps into my cold heart, reigniting the space he had claimed so many years ago.

"I miss her so much, Kaeleb," I mumble into his chest, finding my way back to the present. I watch from afar as the door closes, shutting the past away but not the pain. It's still very much here and alive within me. "It hurts."

"I know it does." Sobs escape me and his arms tighten around my body. "Let it out, Bree. You have to. You need to."

Unable to fight this memory any longer, I have no choice other than letting the emotions flow. Each replay of her lying on the cold floor shreds my chest. The pain is agonizing.

I cry my way through until the memory finally recedes, and there are no tears left, and still my body shakes with silent sobs as Kaeleb continues to hold me.

By the time I'm completely done, I'm sitting in Kaeleb's lap with his arms still around me and his chin upon my head. With my cheek lying against his chest, I listen as the rhythmic beating of his heart draws me dangerously close to sleep.

Through the slits in my eyes, it becomes obvious that I've been taken to an office of sorts. I'm assuming it's an office, based on the diplomas and certificates hanging on the wall, but I haven't read them. I've been focusing on the cracks in the leather couch we've been sitting on and the blanket wrapped around me, offering a small comfort within its warmth.

After a while, I let out a long breath.

"Do you remember her?" I probe, my voice thick.

"Hmm?" Kaeleb's chest vibrates against my cheek.

"Adley. Do you remember her?"

My head rises with his deep breath. "I do."

Finding security as I twist the fringe of the blanket around my index finger, I ask, "Do you remember me?"

His answer is instantaneous. "How could I ever forget you?"

My breath stills with the candor of his statement and guilt floods me, all too aware of how I willingly banned him from my memories long ago.

"When did you know?"

Another inhale. "The first night I saw you in the dorm."

I run through our interactions since that night and immediately want to smack my forehead for being so oblivious. His constant emphasis on the name Raven, the fact that he never once asked me about my family or my past, the stupid skating accident where he took many dishonest liberties while recounting—every one of them so obvious now.

"Why didn't you just tell me? I feel so stupid."

The leather creaks under Kaeleb's weight as he shifts underneath me, nudging me from his chest and curling his fingers over my shoulders. His thumbs dig into my flesh, and his eyes are firm when they lock onto mine. "I couldn't *just* tell you."

He clenches his jaw tightly and shakes his head. "Jesus, Bree . . . I had to keep it to myself until I felt you could handle it. Handle *me*. And you *still* passed out even though it's been months now. Can you imagine if I'd said something to you that first night, without giving you time to know me again?"

Point taken.

"I dropped hints here and there, but when you didn't catch on, I made them more obvious, hoping you would figure it out on your own. But you didn't. Or *wouldn't*. So I decided to tell you. I couldn't keep it inside any longer. It wouldn't be fair to either of us."

I nod slightly, accepting his answer. How can I not? He's absolutely right.

"I knew," I respond through a ragged breath. "When you saw the scar, I knew. Deep down. I didn't want to admit it to myself. It was too much. It's still too much, actually."

Kaeleb releases one of my shoulders and runs his hand through my hair while giving me a soft smile. "Hey . . . you survived me telling you. That's a start." His knuckle grazes my cheek, and he adds, "God, I've missed you. So much."

His arms circle me once again, pulling me into a tight embrace. Hesitantly, I settle my cheek on his shoulder, the whole encounter this morning running through my mind. As I mentally recall his actions and words, a couple of statements jump out at me.

"Did you call me sweetheart?"

Kaeleb's shoulders bob with silent laughter. "I did."

"And babe?"

"As I recall."

This time it's me who pushes away to get a better view of his face. My left eyebrow rises. "Why would you do that?" He continues laughing. "Seriously, Kaeleb. I'm not one of your harem. Don't expect me to follow you around, fanning you with feathers just because you called me some patronizing terms of endearment."

"Okay," he relents, tapping his finger against his chin in thought. "I'm assuming *gorgeous* is off the table?"

I cock my head and give him a deadpan expression, resulting in more of his obnoxious laughter until his lips settle into a thoughtful smile. "What if I call you *Sunshine*? It's not demeaning in the least. And I'll go ahead and keep that one specifically reserved for you, since, you know, you're not part of my *harem* and all." His eyes tighten a fraction when he adds, "I'm officially offended by the way."

My head jerks a little at his suggestion. *Sunshine?* I'm anything but a warm ray of sunshine. I'm dark, dreary, morbid. Definitely *not* sunshine material.

As though reading my mind, Kaeleb offers, "You've always been my sunshine. Ever since we were kids." He tightens his gaze. "I know you're still in there, Bree. And I *will* find you."

As the intensity peaks, he offers me a crooked smile. "You *are* gorgeous by the way." His grin widens as his thumb brushes lightly across the tiny skull pierced into my dimple. "Even though you jacked up your face with all these piercings and dyed the shit out of your hair. Don't even get me started on the contacts."

I narrow my eyes, but I can't fight the smile that breaks across my face as I punch him in the shoulder, his infectious laughter filling the room.

Sigh.

I've missed you too, Kaeleb.

Chapter 12

Sessions

Session 1:
(Two months ago, approximately two and a half seconds after Kaeleb was forced out of Palmer's office)

Palmer: So what happened out there?

Me: (shivers and wraps blanket tighter, noting it still smells like Kaeleb) No idea.

Palmer: I think you do have an idea. What happened?

Me: I had an out of body experience. (*which regretfully, I did*)

Palmer: Is this because Kaeleb referred to you as . . . *Aubrey*?

Me: (grips blanket tighter) What? How did you know about that?

Palmer: (emotionless) I know a lot about you. (sighs) You see, your guardian, Linda, and I are friends, lifelong friends actually, and you taking this course was no accident. She contacted me once you received your acceptance letter, asking me to keep an eye on you. She filled me in on your history as well as your refusal to continue with therapy. She was worried about you making a successful transition, so I suggested the course as a means of monitoring you from afar while here at Titan.

Me: (*sneaky, Linda, real sneaky*) My history? Am I your patient now? What are you anyway?

Palmer: Yes, I am a psychologist if that's what you're thinking. But no, you're not my patient. I no longer practice formal therapy.

Me: So what the hell am I doing here?

Palmer: (leans forward in chair, elbows on knees, fingers interlaced and hanging) Well, if I remember correctly, you passed out on the lawn during the Bubble Exercise. You were brought to my office as a means of recuperation. Mr. McMadden was adamant in his refusal to leave until you came to, so I allowed him to stay while I finished out the remainder of class. When class was over, I came back. You were awake, and now we're here, discussing why you lost consciousness during this particular session of class. (cocks head) How's that?

Me: (*wow, Dr. Palmer is feisty*) It's nothing. I just didn't eat all day, and it was freezing out there. It was too much for my body to handle.

Palmer: Bull.

Me: Bull?

Palmer: Yes, bull. (sighs) Listen, I can't make you tell me anything you aren't comfortable sharing. What I can do is tell you I'm here, every day from twelve o'clock to three, and five o'clock to seven. If you would like someone to talk to, if you *need* someone to talk to, I am here and readily available. No patient bullshit, just here. To listen.

Me: (nods blankly) Um, thanks. (grabs backpack) But I wouldn't plan on it. Things are going well and I'm doing fine.

Palmer: (nods back) Well, if anything changes . . .

Me: It won't. (throws blanket onto the floor and leaves)

Session 2:

(The very next day, 12:00 on the dot)

Me: (knocks)

Palmer: Hello . . . Aubrey. Come in.

Me: (steps in and plops down on couch, grabbing my new favorite blanket and wrapping it around me) Um, so this is just like a venting thing? No prescriptions written, no notes or recordings, none of that jazz?

Palmer: (takes seat across from me, strokes his stark-white beard while eyeing my hold on the blanket) Yes.

Me: (breathes in deeply and also notes how much he looks like Santa Claus in his red sweater) Okay, um, well . . . it's just . . . with Kaeleb knowing who I am, it's becoming more difficult to block things out. Like, certain feelings and thoughts about my past.

Palmer: And who is Kaeleb to you exactly? Linda never mentioned him.

Me: She wouldn't have. She only met him a few times when we were kids. She doesn't even know he's here. (sighs) I guess I figured you knew something though, since we were always assigned together. Either that or because of our last names.

Palmer: (smiles and reclines in his chair) No. I assigned you together because you seemed to trust him more than the others in the class.

Me: Hmm . . . I guess that's true. I knew Kaeleb before my parents died, before I went to live with Linda. We were best friends.

Palmer: Yes, he mentioned the same thing yesterday when I approached him.

Me: (mouth wide open) Then why did you ask?

Palmer: I just wanted your perception of the relationship.

Me: (narrows eyes) Anyway . . . When he used my name yesterday, I remembered something about my sister. And that memory haunted me all night last night and this morning. I used to be able to block out the pain, but I can't seem to push it away this time. I just . . . well, I just wanted to tell someone about it.

Palmer: (nods) Well, I told you I was available. I'm glad you decided to take me up on my offer.

Me: (shrugs shoulders)

Palmer: And what about Kaeleb? Do you also trust him enough to discuss your past? To let him into that part of your life?

Me: Yes, he was there. It's not like he doesn't know what happened . . . to *them*.

Palmer: Well, it seems to me that Kaeleb has triggered something within you that refuses to let you escape the past any longer. Perhaps it's time to allow yourself to experience the pain of your family's deaths and come to terms with them. Perhaps you need to let go of *Raven*, and reacquaint yourself with *Aubrey*. With who you really are.

Me: No, I can't. That's not a possibility.

Palmer: Why is that? What's wrong with Aubrey?

Me: Aubrey is dead.

Palmer: (nods) I see. And Raven?

Me: (twists fringe on the blanket around finger) Raven saved me. Saved many people actually. (looks Palmer directly in the eyes) Aubrey caused death. Raven prevents it.

Palmer: How so?

Me: As long as I'm Raven, I'm labeled a freak. People typically won't get within a five-foot radius of me. I have no relationships; therefore, I can't cause any more death.

Palmer: (inhales and exhales) What about Kaeleb?

Me: I tried to keep him away. (chin quivers) And Quinn too. My roommate.

Palmer: I see. (sighs) Humans by nature are social creatures, Aubrey. Relationships are needed to sustain life and happiness. Perhaps your inability to avoid Kaeleb and Quinn is merely your inherent need for human interaction.

Me: I guess. Or *perhaps* Kaeleb and Quinn just wore me down until I had no choice other than to let them into my morbid existence.

Palmer: (chuckles) Perhaps.

Me: So . . .

Palmer: So . . . back to why you're here. (clears throat) These feelings you're experiencing, which you're unable to repress, I think it's time to acknowledge them. Life is about balance, Aubrey. You have moments in your life that have been too painful for you to mentally accept and overcome, so you block them for your own protection, but there is so much that you also suppress along with them. Life, love, relationships, happiness . . . these are all things that can counter the negative, making the pain bearable, and I think once you find that balance, you will be able to cope with your past.

Me: (swallows) This is starting to feel dangerously like a therapy session.

Palmer: No. That's just my advice as your friend. Take it or leave it.

Me: Friend?

Palmer: Yes, imagine that. Three new friends all in a matter of months. There may be hope for you yet, my dear.

Me: (smiles) Maybe. But don't count on it.

Palmer: (laughs)

Session 12:

(One month ago)

Palmer: Thank you for trusting me with the actual story of your sister's passing. I know that was difficult for you.

Me: (wipes tears and pulls blanket tighter around shoulders) It was. It's still painful, though. It physically hurts to talk about it.

Palmer: Which is to be expected. The wound is still very raw, but the more you acknowledge the memory and discuss it, you will find the experience to be less trying. Now let's balance.

Me: (clears throat) Well, um, she was very beautiful. Angelic almost with her huge blue eyes and her golden-blonde hair. She was filled with so much life. It encapsulated her. And energy . . . God, I used to laugh so hard at her. She would always shake her tiny bottom in my face and giggle. Her laughter. Her giggles. They were absolutely contagious. (smiles widely) Still are evidently.

Palmer: (grins back) Yes, it seems they are. How do you feel now? Talking about her in a more positive light?

Me: (inhales) Better.

Palmer: Good. Let's try diving into uncharted territory. Your mother. Her death. Do you think you can discuss it?

Me: Not sure, I'll try though. (exhales) Um, she died, obviously.

Palmer: (expressionless)

Me: My father said she died of a broken heart. Not too long after Adley. I didn't see her much after that because she locked herself in their room and wouldn't come out for days at a time. She refused to eat. She wouldn't talk to me or my father. She just ceased to exist until one day she just . . . didn't.

Palmer: (inhales and exhales deeply) And your feelings about that?

Me: (shrugs shoulders) It hurts, you know? That she chose that path, that I wasn't enough for her to want to live. But in essence, I was the reason Adley died, so I guess I can see why. And I guess you can say that I'm the reason my mother died as well.

Palmer: (shakes head) You were *not* the reason Adley died. Accidents happen. This one, unfortunately, ended in a regrettable way, but they do happen. There were many other factors involved. Your parents, for instance, should have been watching her. You were six years old, Aubrey. That responsibility was not yours to bear. And like you already stated, your mother's death was her choice. Hers. Neither were your fault. You need to come to terms with that and accept it, or we will never be able to get you past this atypical fear of death.

Me: (sighs loudly) Well, I guess we'll just have to agree to disagree on that.

Palmer: (growls) Okay. For now. (steeples his fingers) Can we move into your father's death then?

Me: No.

Palmer: (eyebrows raise) No?

Me: No.

Palmer: Do you know when you will be comfortable discussing his passing?

Me: Never.

Session 23:

(Two days ago, right after final exams)

Palmer: Your hair is lighter today. And the brown contacts could actually pass for normal. It's a good look for you.

Me: (fingers bottom of hair)Yeah. I just wanted to try something different.

Palmer: (fails miserably at hiding his grin) So how did your exams go?

Me: They went well, I think.

Palmer: Your coursework . . . not easy classes. Why did you choose them?

Me: Honestly?

Palmer: (nods)

Me: Well, I've always excelled in the sciences, so the courses just seemed the obvious choices.

Palmer: (cocks eyebrow)

Me: (sighs) And the fact that I wouldn't have to work with other people, or depend on their participation in stupid projects, definitely was part of the reason I chose them.

Palmer: I see. Well, have you thought about going pre-med? You undoubtedly will have the core curricula to continue down that path.

Me: (flashes palms) Whoa there, Doc. One step at a time. I'm just trying to survive my freshman year.

Palmer: (chuckles) Which you are successfully managing to do. And Kaeleb and Quinn? How are they faring?

Me: (rolls eyes) Kaeleb is annoying. He's been whistling "You Are My Sunshine" when he sees me. Has been for months now. Even in front of his girlfriend of the week. She hates it. And Quinn continues to be oblivious to my history with Kaeleb. (bites bottom lip) She's still not eating very much, and under Sabrina's influence, it's becoming less and less while her marathon miles continue stacking up. I'm worried about her.

Palmer: (grunts) I can see why. (leans forward) Are you still considering telling her about you and Kaeleb? Your *history*, as you call it?

Me: (nods) Yes. Every time she calls me Raven, I cringe. And Kaeleb snickers. Which is annoying enough to push me over the edge. (nods again) Soon. We will tell her soon. I think I'm at the point where I can discuss certain aspects about my past with her that I couldn't before.

Palmer: Excellent. I think that's a very large step in the right direction.

Me: (smiles)

Palmer: Will you allow her to call you Aubrey? Or will you maintain Raven as your identity?

Me: Um, I'm not sure yet. Raven is a part of me, but I'm learning to accept that Aubrey is a part of me, too. Am I ready to become Aubrey? No, not fully. But I think using my birth name may help get me to that point eventually, right?

Palmer: Yes, I think so. The more association you have with that part of your life, the more it will help you cope with your fear of death and to move forward. In doing that, you will eventually be able to combine Raven and Aubrey. You have to remember that you are not either/or but comprised of both entities.

Me: (nods)

Palmer: (smiles) Good. So . . . you heading home over winter break?

Me: Yes, I can't wait to see Linda, actually. I miss her.

Palmer: I'm sure she misses you too. I know she will be glad to see you.

Me: Well, that remains to be seen.

Palmer: (stands) Will I see you after the break?

Me: (stands) Of course, Doc. I love our chats. (punches him in the arm)

Palmer: (laughs) Well, I guess we'll be seeing each other soon then.

Me: Yes, sir. (smiles shyly) Um, thanks, you know, for taking the time to talk to me. To help me.

Palmer: (places hand on my shoulder) You're very welcome. We can continue next semester working through anything else we come across. But you really should be thanking yourself. You're doing all the hard work. (squeezes shoulder) I'm proud of you, kiddo.

Me: (blushes) Okay, well, see you mid-January then.

Palmer: I look forward to it.

Me: (reflects internally) Me too, Doc.

Chapter 13 ✳

Bonds

Closing my suitcase, I quickly zip it shut, slide it off my bed until it hits the floor with a thud, and lug it in front of my closet. I'm surprised with the feeling of nervous excitement thrumming through my stomach.

"You packed and ready?" Quinn asks from behind me.

"Yeah, I think so. You?"

"Yep." A pink (of course) suitcase slides its way right next to mine. I can't help but grin. The girl loves her pink.

I turn to face her, the smile still present on my face. "Good."

My phone buzzes, causing me to jump and pull it out of my jacket. After reading the message, I quickly stuff it back in my pocket. "Kaeleb's on his way up."

Quinn laughs. "That boy never has any trouble breaking into the girls' dorm, does he?"

"Except that one time." I giggle. "Remember? When he got caught in Amanda's room? I've never seen him move so fast."

Quinn's eyes light up at the memory. "Well, he was wearing those ridiculous Hulk boxers, and they helped with the speed factor, I'm sure."

"Idiot." I shake my head as I watch her go into the bathroom. Kaeleb's made no secret about his reasoning behind the *Hulk* boxers, offering the implication that there's something *superhuman* hidden inside them that grows exponentially in strength and girth when stimulated. Ridiculous doesn't even come close to describing it—or his delusions.

A knock at the door saves me from all thoughts of Kaeleb's, um, *superpowers.*

Snapping out of it, I open the door. Kaeleb's eyes are bright with excitement as he shakes the snow from his unkempt, yet extremely sexy, hair before sliding out of his bomber jacket and throwing it onto my desk chair.

He has a mischievous smile when he turns to face me, and he appraises my appearance from head to toe before whispering in my ear, "I like the hair. And the eyes. Brown suits you."

My heart picks up, racing steadily as his cheek brushes against mine. "Next thing you know, I'll be seeing you in something other than your standard Doc/Dickies/concert tee uniform. I'm looking *very* forward to that."

Idiot.

My eyes roll into the back of my head and I push him away, his silent laughter only making me more annoyed. "Save the wooing for Trixie."

His eyebrows shoot up and the smile on his face broadens. "Tracie?"

"Whatever," I scoff. "Does it really matter? I'm sure there will be a new victim falling for your pathetic pickup lines by next week. I stopped trying to remember their names months ago." I throw in an evil glare to further drive my point.

"Hmm, interesting." He chuckles, rubbing his hand along his jaw. "I wouldn't have pegged you for the jealous type."

"You won't be pegging me at all. Ever."

Kaeleb throws his head back in laughter, then lowers his eyes and locks them onto mine.

After inching his face closer, his breaths hit my mouth as his wide smile falls into an arrogant grin. "Never say never, Sunshine."

I narrow my eyes more but feel my annoyance start to crack. I don't know how he does it; it's impossible to stay angry at the man. Within seconds he manages to simultaneously infuriate me, challenge me, and humor me as I fight back the laughter. The scary thing is that, over the last couple months, I find myself enjoying it. Craving it actually, but of course, I don't tell him that. I just knock him in the shoulder.

"Can we stay on track here?" I growl under my breath as Quinn makes her way out of the bathroom. She eyes our closeness with curiosity, which is the exact reason we're having this meeting.

Kaeleb and I have decided that it is finally time to tell Quinn the full story behind our relationship. After my last meeting with Palmer, I realized it wasn't fair to keep her in the dark any longer. So we made the decision to enlighten her. Together.

But now that the time has come, my throat becomes parched and thick, and my previous excitement transforms into anxiety, churning in my stomach. There's an obvious tension shift in the room, which I'm sure is completely my fault because as I look at Kaeleb, still grinning, and then to Quinn, still surveying both of us, I realize mine is the only mood that has drastically changed. A warm hand soon envelops mine and gives it a light squeeze. I guess Kaeleb senses it too. Quinn's eyes widen, brimming with unspoken excitement at the sight of his gesture.

And with that, I decide it's time to just get this over with.

"Um, yeah," I sputter. "There's . . . uh . . . something we need to tell you, Quinn."

Kaeleb starts whistling "You Are My Sunshine" next to me, and I elbow him in the ribs. He grunts but covers it with laughter while I motion for Quinn to sit on her bed. Shooting him a sideways glare, he nods and blanks his expression. He jerks his chin in Quinn's direction, and I release his hand and head to my own bed, taking a seat across from her. Kaeleb grabs Quinn's desk chair and spins it around. He straddles it, elbows down and fingers curled over the top. After setting his chin on his knuckles, he sits calmly, waiting for the event to unfold.

Clearing my throat, I turn my attention back to Quinn, whose green eyes are wider as she gasps and covers her mouth. "You guys are dating, aren't you?"

Kaeleb snickers, but I keep my eyes on Quinn. "No, we're not *dating*." She drops her hands and her mouth curves toward the floor. "*But*," I add and watch as her eyes light back up, "we *do* have a relationship of sorts." I quickly raise my hand and point to her before she gets the wrong idea. "Don't get too excited, it's *nothing* really."

"Damn, Bree. That hurts." Kaeleb clutches his chest, and I roll my eyes.

"Bree? Who's *Bree*?" Quinn asks. I tighten a glare at Kaeleb, who's given up on the whole not-smiling thing, before turning back to Quinn.

I give her a shy grin and shrug my shoulders. "Me. My name is Aubrey. Not Raven." The statement shocks my system. Although I'm working through it, the sound of *Aubrey* passing from my lips still sends a startling blow throughout my body. But as Palmer said, I guess that's part of the process.

"What?" Her expression morphs slowly from excitement, to uncertainty, to realization, before finally landing on disappointment. "Why didn't you tell me? I asked you months ago about your name. Did you not . . . *trust* me?" Hurt spools off her and slams into my chest, prompting me to rise from my seat and settle next to her.

Shaking my head, my tone is emphatic. "No. Nothing like that, Quinn. I trust you implicitly, which is why I am able to tell you this now. At the time, I wasn't able to discuss certain aspects about my past, but over the last couple months, I've been learning how to handle it. As soon as I realized I was ready, I told Kaeleb it was time to tell you."

I take her hand into mine. "No secrets between us. *Any* of us, anymore. I promise." Kaeleb nods and Quinn's face softens.

Looking down at our joined hands, she squeezes softly before stating, "Okay, I believe you." Her eyes meet mine. "Now spill."

I begin by telling her about knowing Kaeleb as a child and how I was forced to leave after the death of my parents, never thinking I would see him again. I speak freely for the first time about the creation of Raven and the death of Aubrey. Kaeleb takes over and explains how he knew it was me the first night we met and continues until my unconscious exit from the Elements of Trust class. I end the discussion with an explanation about my meetings with Palmer and our nontherapy sessions, bringing her into the present. When we're done, she looks at both of us, first Kaeleb and then me, with tears in her eyes.

Then she breaks into an enormous smile. "You guys are gonna get married, I just know it."

Stunned, I drop her hand, and Kaeleb falls forward from his balancing act, sending the front legs of the chair crashing to the floor.

"Quinn, no, we're just *friends*. That's all," I warn, tearing my stare from Kaeleb. I'm kind of insulted actually by the melodramatic display.

My eyebrows slam together, but I let the offense go for now because I know that dreamy, love-struck look on Quinn's face. I see it every time Josh picks her up for a date. My dear friend is, and always will be, a true romantic at heart, but this? Well, this is definitely not *that*.

But she's relentless once she gets something in her head. "If you say so," she sings, her full grin still in effect.

Kaeleb barks a laugh, and I shoot him another dirty look. Is it really that ludicrous of a notion? And didn't he just proposition me like two seconds ago?

Idiot.

Quinn's smile fades. "Seriously, thank you for trusting me with that . . . *Aubrey*." The tone in her voice is uncertain as she speaks the name, but before I can give it too much thought, she walks past Kaeleb, not stopping until she's in front of her desk. We both watch her as she stands there, deliberating for some time before glancing over her shoulder. "Since there are no more secrets, I would like to share something with you as well."

My heart thuds because I know what she's doing before she even opens the drawer. I glance at Kaeleb, who's eyeing her with interest as she turns with the envelope in her hand, and he continues to do so until she dumps the photos on the bed.

Kaeleb stands next. The legs of the chair screech along the floor as he pushes it aside and braves his way to the edge of her pink comforter. Jaw clenched tightly, he spreads the pictures across the bed. "Quinn . . ." he breathes.

Her chin quivers. She wipes a tear just as Kaeleb puts his arm around her and pulls her into his frame. He sets his chin on her head, and she loops her arms around his waist before she speaks.

"My parents sent me to fat camp five summers in a row, starting when I was in fourth grade. Being overweight was unacceptable in my house." I swallow the lump in my throat when another tear rolls down her cheek. "After the final summer, when I was able to finally lose the weight, my mother started putting me in pageants to make sure I stayed that way. She was always monitoring my calorie intake, making me get up an hour early to run. I started taking diuretics and laxatives, anything I could do to get the food out of my system."

She tears her gaze from the photos to look at me. "I *hate* the girl in those pictures. But no matter how hard I try, she's still there, in the mirror looking back at me or squatting inside my head. Taunting me. Whispering." She breathes in deeply. "Size zero or size sixteen, she's always there." Kaeleb squeezes her tighter, and she buries her head in his chest. "I hate her."

My heart breaks for her because I know that hate. It's possible that a hatred so strong and so tangible will eventually take over her life, and there will be nothing I can do to help her. Except . . . "Palmer. Why don't you talk to Palmer? I mean, it's just a thought," I offer.

Resting her cheek against Kaeleb, she gives me a weak smile. "Maybe."

I release a defeated breath because the look in her eyes tells me she won't be calling on Palmer anytime soon.

Kaeleb picks up on her hesitation as well. "Quinn, you should give it a try. I mean, look at Aubrey. She could pass for almost normal now. Evidently he's a miracle worker."

Quinn laughs and Kaeleb just smiles, pleased with her reaction. I let his snarky comment slide, because I figure that's what he was going for.

After wiping her face, she releases him and steps away, giggling. "True."

My lips purse, and I cross my arms, sending them into more laughter.

Once their antics die down, Kaeleb takes a deep breath. "Well, since we're under the sharing tree, I guess it's my turn."

Stunned, Quinn and I look at each other before directing our stares at him. "Don't look so surprised, ladies." He chuckles before locking eyes with me. "There's an actual reason I'm in the Elements of Trust course with you, Bree."

I frown, dumbfounded. The idea of him having *any* problems comes as a complete shock to me. He maintains my stare, his expression no longer playful and lighthearted, but now tinged with unmistakable regret.

He dips his head. "I lost my *own* parents when I was fifteen." Blood rushes to my face and my heart hammers with his admission. Kaeleb lifts his hand to pause my reaction. "But not how you're thinking."

He barely speaks above a whisper as he continues. "My sister was a really good swimmer. Very competitive. At only thirteen years old, her times rivaled some of the high school girls', and some even called her a swimming prodigy." A breath catches in my throat. His sister. I can't believe I'd forgotten about Katie. She was the same age as Adley.

He covers his face, his fingers and thumb digging into his eyes to clear the moisture pooling within them. His chin continues to tremble long after he drops his hand. "But she was never good *enough*, you know? My parents constantly pushed her. They made her practice after hours, swimming endlessly day in and day out. Every lap in the pool had to be faster than the last."

Quinn clears her own tears, her bloodshot stare remaining on Kaeleb as he speaks. "I tried to get them to ease up, you know? Because what they were doing was killing her. Mentally, physically, emotionally . . ."

My lips quiver with the feebleness in his tone. "I fought them, I screamed at them, I warned them, until they finally ended up kicking me out of their house. Sent me to live with my grandparents and never looked back."

His reddened eyes fall to the floor. "She had a complete mental breakdown one year later. Had to be hospitalized."

A gasp escapes me, and I cover my mouth. Kaeleb simply shrugs his shoulders. "It was about six months before she was released. She stayed with me and my grandparents for a while but eventually moved back in with my parents. I, however, haven't spoken to them since."

He looks at Quinn. "So I understand never being accepted by your parents and never being good enough. I fucking watched it happen. Right in front of me. *To* me."

Wild eyes find mine, his face flushed with anger. I can tell by his clenched fists he's trying to maintain his control, but it's useless. His voice rises in volume. "I was her big brother for Christ's sake and I couldn't do shit for her." His arms fly into the air and Quinn breaks into sobs.

Kaeleb leashes his sorrow, collecting himself before continuing, "Some would say I really haven't dealt with that anger. That I haven't forgiven myself for leaving her with *them*. Some might even say I use women to help alleviate some of that guilt, to take some of the hurt away and forget, even if it's only for a night. But regardless of what I do, the pain always remains."

I nod because I know this pain. We all do. And in this moment we become forever bonded by it.

Quinn steps back into his embrace. I walk over to where they stand and wrap my arms around both of them. We hold onto one another closely, silently reflecting on our own sordid pasts. Each of us lost in our own darkness, trying to find our way to a lighter place.

We stay like that for a long while, until sniffles subside and breathing returns to normal.

Kaeleb eventually clears his throat. "Well, I guess *sharing time* is over?"

Quinn and I give each other a small smile before releasing our hold, breaking our circle. As we step away, I dry my face while Kaeleb and Quinn do the same.

Once we're composed, I look at Kaeleb, who's slinging his jacket over his shoulder, obviously *very* done with sharing time. "Kaeleb?"

"Hmm?" he hums.

"Um, *you* might want to talk to Palmer. You know, before your dick falls off." Quinn snorts from behind me, and I can't help but grin.

He returns my smile and adds a wink. "Sunshine, I always protect the *Hulk*. No need to worry about that." Shaking my head, I watch him stride to our door. Just as his fingers touch the knob, he turns and with solemn eyes offers, "You'd be the exception, you know. With you, it would be real, not an escape."

I continue to eye him, struck silent as he pivots around and leaves the room, quietly shutting the door behind him.

Slowly, I turn back to Quinn, only to find her donning a wide, knowing grin.

"See?" She giggles. "You two are totally getting married."

Sigh.

My poor, dear friend.

Quinn bounces away, skipping happily as she heads into the bathroom. Once the door shuts, I move to my bed and sit on the very edge. As I wait for Linda, a new excitement builds.

Maybe it's the fact that I'm about to see her after months of not realizing how much I've missed her.

Maybe it's the moment I just shared with my two best friends, a moment I know has officially solidified our three-way bond into a lifelong promise.

Or maybe, just maybe, it's the fact that Kaeleb's parting words have ignited something in me that I never knew existed. Or wanted.

Regardless, I know that my life has forever been altered, and for the first time in ten years, I've finally found a new path.

One that isn't completely saturated with darkness and fear, but dimly lit with newfound courage and optimism.

And as I cautiously take that first step, a splinter of hope ignites in my heart.

Chapter 14

Freshman Firsts

The rest of my freshman year happened so quickly, it's hard to list everything of importance. But that being said, there were many moments that happened that will forever stay etched in my mind. So many firsts that should be noted:

The first time I laughed so hard I nearly peed my pants. There's just something about trying to remain quiet in the library that fuels the need for an outlandish fit of laughter. Kaeleb and Quinn were absolutely no help.

The first time I got drunk, unabashedly, in the company of my friends.

The first time I attempted The Robot, which unsurprisingly accompanied the above listed first.

The first time I gave in and ate my first burger in months. Best. Burger. Ever. Definitely wasn't the last.

The first time Kaeleb lasted a whole week without a lady friend. And then a month. And then the rest of freshman year. I'm pretty sure he had a raging case of blue balls.

The first time that Quinn allowed herself the simple freedom of eating a piece of chocolate cake at an impromptu celebration for Kaeleb's nineteenth birthday. We cheered her on in the privacy of the corner booth of a local restaurant.

The first (and only) time that I took the Leap of Faith in Palmer's trust class. Plunging to my possible death from three stories in the air once was enough for me, thank you very much. Kaeleb, however, did it twice.

The first time I ever achieved the Dean's List, and with a solid three point nine GPA.

The first time I skated, actually skated, at the infamous death trap known as Skate Place. I fell a lot, of course, but Kaeleb was there to help. No chins were busted this time around in case you're wondering.

The first time that I allowed Kaeleb to hold my hand for longer than a second. But he kind of had to. Again, please see above listed first.

But most importantly, there were a string of firsts that served to remind me of how far I came my freshman year. Remembering my first day at Titan, there's an insurmountable amount of pride that I found the strength within myself to giggle with my peers, walk arm in arm with my best friend and hand in hand with the *possible* love of my life, and just allow a contented smile to cross my face.

Sophomore Year

Chapter 15

Transformations

"Hmm . . ." Quinn hums.

"Err . . ." Kaeleb sputters.

I, however, have no riveting commentary to offer as we all congregate in my bathroom with our heads angled in the same direction, staring at my reflection in the mirror. Kaeleb and Quinn sit opposite each other on the countertop. I'm right in between them on a barstool.

It's almost October, and classes started about a month ago, right after Quinn and I settled into our very first apartment. Linda wasn't too keen in the beginning, but after spending the summer together, I was able to eventually sell her on the fact that I was ready. Ready to be off campus and living with my best friend, with no RA, or curfews, or *rules* for that matter. I could understand her hesitation, but I also knew she could see how much I had changed during my freshman year.

The summer with her was, well, the absolute best summer of my life. We laughed until we cried, we visited every single amusement park within a three-hundred-mile radius, we watched sappy movies and sighed as girls often do, and we went camping in the rugged outdoors. I even squealed like a girl when she presented me with my very own car, and the look on her face was one of pride and pure joy when she handed over the keys—it's a moment I never want to forget.

Actually, the whole summer was full of those moments. I never knew how much I adored her until I was finally brave enough to accept her into my heart. And honestly, I'm proud of that. I'm proud of myself. I don't think I could love any person more than I do her.

Well, except the two goofballs still staring at me in the mirror.

"It's not that bad, guys," I sulk, setting my hair dryer on the counter.

"It's unfortunate is what it is," Kaeleb deadpans while Quinn stifles a giggle.

"It's definitely *not brown* now," she adds, hopping to the floor.

I decided today to step away from my brown dye job and try something different. While I'm not quite ready to see myself as a blonde, I wanted something, something less gloomy, so red with my go-to electric-blue streaks is what I tried. When the color didn't take the first time, I bleached it and tried it again with a more intense hue. The result? Cinnamon-colored hair with blue streaks.

Well, it could be worse.

Maybe.

"I'm thinking I should call you Rainbow Brite instead of Sunshine until this situation," Kaeleb circles his hand around my head, "sorts itself out."

"Shut up, ass. Besides, Rainbow Brite had blonde hair."

"As do you," he replies, a cocky grin on his face.

Rolling my eyes, I shove his shoulder, almost knocking him off the counter. He chuckles and repositions himself closer to the mirror.

"You know what would make it better?" Quinn asks, fingering through my hair, fluffing it and fanning it across my shoulders. "I mean, you don't have to, but it would tie in with the blue if you," she shoots a timid glance to Kaeleb before looking back to my reflection, "took out your contacts."

I caved last year and told her my natural hair and eye color, and there isn't a day that goes by that she doesn't mention one of them.

Threading a section of hair between my fingers, I flip it up for examination, finding myself surprised that I'm actually considering this option. The black box sitting on my counter catches my eye, and I glance at my face in the mirror.

One month ago, I removed every one of my piercings. Every single one. No more barbells, no more skull studs in my dimples, no more loops lining the shell of my ear, and no more ring dangling from the septum in my nose. A small hole still remains where it once speared through the skin, but the others seem to be healing nicely and are barely noticeable. My long hair and bangs tend to cover a lot of them anyway.

But removing the contacts? Well, the thought fills me with apprehension. Eyes, they say, are the windows to the soul, and regardless of the progress I've made the last year, there's still a part of me that fears my soul is nothing more than a black shadow lurking inside, ready to strike down and devour those who mean the most to me.

In my own warped mind, I fear their removal will only serve to open the doorway, releasing death and allowing it to run rampant, once again giving it free rein over my life while endangering the lives of others.

"Death just is, *Aubrey. In Raven, you seek to control something that is not meant, or able, to be controlled. And in doing so, you are harnessing your own life. Forbidding yourself the full experience of it."*

Palmer's words race through my mind, and I'm reminded of the vow I made to myself at the end of last year.

I will not let the fear of death rule my life any longer.

Glancing up, my eyes find Quinn in the mirror, nibbling her bottom lip and bouncing nervously off the floor, then slide over to Kaeleb, still sitting on the counter as he looks at me. His knee is propped up, his arm draped across it casually, but his eyes are watching me intensely. Our stares lock as he dips his head in my direction, scrutinizing me. His face is full of determination; it's a couple seconds before I can tear my gaze away from his and focus on my reflection.

I pause, take a deep breath, and exhale forcefully. My hand trembles as I bring it to my right eye. Using my thumb and forefinger, I pinch the surface of the contact and slowly extract it. After blinking a couple of times, I open both eyes and stare. Quinn covers her mouth behind me and Kaeleb grins like it's Christmas.

One blue eye, one brown.

One down, one to go.

Still shaking, I perform the same ritual with the left eye. Once the contacts are removed, I set them on the counter and take a step back. The chair moves along with me, and Quinn steps around it, taking her place by my side.

"They're beautiful, Aubrey. Just like a clear blue sky." A smile forms as I meekly accept her compliment. "And they go much better with the hair." She giggles.

Placing her hands on my shoulders, she turns me to face her. Her eyes rake over my entire appearance before she nods her head. "It suits you. Raven suited *Raven*, but this suits *you*, the person you are becoming."

And then she blows me away by pulling my body into her tiny frame, embracing me. "I'm so proud of you." She jostles me with a monstrous hug before releasing me from her hold. Stepping back, her eyes drift to mine once again before looking over my shoulder. Her smile broadens and she clears her throat. "I, um . . . I'm gonna go call Josh and see if we're still on for tonight."

Before I can say anything, she disappears from the bathroom, shutting the door behind her and leaving me alone with Kaeleb. Once she's gone, an electric current charges the air, and soon after, his presence warms the back of my neck. My heart pounds, my hands get clammy, and my throat dries as I stand with my back to him, deathly afraid to turn around.

What if he sees only darkness when he looks into my eyes?

What if he sees what I fear most?

"Turn around, Sunshine. Let me see you." My heart anxiously ricochets in my chest. Panic sets in, and my legs suddenly feel as though they weigh one hundred pounds each. I start to shake my head to tell him I can't do it, when his fingers graze the base of my neck as he slides my hair onto the opposite shoulder.

Leaning forward, he breathes into my ear, "Bree. Please."

I tremble, having his body so close to mine, shaking loose the iron shackles weighing down my feet. Hesitantly, I turn until I face him, and he takes a step back, giving me room to breathe.

Not that I'm breathing.

In fact, as our eyes meet, the moment is so intense there are no breaths between us. His pained expression is pleading as his stare roots into mine, searching desperately for the girl he once knew. Tears brim my lower lashes, and my throat tightens painfully while he continues his pursuit, knowing that my ultimate fear has come true. What he's looking for no longer exists.

Just as I'm about to break contact, he cups my face gently, and his lips lift into a full smile. His features soften as he strokes a falling tear from my cheek, releasing a light breath before he speaks. "There you are."

Kaeleb lowers his chin and his heated breaths fan my face as he whispers, "Now that I've found you, I'm going to do something I've wanted to do since I was eight." He quickly closes the distance between us, brushing his warm lips gently across mine, and the pure tenderness of the kiss sends my heart soaring. There is no gloom, no fear, no anguish . . . only joy fluttering from my heart, taking flight, rising out of the darkness and into the light. Strength and vitality flood my being as his lips continue to deliver the breath of life into my very soul.

As I meld into him, his hand lowers and joins the other one underneath my thighs, and I'm suddenly whisked onto the countertop. Once I land, he breaks the kiss with a smile, but keeps his forehead against mine. He moves between my legs and slides his hands up my arms, curling his fingers around the nape of my neck, stroking his thumbs just beneath my jawline.

"And I've wanted to do *this* since I was eight . . . *teen* . . ."

Tightening his hold, his tongue darts over his lips before he brings them to mine, deepening the kiss. As my lips part, his tongue slides past them ever so gently. My head tilts on its own accord, and my body goes limp as I sink into his hold, allowing his strength to keep me upright.

I have no idea what I'm doing. I've never been kissed like this before. Sad, I know, but when you spend a lifetime fending off any type of personal connection, this is what you end up being: a nineteen-year-old, never-been-kissed virgin with deep-rooted issues.

But luckily, Kaeleb seems to have mastered the art of *the perfect kiss*, so I just let him take control.

With our mouths fused, his tongue softly caresses mine as though it's the most natural thing in the world. It's not forced, it's not hurried, it's not aggressive; it's just . . . *perfect*. His fresh scent invades my senses, and I take every bit of it in, allowing the comfort of its familiarity to bind me to him. A sigh passes through my lips, the emotion bubbling within me forcing its escape. Kaeleb chuckles under his breath and pulls back, ending the kiss with a light peck on the lips.

Timidly, I reach up and run my fingertips over my mouth, the remnants of his warmth fading as my eyes slowly drift to his. I can't imagine what my face looks like, but I have a feeling it's an impressive mixture of absolute bliss and utter bewilderment.

Kaeleb's expression is steadfast, until he smiles and leans the palms of his hands against the edge of the countertop. "And so the wooing begins."

A familiar giggle from just outside the door causes me to jump and Kaeleb to press himself off the counter. Giving me a wink, he turns and grabs the knob, whipping it open to expose the wide-eyed guilty offender. Quinn remains planted as Kaeleb leans in and kisses the top of her head then heads to the front door.

"Call ya later, Rainbow Brite," he shouts before the door shuts behind him.

Quinn's eyes are huge, but she manages to cover her smile when I shake my head and tighten my gaze at her. I know she wants to say it. She's probably foaming at the mouth behind that hand of hers.

But there will be no mention of any marriage today.

There will only be me, in this moment, as I shut myself in the bathroom alone and relive my very first kiss.

A kiss that will forever alter my life and revive my soul.

Chapter 16
Tears

The wooing (if that's what you want to call it) began later that same night via text:

> KAELEB: 1651 Vinebrook. You can leave Starlight at home. I'm picking you up at 7:00.
>
> ME: Um, you know the name of Rainbow Brite's horse? Really? :/
>
> K: I possess an ungodly amount of random knowledge. Be impressed. ;)
>
> ME: I'm not impressed. I'm concerned.
>
> K: As you should be.
>
> ME: Where are you taking me btw?
>
> K: Not telling. You're going to have to leave Rainbow Land and the sprites for a bit though. Be sure to leave them food and water.
>
> ME: You realize I can google the address, right?
>
> ME: And really? :/
>
> K: You seem to know a lot about Ms. Brite yourself.
>
> ME: Shut up.
>
> K: ;) See ya at 7.

Our first date . . . well, it was typical. Kaeleb asked that I wear anything but my usual attire, so I happily answered the door in my Docs and my baggy, olive-green cargo pants, along with my favorite Minipop concert hoodie. He just grinned and shook his head, looking as hot as ever with his sexy, lopsided grin, spiked hair, and navy Henley over white T-shirt combo. The bottom of his dark jeans covered his blindingly bright red Nikes, which I made fun of the entire evening.

Our usual banter continued as we ate our pizza, and he filled me in on his life plan. He officially decided to major in kinesiology, working his way into sports medicine or physical therapy. I thought it had something to do with his sister, but he made no such correlation. He seemed content with the decision, which made me smile. I, of course, had nothing to add. After all, I still had no idea where to concentrate my classes. This year is still the basics like Physics, Chem II, Biology II, Microbiology, etc., but I still haven't discovered my direction.

That was the first night we held hands, like *really* held hands, and it was nice. Comfortable.

We walked the streets for a while, our fingers interlaced as we discussed anything and everything. By the end of the night, my face hurt from smiling, and when we ended the date, he gave me a kiss that curled my toes. I've never quite understood the expression, but after that night, I'll never forget the feeling.

It's been a little over a month since our first official date, and for someone who recently reentered my life, I can't picture him ever being out of it. I hope to God I never have to.

Quinn is still going strong with Josh and has recently been quoted as saying he might be "the one" because she "just has a feeling."

Sigh.

I don't see him much, except when he picks her up to take her out. They go out often, and I'm pleased to see her gaining some weight in her blissful state. I can tell it makes her uncomfortable though, by the way she changes a gazillion times because something's "too tight" or "makes her look fat," but she looks better to me. And when she's with him she seems happy, which makes me happy for her.

But now, as she stands on my bed with her feet on either side of my waist, bouncing up and down and singing "Happy Birthday," I find myself wanting to knock her happy ass onto the floor. Pillow over my face, I hold it tightly against my ears, trying to muffle the horrid sound until she unexpectedly yanks it away. My hands shoot up to my face and I roll on my stomach, which earns me a swift swat on the ass.

"God, Aubrey, you're such a freaking vampire." She falls to my side and starts poking her finger in my ear. "Get up. The sun is shining, it's Saturday, and it's YOUR BIRTHDAY." I turn my head in the opposite direction, but she continues with her finger assault.

Slapping at her hand, I groan and slowly rise, stretching once I'm finally upright. My eyes feel as though they're sewn shut, but after a good head shake, I peel them open. They immediately meet Quinn's, full of excitement, and her smile, brighter than the sun.

I squint.

"What are you doing up so early?" I ask, my voice raspy.

"It's your birthday, dummy. I have a whole day planned, and we need to get started. November 2nd only comes once a year, so it's time to par-tay," she says as she performs some ridiculous sashay with her shoulders.

"Stop. Yelling. Please." I scrub my face, assisting in this waking up shenanigan she insists upon. "Besides, we partied last night, remember? Halloween party in apartment 254?"

"Yes, I remember, but like I said, it's a new day. Now get up! We have plans."

"God, Quinn, I will do anything if you just stop screaming. You're like an inch away from my face." The bed jiggles as she hops off, giggling. She leaves the room, but not before poking her head back inside.

"We have an appointment at ten. Get your ass up."

"An appointment? What?" My brain is not working yet this morning.

Silence follows, and I glance at the doorway. My hyperactive roommate has abandoned me in my clouded mental state.

Fine.

As I'm about to force myself out of bed, my phone vibrates on the table next to me. A small grin breaks my muddled expression at the sight of Linda's name.

"Hello."

"Happy birthday, honey! You're officially in your twenties. Can you believe it?"

I pull the phone away until her shrieking stops. Once I hear silence I place it back against my ear.

"Thank you. I'm officially awake."

Her laughter rolls through the line until she releases a sigh.

"Quinn hasn't woken you already? Surprising."

"No, she did. She started the process and you officially ended it. I am now . . . *fully* awake."

More laughter. "Great. Well, enjoy your day. I hear Quinn has a special event planned."

My gaze shifts to the door as Linda exhales deeply, and for the first time since she called, I hear exhaustion in her voice.

"Are you okay? You sound wiped."

Another long breath follows. "Oh, I'm fine. Long shift at the hospital. No biggie."

"Okay. I miss you."

"Aww, I miss you too, honey. Not too long until winter break. I'll see you soon, yes?"

"Yep. Soon."

The shuffling of her sheets lets me know she's finally made her way to bed. "I'm finally going to sleep. I just wanted to call you first thing."

A smile stretches across my face as I repeat something I said for the first time this summer. It just never gets old. "I love you, Linda."

A small sigh hits my ear before she responds, "I love you too, Aubrey."

Once we hang up, my feet hit the floor and I shuffle to the bathroom. Laughing, I recall the Halloween party last night while brushing my teeth. Kaeleb was in full costume as the Hulk, which, unfortunately, lead to several suggestive comments. As for me, I wasn't dressed up *at all*. And Quinn donned a very revealing fairy getup, earning her an early exit with Josh. No wonder she's all bright-eyed and bushy-tailed this morning.

But the main source of my laughter is the fact that Sabrina and Candace showed up scandalously clad in Playboy Bunny costumes, complete with cotton tails, accentuating their lackluster behinds for the entire world to see. Kaeleb overtly suggested a skeleton unitard would have made a much more believable and appealing costume, resulting in a burst of laughter from me and a death glare from the two hungry hares.

I haven't really spoken to either of them since last year's cereal incident, but since Quinn refuses to tell them to go to hell, I've been forced to see them from time to time. I've managed to keep my mouth shut, but Kaeleb . . . *obviously hasn't.*

Grinning, I exit the bathroom dressed in my plaid pajama bottoms and white tank top. As soon as I reach the kitchen island, Quinn turns me in the direction of my room with instructions to not come back until I'm dressed. Trudging away from my morning tormentor, I yell, "It's MY birthday!" and complain about the lack of coffee.

She promises my morning dose of caffeine once I'm dressed and ready.

I get dressed in a matter of seconds and meet her in the living room. She hands me a warm, delicious cup of coffee and a toasted bagel covered in cream cheese.

"Let's go," she says, after shrugging on her jacket and snagging her keys off the entryway table.

"All right, all right," I mutter. Makeup free, I open the door and she bounces through. I don't miss my morning ritual of blackening my eyes, paling my face with powder, and applying my dark lipstick. I haven't missed it for a while, actually.

Reveling in that fact, I smile and head to the car.

Quinn drives to a random parking lot, the car idling quietly as we sit directly in front of . . . *Daybreaks Salon and Spa.*

My eyebrows lift as I meet the gaze of my roommate, who's grinning from ear to ear. "HAPPY BIRTHDAY!"

"What are you doing?" I ask hesitantly.

Amazingly her smile widens even more. "We're getting makeovers today. The full treatment. Manis, pedis, massages, hair, and makeup. Then we're going *out.*"

I glance from the salon and back to her. "Um, I have no money," I state, because it's true. I have like twenty dollars in my bank account, and I won't have any more until Linda makes my monthly deposit next week.

"No worries." She sets my coffee in the cup holder. "It's my birthday present to you."

"Quinn. You don't have—"

She cuts me off with a fierce wave of her hand. "I want to. Plus, what's the use in winning pageants if I don't get to spend the fun money?"

Oh, my reigning Princess Fi-Fi. Who was indeed just crowned Miss Collegiate America.

I eye the salon a while longer before opening my car door. Quinn yips with excitement as she steps out, and before you know it . . . my nails are buffed, filed, and coated with a very light beige nail color that matches my toes; my muscles are limp and soft from the massage; and I'm sitting in Sergio's hair station, who tsks and shakes his head when he sees me.

Not long after his blatant disapproval, he and Quinn are deep in conversation, sporadically pausing only to give me scrutinizing glances, while I sit in the chair feeling like a science experiment. Once they finish their assessment, they both smile and nod in agreement, and I'm turned away from the mirror. Sergio coats my hair with some god-awful smelling colorant while lining several sections with foil packets.

Quinn is captivated by some celebrity magazine, so I make use of my time by texting Kaeleb.

ME: Help. Me.

KAELEB: LOL What's up, Sunshine?

ME: Quinn kidnapped me for my birthday and my hair is being accosted by a very hot gay man.

K: Birthday? It's your birthday?

ME: Shut up. You know it's my birthday.

K: How could I forget? ;) Happy Birthday. I wanted to let you sleep in or I would have called you earlier.

ME: There's no sleeping in with Quinn Matthews having access to my room.

K: I also have access to your room. Although my waking you up would have been much hotter than Quinn's. Unless . . .

ME: You're such a dude.

K: That I am.

κ: Shit. So does this mean no more Rainbow Brite jokes? I had a whole slew of material for tonight.

ME: Aw, darn.

κ: I'm sensing sarcasm.

ME: You ARE a self-declared infinite well of knowledge.

κ: And there it is again.

ME: :)

ME: Shit. I've gotta go. He's yanking the foil out of my hair.

κ: Can't wait to see you gorgeous. Still on for tonight?

ME: Tonight? We've got plans tonight?

κ: Touché

I grin at my phone and hand it to Quinn as I'm dragged to the sink. Once I smell like a coconut, I'm back in the chair, once again turned away from the mirror while hot Sergio begins combing and pinning my hair in sections.

"You've managed to fry your hair, darling. I put a treatment pack on it, but I'm still going to have to take some length off," he states while waving a comb dangerously near my eyeball.

I glance to Quinn, whose eyes are following his every move as though she's memorizing them. Her hair looks great, of course, with multiple shades of blonde streaking through it. Her makeup has been applied to bring out her natural beauty. The light-brown shadow on the top and the matching hue lining the bottom is accentuated by her long, dark lashes. Her cheeks are rosy pink and her lips shine with a neutral gloss. She looks stunning. I hope they can do the same for me.

"Go ahead, boss. Chop away."

And he does. For an extensive amount of time.

Every snip and stroke of the brush seems to serve a purpose. When he's done, he steps back and clasps his hands in appreciation of his masterpiece. Quinn gasps. I just want to be turned so I can see.

I don't have to wait long.

After Quinn and Sergio share a grin, I'm whirled around at warp speed. Once I come to a jarring stop, my eyes land on the person in front of me. At first sight, tears sting my eyes, and Sergio gasps in confusion at my reaction.

"What are those tears? You love? Or hate?"

I have no words. I can only manage a slight nod. Tears spill over and my chest begins to thrum while I take in the person staring back at me.

Her bright-blue eyes are wide and the shade of her hair is almost identical to the eight-year-old version of me, the only difference being the darker blonde strands masterfully threaded throughout, now shoulder-length with bangs forming a frame of layers around her face.

My heart lurches as I'm brought face-to-face with the little girl I buried so long ago.

I know that girl in the reflection.

It's Aubrey Miller before she died, twelve years later.

With tears trailing down my cheeks, my eyes remain glued to the mirror as I let out the breath I've been holding and smile, stating with absolute resolution . . . "I love."

Chapter 17

Normalities

"I would like to thank the Academy . . ." I trail off, losing my balance on Quinn's bed. Readjusting the tiara on my head to its proper position, I blow the bangs out of my face, clear my throat, and try to wipe the smile off my face. "Whoops. Wrong speech."

Quinn sits cross-legged on the floor, giggling and looking at me, fully engrossed in my performance. We're both feeling a bit toasty from the champagne she illegally purchased on our way home. Just the right amount of giddy and numb.

Lifting the flute and bringing a dried bouquet of roses to my chest, I continue with my acceptance speech. "I would like to say *thank you*. Thank you from the bottom of my heart. Wearing this crown," I break to add a whimper, "means the world to me. I am proud to represent you as . . . Miss Rama-lama-ding-dong." I roll my tongue and wiggle my hips along with my announcement. Quinn covers her mouth, laughing hysterically. "And I would also like to thank you for the nomination of Kick Ass Friend. I am humbled and unworthy of such an honor. But thank you for that, Quinn." I end with a royal dip of my head in her direction.

She smiles warmly and nods back. "It's well deserved."

I swipe the hair out of my face before kicking my feet, landing my ass on the mattress while ensuring not one drop of champagne is spilled. Bouncing a couple times, I finally settle as Quinn bolts to her feet.

"It's hot in here," I remark, fanning myself. Quinn stumbles to her closet door.

"I think we're drunk!" She laughs, then slides the door open, exposing a sliver of her shimmering formal attire. Fingering through them, she finds the one she's looking for and pulls it out. Facing me with a huge grin, she extends a hanger, shaking it back and forth. Little rainbows dance along her white walls, reflecting the intricate beading of the dress. Navy and strapless, it contains a crystalline silver sash, which beautifully accents the empire waistline. The bottom half of the dress has several layers that flow gracefully as she walks toward me, waving it in front of my face.

"That's pretty, Quinn. Are you wearing it tonight?" I ask, reaching forward with outstretched fingers and grazing the sheer top layer.

"No," she giggles, "you are."

"What?" I screech as the gown lands in my lap.

Undaunted, Quinn turns and approaches her closet, snagging another gorgeous dress. She slides the hanger over her head and moves in front of the mirror, fanning out the skirt before meeting my eyes in the reflection.

I avoid her gaze and focus on her dress. Pink and sparkly. Big surprise.

"You. Are. Wearing. That. Dress." She emphasizes each word as I glare with disdain at the offending garment in my lap.

"Um, no." Taking the hanger in my hand, I turn to set it on her bed, reverently smoothing the dress with both hands.

"Aubrey Miller, it's your birthday. And you are wearing a goddamn dress if I have to wrestle you to the floor, pin you down, and force you into it." Quinn pivots around and with her dress still draped across her body (hanger included), she marches to her bed, knocking me aside. She grabs the dress and forces it into my chest, her fist colliding with my shoulder.

Mouth open and offended, I rub my now aching muscle. "Ow, *bitch*. That hurt."

"You haven't *seen* bitch yet. And you don't want to. So I suggest you put on that dress *now*, and then I will touch up your makeup." She knocks my already aching shoulder with hers and I give her a dirty look, but it soon disappears when she smiles softly. "You look so beautiful, Aubrey. You really do. I'm so proud of you."

My throat squeezes shut and tears surface.

Damn you, alcohol.

Her grin widens. "Plus, I really, *really* want to see Kaeleb's face. Come on, Aubrey. You have to or I will officially take back my Kick Ass Friend nomination." With that, her face falls serious, but the anticipated excitement of seeing Kaeleb's reaction still twinkles in her eyes.

Looking at her half-drunk, half-pleading expression, I can't do a damn thing but smile. Again, I blame it on the alcohol and the fact that I'm also curious as to what Mr. McMadden will think of my makeover.

My heart rate picks up, and before I know it the hanger is hooked over my finger and I'm heading to my room with a ridiculous grin on my face, bouncing off the balls of my feet. Kinda like how Quinn does constantly.

Shutting myself in my room, I drape her gown across my bed and glance in my dresser mirror. My reflection isn't much different than when I left the salon, with the exception of makeup applied to my face. My hair is still very blonde, and my cheeks are rosy and warm. Reaching up, I push my bangs away from my eyes, surprised at the life that emanates from them—life I never thought I would find the courage to allow myself to experience.

Yet here I am.

My eyes drift to my dresser and land on the picture frame on top: a photograph of Kaeleb, Quinn, and me. My mind reels over how much my life has changed over the last year.

I remember the day the picture was taken like it was yesterday. Blackened hair with blue ends, those freaking cat-eye contacts, blood-red lipstick, my eyes caked in black putty-like shadow, and my face expressionless with the refusal to let myself smile.

Saddened by the person captured in the image, I set the picture aside. I've denied myself so many experiences, so many innate emotions and connections, so many things that constitute . . . life. Too much energy wasted, fending off every single thing needed to nourish and sustain my soul.

Hope drowns out the sorrow, drawing one very important conclusion.

I was dead.

But now, I am very much alive.

My eyes rake over the navy dress, and I find myself smiling because I know for certain that Kaeleb McMadden is the reason. He saved me.

And he's on his way over here.

I need to get dressed.

Shimmying out of my cargos and yanking my T-shirt over my head, I grab the dress, only to pause in question.

Does this go over my head? Or do I step into it? And what about my underwear? And bra? What about shoes?

"Quinn," I screech. "Help!"

I'm approaching full panic mode when she makes her appearance.

"You okay in there?" she asks through the door.

"No, I'm definitely *not* okay. How the hell do I get this thing on, and more importantly, what do I wear under it?" Jesus, who knew being normal would be so difficult?

"Are you decent?" The knob turns, and I quickly grab a towel to cover my pitiful excuse for a bra and panty set.

Quinn enters my room with a freshly filled glass of champagne . . . and a box wrapped in yellow birthday paper, topped with the biggest bow I've ever seen. Setting the flute on my bedside table, she states, "Happy birthday . . . again."

"Quinn, the salon was more than enough. I can't accept this." I push the present into her pink terrycloth robe, only to have her shove it back in my direction.

"You can and you will. Open it." Sighing outright in protest, I tighten the towel around my chest and sit on the bed next to the dress. The bow unfolds slowly before I peel the wrapping off. The solid pink lid and the alternating pink-and-white stripes of the box underneath it tell me all I need to know.

I give her a shy smile before removing the lid. Sitting right on top is a simple cream-colored bra with matching lace lining the edges. I hold it by the straps, eyeing its beauty. I've never had anything so . . . feminine.

"What about the straps?" I inquire, still in awe that my friend was able to get my sizing correct without asking. Which most likely means she raided my boring array of white cotton everything.

"You can take them off, dope. Look."

She takes the bra and removes the straps, confirming my suspicions when she strides over to my undie drawer and drops them in. I narrow my eyes in her direction, then lower my gaze to the box on my lap. Coordinating panties lie on top of the white tissue paper, and when I pull them out, I'm surprised to find there's no back to them. Just a half-inch-wide piece of fabric.

My brows rise in question. Quinn giggles. "Time to try something new, Aubrey. They're more comfortable than you think. You get used to them," she adds, grabbing the champagne flute and handing it to me before stepping toward my doorway.

"Put them both on *under* the dress. Then step *into* the dress." Her laughter is unconcealed. "Pull it over your hips, and call me when you're ready. I'll zip ya in."

She blows me a kiss and disappears before I have time to thank her.

I sit silently, deliberating, before deciding Quinn is right. It's time to try something new.

So after hooking the bra and situating myself into the panties, I step into the dress and slide it over my hips as instructed, clamping the top underneath my arms before calling Quinn once again.

I fluff and finger through my hair while I wait, sipping champagne. She returns with a suitcase full of makeup and her own flute of bubbly.

After tossing the makeup on my bed, she quickly zips me, then I turn to face her.

She's fully dressed, and I take in her appearance with appreciation. She's absolutely stunning.

Her makeup is still the same as earlier, her long blonde hair twisted in tousled, relaxed curls, and her light-pink dress from before is now on her body instead of the hanger around her neck. It flows beautifully, satin hitting her knees as she walks.

It's no wonder my best friend is the reigning Miss Collegiate America. My face falls as my heart breaks—she can't see what everyone else does, but inside and out, Quinn's truly the most beautiful person I've ever met.

Taking a seat on my bed, she curls her feet underneath her legs and points to the space in front of her. "Sit."

I do as I'm told and brush the hair off my shoulders as I relax. She digs through the mountain of cosmetics, setting aside an eye shadow palette, a tube of mascara, and lip gloss. She pushes the box aside and scoots closer to me.

"Close your eyes. Chin up. Don't move."

"Okay," I breathe, suddenly nervous, seeing my alarm clock.

Kaeleb will be here in less than five minutes.

I shut my eyes and try not to blink as she dabs shadow along the top and bottom of my lids. Her finger brushes lightly against them before she applies more in the crease of my eye. After smudging it a bit, she exhales. "Okay. Open."

My eyes open and flutter a bit before settling on her smile. "Gorgeous," she says before tilting my head back. "Now don't blink." A mascara wand makes its way to my face, and not long after, both sets of lashes are coated with what must be at least the third coat of the day.

"Perfect." She pumps the lip gloss before giving my lips a healthy application, then sits back and appraises her work.

A very pleased smile crosses her face as she nods. "You. Look. GORGEOUS," she shouts, handing me a mirror. "Kaeleb is going to shit himself. I can't wait." She jumps off the bed and grabs her champagne.

I examine myself and have to agree. She did a beautiful job. My eyes look sultry but natural with their shimmery, light-brown shadow, and the deeper brown at the corners makes them pop a brighter blue than I ever remember them being. My lips shine with a nude gloss just like hers, and they lift into a relieved smile before I set the mirror aside and accept the champagne she offers.

"Thank you so much, Quinn. This day has been . . . unbelievable. And I owe it all to you. You have no idea." My voice trembles a bit with the admission, because she really has *no idea* what she's done for me today.

I feel normal.

A normal girl, about to have a normal birthday celebration with her friends, in a normal (albeit spectacular) dress, with normal hair and makeup.

The only thing that's missing is a pair of normal shoes.

"Shoes—I need shoes," I exclaim.

"No, you don't." Quinn giggles and reaches for the knob of my bedroom door.

"What? Why wouldn't I need shoes?"

That makes no sense.

She's drunker than I thought.

That's it, I'm officially hiding the champagne.

"You'll see," she says just as there's a knock at the front door.

Quinn winks. "Trust me. Just, stay in here. Don't come out until someone comes to get you."

She quietly shuts the door and I remain seated. Kaeleb's murmur filters into my room, and a nervous excitement flitters through my belly and spreads into my chest. My joy takes flight, and I breathe in deeply, contentment pumping enthusiastically with each thrumming heartbeat.

Damn, it feels good to be alive.

Chapter 18 ✳

Dreams

I don't have long to wait. After a very loud squeal from Quinn in the other room, there's a knock at my door. My pulse kicks up and I stand, smoothing out my dress. With a glance in the mirror, I plump a couple sections of my new hair with my fingers. "Come in," I remark, turning in the direction of the door.

Kaeleb pokes his head around the corner, his eyes finding mine. His brows rise and his mouth falls open before he shifts his focus to take in my hair, my exposed neck, and the line of my dress. He holds his stare briefly at the crystalline sash lining my waist, and then allows it to slowly drift down my legs to my perfectly painted toenails. The left side of his mouth quirks up as he clears his throat, frozen in place. He tears his scrutiny away from my feet, fully stepping into the room and shutting the door behind him.

I take advantage of the seconds his back is turned and survey him from head to toe. His light-blue button-up is folded to his elbows, displaying flexed muscles along his forearms. He places both palms on the door and leans in, and his shirt rides up just enough for me to see the designs on the back pockets of his dark jeans. They hug his ass perfectly, and I itch to slide my hands into those pockets so I can feel the hardness of his toned body.

My fingers curl, needing to touch him, but I maintain control while Kaeleb braces against the door, breathing deeply. He remains there, completely silent, his breaths the only sound in the room. I begin to feel self-conscious, running my hands over my hair and dress to make sure everything is as it should be.

Just as I start to ask him if he's all right, he whips around with a full smile on his face. A few long strides, and he's standing in front of me. Raising both hands, he traces the tips of his fingers along the sides of my cheeks, leaving a scorching trail as they run down my neck and thread themselves into the hair at my nape. With his thumbs, he tilts my head back and looks me directly in the eyes.

"You look amazing, Sunshine. Truly breathtaking." His head dips slightly to graze his lips tentatively along mine, the movement so sensual I can't keep my hands off him any longer. Fisting his shirt, I pull him into me and press my mouth hard against his, the need to taste him overriding my caution. A whimper rises in my throat and escapes into his mouth as his tongue parts my lips, deliberately stroking and caressing mine. His hold tightens, his fingers curling deeper into my hair, the tinge of pain sending shockwaves of pleasure coursing through my body.

After another gentle sweep of his tongue, he lessens the kiss and pulls back. His lips brush against mine before sliding over to the corner of my mouth, up along my cheek, until finally coming to rest against my ear as he breathes, "Happy birthday. The dress is phenomenal."

I smile, and as his cheek presses into mine, I know he's smiling too.

"Thank you," I reply, my voice deep and throaty. He releases me, taking a step back. His fingers are warm as they trace my neck and trail down my arm, leaving a rash of goose bumps in their wake. Once they glide over my wrist, he takes my right hand into his, lifting it in the air to twirl me around.

Silence fills the room as I spin. When I finish the turn and our eyes meet, he breathes out a sigh and lowers my hand but doesn't let go. "Damn, Bree. I just can't get over it. You look—"

"I know. I look like Aubrey again."

"No," he stutters, "I mean, yeah, you do. But it's just . . . the girl I lost all those years ago is standing right in front of me. It's a bit surreal."

A blush creeps into my cheeks and I instinctively run my fingers over the material of the dress. Fanning it out at the bottom, I respond, "I'm pretty sure I didn't wear dresses like this when I was eight years old."

He shakes his head and laces his fingers through mine. "No, you didn't."

Tightening his grip, he draws my body flush against his and nuzzles his nose into my neck. His lips tickle my skin as he adds, "But you should've. It would have been a nice change to see you in something other than your ratty jeans and oversized Super Mario Bros. T-shirt in my dreams."

I remember that shirt. I wore it all the time.

My nose crinkles and I pull away, an inquisitive grin on my face. "Really?" I ask. "You dreamt about me?"

"I did."

His hand tightens around mine. "You were my best friend, Bree. My only friend." I watch his peaceful expression transform into one fixed with regret. "*That* night, the night you were taken away, wasn't one I could forget. You weren't the girl I knew anymore. Your eyes were so . . . *empty*. Not the eyes I recognized. It was like you were gone before they took you."

Kaeleb shrugs innocently. "I was worried about you. I *needed* to know you were okay, but unfortunately, I never got my answer. And a part of me clung to that need because sometimes a little blonde-haired girl would sneak into my dreams wearing a very familiar Mario Bros. T-shirt, her big blue eyes full of life, and smile like you used to. Like I remembered. Like you are now, in fact."

Right on cue, a smile fills my face, and his troubled expression eases into a comforted grin. "*That's* what I can't get over. You are quite literally my dream come true."

A gasp lodges in my throat, his words stealing not only my breath but my heart. Casting me a knowing look, he adds, "Like I said, absolutely breathtaking."

Still unable to speak, I do the best I can to demonstrate my gratitude for his beautiful words by rising on my tiptoes and kissing him heartily on the mouth. An odd yip sounds from the living room and I drop down onto my heels, eyeing him curiously as I inquire, "What's going on out there?"

Kaeleb releases my hand and drapes his arm over my shoulder, guiding me to the door. He leans into me and whispers, "Ready for your present?"

Grinning ear-to-ear, I nod. He quickly brushes his lips across my forehead, gives me a wink, and opens the door. Kaeleb takes both of my hands in his and pulls me so I'm directly behind him. Quinn's giggles fill the air with our approach, and he drops his hold with a slight squeeze to indicate that I should stay put.

"Boo, I wanna play," Quinn pouts and hands him what I can only assume is my gift. Kaeleb's head dips a bit, nestling what is now in his arms. He pivots slowly and when my eyes fall to what he's holding, a gasp stills in my throat.

Because there, cuddled ever so comfortably in his arms, is a puppy.

But not just any puppy.

This puppy is the spitting image of *Walter*.

A lump forms when I try to swallow and my eyes tear as I look him over. Same golden fur, same deep-set brown eyes, same black whiskers on his cheeks. Same everything.

And as I stare at him, realization crosses my mind.

Kaeleb not only gave me life again, but it seems he unknowingly brought Walter along for the ride.

Talk about surreal.

Moisture builds in my eyes, causing Kaeleb's brow to furrow. "Are you okay?" he asks. I stroke the puppy's soft, furry head. He nuzzles my fingers with his cold nose and begins to gnaw on them. I wipe the tear running down my face, give a sniffle, and turn my eyes to Kaeleb. His head slants slightly, clearly not understanding my reaction.

"Can I hold him?" My voice is shaky and unsure as I reach out. Kaeleb silently hands him over, and once he's comfortably situated, I hug him close to my chest. He licks my nose and I giggle, smiling down at him.

Puppy breath.

Love.

Once the puppy is done bathing my face, I kiss his head gently and look at Kaeleb, who's still watching me curiously.

"He's . . . perfect."

Kaeleb's brow dips as he wipes another tear from my cheek.

I don't tell him about Walter. I don't tell him how my heart broke the day he died. The day I killed him by accident. Fear spikes and riles every nerve throughout my system, but I try to push it aside. The terror is shoved safely back into my memory bins, along with the memory of his loss. There's too much happiness in this room right now to taint it with the past.

Moving forward the best way I know, I replace his memory with this one.

"Walter. His name is *Walter*," I say on a breath and a smile.

Kaeleb relaxes and runs his hand through his hair.

"I love it. It's perfect." Quinn claps and leans into me, giving the puppy a light kiss and a loving pat before leaving the living room. She reenters holding a cake with twenty lit candles on top. It has chocolate frosting with "Happy Birthday, Sunshine" written in yellow, and a sun covering the corner. With the shaky rays extending across the top, I know it's handmade.

Kaeleb.

I glance up, brows raised. "You made this?"

His face lights up with pride. "I did."

I grin. "Wow, Kaeleb. Thank you. You'll never know how much this means to me."

And he won't.

The look in his eyes tells me he wants to ask, but we're interrupted by a knock at the door.

"That must be Josh." Quinn bounces excitedly, almost dropping the cake. "Hurry and blow out the candles!"

Both watch as I draw in a deep breath, curl Walter tightly into my body, and blow out the candles. One by one they're extinguished, and I'm gifted more puppy kisses for my efforts. Quinn sets the cake on the breakfast table, then bolts to the door to let Josh in. He barely glances at her, too busy texting on his phone. My head jerks with his blatant disregard for the gorgeous girl standing by him. Kaeleb and I exchange stunned stares, but say nothing as Josh ends the text and slides the phone into his pocket.

He saunters over to Kaeleb and extends his hand. "'Sup, man? Good to see ya." After shaking it, he turns to me and states, "Happy birthday." The coolness in his tone is odd, because he's usually more cordial. Knowing he's still close with Sabrina and Candace, I wonder if this is about the unitard comment Kaeleb made last night, but then I realize I don't really care as the memory plays out in my mind. I grin.

Kaeleb smirks and I can tell he's thinking the same thing.

Quinn bolts around the corner, a pink clutch in her hand. "I'm ready, let's go, Josh." Glancing over her shoulder at me, she adds, "Have fun, you guys."

"What? What about us?" My expression turns inquisitive as I watch her hook her arm in Josh's, who *still* hasn't complimented her appearance. My frustration is rapidly churning into extreme irritation.

Quinn is clearly not as upset as I am by Josh's lack of compliments. "You guys are staying in, *obviously*. You can't leave Walter alone on his first night. Maybe you can give him a piece of cake."

"NO," I shout. Everyone in the room jumps, and I struggle to compose myself before adding in a softer tone, "No chocolate. It's not . . . *good* for dogs. Nothing other than puppy food, got it?" I direct my warning at both Quinn and Kaeleb. Their expressions are stunned, but they nod slowly.

I stare until I feel they've grasped the importance of my order. Homing in on Quinn, I narrow my eyes in her direction and purse my lips. "You knew about this all along, didn't you?" Kaeleb laughs out loud, confirming my suspicions. "Why did you make me get all dressed up if we're not going out?"

Quinn gives me a knowing look. "Because dummy, it's your birthday. And your *real* gift from me was the look on Kaeleb's face when he first saw you. For you to feel as beautiful as you are." Her eyes dart to Kaeleb. "While I'm sad I missed it, the way he's looking at you right now tells me that my gift was definitely delivered."

My eyes drift to Kaeleb, standing there with a gorgeous, crooked smile as he gently brushes the hair off my shoulder, tickling my skin with the pads of his fingers.

"Breathtaking," he murmurs under his breath. My face flushes as I recall his confession in the bedroom. I turn away quickly, self-conscious about my involuntary reaction.

Quinn's sparkling eyes bounce between the two of us.

"Thank you," is all I can manage. She gives Walter a pat on the head and turns with Josh to leave.

Just as I'm about to speak, Kaeleb calls out to her, stealing the words from my mouth. "You look gorgeous, Quinn. You deserve to know that as well." They both halt, turning in unison. Kaeleb eyes Josh, his face tightening into a sneer. Josh says nothing, but Quinn's eyes glisten slightly as she gives us a sad smile and a shrug of her shoulders. "Thank you, Kaeleb."

She nods her head and then they're gone, leaving us alone in the living room.

Immediately, Kaeleb's strong arms wrap around my body and gently pull me into his chest, careful to not squish Walter in the process. He kisses the top of my head, my temple, the top of my cheek, and the corner of my mouth. That's as far as he gets before Walter stands in my arms, licking both our faces with his own puppy kisses.

Kaeleb pulls Walter out of my arms, props him along his forearm, and sets him on his hip. He brushes the hair from my face before curling a hand around my neck. He licks his lips and leans in to give me a scorching kiss. My body melts into his as Walter whines in protest.

Our mouths ravenous, Kaeleb wraps his arm around my waist, urging me backward. I willingly comply, retreating under his direction. Memorizing his body, my hands float along the curves of his muscles as they work their way up to his neck. As soon as my knees hit the couch, I thread my fingers through his hair and pull him closer, which earns me a groan in return.

He lowers me, his mouth working against mine the entire descent. Once I'm seated he breaks the kiss, ending with a gentle peck to my lips and a graze of his nose along mine. I savor his scent and taste as he places Walter on the floor. Once his hands are free, he sits on the couch and gently presses me to lie down. Lowering his body, he settles his hips between my legs. His mouth trails down my neck, and my body impulsively begins to grind against his. The friction of our movements surges to the center of my body, and an unfamiliar yearning raids my senses. My entire body thrums, and my heart pounds with nervous anxiety.

My virginity has never been a secret. Kaeleb knew it the first time his hand simply brushed over my breast, the way my body responded to the touch, and he let it be known there would never be any pressure from him to do anything I wasn't ready to experience.

And right now, he's all I want to experience.

Unfortunately, *someone* has other plans.

Just as Kaeleb's lips work their way back up my throat and find my mouth, a cold, wet nose jabs between our faces. Surprised, we disengage, only to find one very eager Walter. His paws are underneath my head as his whines rise in pitch to ear-shattering levels.

Kaeleb's forehead falls; his shoulders shake with laughter. "Well, that's a first. I cock-blocked *myself.*"

Still whirling in euphoria, I giggle as he places a tender kiss against my skin. He reluctantly pushes himself off and, once seated, pulls me up right next to his body. Sighing contentedly, I curl my feet under my legs, watching him help Walter onto the couch. Obviously very pleased with the attention, Walter's yips die down, and we patiently wait as he turns circles, searching for the perfect spot—-a.k.a. Kaeleb's lap—where he plops down with an exhausted grunt.

Yeah.

I feel ya, buddy.

I suddenly find myself *dog-tired* from the mixture of champagne and today's excitement.

The lusty fog begins to clear, and my mind returns to Quinn. "What the hell was that with Josh tonight?" I ask, a yawn working its way through my lips.

Kaeleb curls his arm around my shoulder, and I nestle into his warmth. He sighs before responding, "No idea. That guy is a fucking douche."

"Agreed," I remark, settling my head against Kaeleb's chest.

Listening to the steady sound of his beating heart, my lids become heavy, and all thoughts are relinquished as I slowly drift to sleep.

It was the beginning of many things that should have never been overlooked regarding Quinn.

Many things I would later come to regret.

Chapter 19   ✳

Implications

"I'm very pleased with your progress, Aubrey, but I still have some concerns. For instance, while you may look like your old self, you still refuse to acknowledge the misdirected guilt that eight-year-old Aubrey Miller experienced. I fear that until you do, you can't move past what drove you to become Raven in the first place. And to be quite honest, I don't feel that you are capable of handling any situation in which death, or even illness, occurs to someone you care for deeply without losing yourself again. Just because you choose to avoid them, doesn't mean the guilt and fear have just magically disappeared. They're still very much there and will remain until you come to terms with them. Regardless of your appearance."

My day pretty much turned to shit after that epiphany from Palmer. That was only the beginning. In microbiology lab, I found out I made my first fucking C on a lab report because my dickwad partner contaminated the media, giving us false results. Probably because he couldn't take his eyes off my ass. Then when I arrived home, I was greeted by Walter carrying one of my brand new Chucks in his mouth. Well, what was left of it anyway.

I've lost a lot of shoes over the past two weeks. Thankfully my Docs are still intact.

After a good scolding, and then lots of love, I took him to bed with me where I've been lying ever since. I blame this funk on Palmer. He's probably just pissed. I haven't been dropping by nearly as much, and he must be looking for a way to twist my mind into thinking I need more help. These damn conversations have become actual therapy sessions. Ones I don't need.

I roll over to stroke Walter's soft coat and laugh as he growls in his sleep. He's most likely wrestling with my other poor, defenseless shoe.

My phone vibrates on my bedside table. Picking it up, I smile and answer the text.

KAELEB: On my way. Need anything?
ME: You
K: I'm all yours.
K: Everything okay?
ME: It will be when you get here.
K: I'll be there in five, Sunshine. :)
ME: K

I pet Walter until Kaeleb arrives. Quinn and I gave him a key long ago, so it's no surprise when I hear his backpack hit the living room floor. My darkened room is dimly lit as he opens the door and steps inside.

That is until he flips on the light.

"AH, NO! Turn it OFF." My arm immediately covers my face.

"God." He snickers. "Quinn wasn't joking. You really *are* a vampire."

Walter barks and whines, the high pitch bouncing off the walls around me. "Make it stop," I groan, rolling over and planting my head firmly in my pillow. I pull it securely to provide a barrier from uninvited light and sound.

I hear muffled footsteps before the pillow is whisked away and replaced with Walter's tongue. I try to block his assault, but he's relentless. I'm forced to roll over and pull him onto my chest.

Kaeleb grins at me, then pulls a treat out of his pocket, waving it in Walter's face. I'm instantly forgotten. Walter eagerly scampers over my body, snagging the treat from Kaeleb's fingers. In one swoop, he's lifted off the bed and placed on the floor.

The bed dips with his weight before Kaeleb forcefully scoots me over. I watch with feigned anger as he sprawls out on his stomach next to me.

"Seriously? There *is* another side to the bed."

He reaches over and grabs the thrown pillow, snickering while folding it under his head. "Yeah, but this side's already warm."

I roll my eyes and elbow him in the ribs, satisfied with the resulting grunt. I see Walter happily gnawing a chew toy before I recline back into my original position. Grabbing the only pillow left and tucking it under my head, I twist to face Kaeleb, then stare into his eyes as he does the same. The side of his mouth turns up as he reaches forward and moves my bangs away from my brows.

"There you are," he states softly on a contented breath.

I breathe out the stress of the day. "I'm here."

"What happened? Wanna talk about it?"

Rolling onto my side, I slide my hands under my cheek and shake my head. "No, I want to just get lost in you."

"You can do that." He pushes up on his elbow and strokes my cheek. His fingers trail over my lips then, leaning forward, his mouth hovers over mine as he inquires, "How lost are we talking here, exactly?"

His head dips as he barely touches his lips to mine. "Lost enough?"

My eyes fall to his mouth and I shake my head.

"Hmm . . ." he hums. "How about this?"

He rests his chest flush against mine and draws his tongue slowly across my lips. They part for him, and he delves in deeply, drowning me in the taste I crave. He pulls back after one sweep, a smug grin on his face. "Enough?"

"More," I state. I thread my hands through his hair and tug him back down. He obliges. My moans fill the air as he repositions his body snug between my legs.

Breaking the kiss, his elbows press into the mattress as he brushes his fingers through my hair. Tenderly, he gazes down at me. "More?"

I barely nod, lost in need as he lowers his head. His hair tickles my jaw and his warm lips part, nibbling and lapping my neck as he makes his way down. My back arches when his teeth nick my collar bone, searching for some sort of release.

He drags his body down mine, causing my nipples to tighten. His fingers flip my shirt up, and my skin quivers with his touch.

I gasp as his tongue trails across my lower stomach, undiscovered territory. He ends the torture with a gentle kiss.

"Lost yet?"

"Not quite," I remark. My gruff voice is almost unrecognizable.

His fingers grasp my pants, pulling them off in one swift movement. "I didn't think so."

Leaning forward, he spreads my legs with a feathered touch. Goose bumps cover my body and my breath hitches. Kaeleb pauses, catching sight of my black lace panties. Raking his teeth across his bottom lip, he scrutinizes me.

My lids are heavy with desire, but my heart is racing with anxiety.

We've never been this far before, and I've sure as hell never let anyone touch this intimate part of my body. I feel self-conscious and draw my legs shut, but they're met with the resistance of Kaeleb's body. His eyes are full of understanding as he hovers above me and whispers, "We can stop if you want, Bree, if you're not comfortable. I want to make sure you're ready before we take it any further."

Looking into his eyes and feeling his soothing warmth, I know there's nothing I wouldn't want to share with him.

I trust him, absolutely.

Nodding slightly, I place my fingers over his lips. "There's nothing I want more. I *need* this, Kaeleb. I need *you*."

A low growl escapes as he brings his mouth to mine, and our tongues tangle with a hunger like never before. He pulls my tank over my head. I shove my fingers into his hair, directing him to my throat. Warm lips trail down my breasts, showcased in my new black push-up bra. Another moan from Kaeleb as he runs his tongue over the swells.

My body grinds against his, the need for relief building between my legs. His hand cups my left breast, stroking my nipple through the fabric. A groan passes through my lips. He hooks his finger over my bra, pulling it down to free my breast. My back curves off the bed as he takes the nipple into his mouth, flicking and teasing.

"Feel good?" he asks.

"Mmm-hmm," I moan, directing him to the other side. He performs the same ritual on my other breast. Pure ecstasy takes over my body as I grind against his jeans. I run my fingertips over his shoulders, brushing his upper back. His muscles clench as he drags his lips slowly down the center of my body. As he inches closer, my thighs tremble and my core throbs for his touch. I shut my eyes when his mouth stops at my panties. My body clenches with need.

"God, Kaeleb," I groan. "More. I need more."

Kaeleb hooks my panties and slowly slides them down my quivering legs, leaving me completely exposed. His fingers brush my sensitive inner thighs before parting my folds.

"Sunshine," he asks, scooting his body to the end of my bed, "you need to get lost? Come to me. I'll take you to places you never knew existed."

My chest heaves and I gasp loudly when his tongue strokes the one area yearning to be touched. Yanking my pillow, I cover my face, stifling my uncontrollable sounds.

Warm lips surround my core and I can no longer control my voice. I moan into the pillow with each flick of his tongue, and just when I think my body can't take anymore, he dips his finger inside of me. The sensation of stroking and lapping sends me over the edge. My body tenses as I explode with a scream. Waves of pleasure roll through me, and with each one, his tender caresses grows softer.

My muscles finally relax. My heart pounds harder than ever, and my skin tingles. Kaeleb chuckles, releasing my legs and gliding until his chest settles against mine. I lie there, reveling in my bliss, our heavy breathing mingling together. Staring into my eyes, Kaeleb's lips curve into a sexy grin as he brings his mouth to mine.

"Hey, are you guys in there?" Quinn yells, pounding on my door.

My eyes widen and a startled screech escapes my throat. I shoot straight up, accidentally throwing Kaeleb; the sound of him hitting the floor causes us to break into laughter. I swiftly pull my bra down and grab my tank, yanking it over my head. Grabbing my panties and cargos from the edge of the bed, I slide them on as Quinn continues beating on the door.

"I hear you in there, assholes."

Our laughter bellows through the room. Kaeleb releases an undignified snort and I see his shoulders shake, trying to contain his laughter. Smiling, I slip off the bed, my hands hitting the floor. Crawling next to him, I give him a quick kiss just as Walter jumps up. He runs over to us, his tail wagging happily, jumps, and lands on Kaeleb's chest. Kaeleb snags a sock to distract Walter as Quinn shouts again.

"We're leaving in an hour to go to the club. You're *coming*, right?"

Kaeleb opens his mouth, and I slap him on the shoulder. "Shut up."

He chuckles and holds the sock out for Walter, who jumps back and growls ferociously.

"*Yes*, Quinn. We will be accompanying you this evening," I yell back.

"So you're definitely coming, then?"

Kaeleb bursts into laughter and a smile crosses my face.

I just can't help myself.

"We'll be ready, Quinn. Go get dressed," I shout, still trying to curb my laughter.

Sounds of receding footsteps fill the hall. I glance at Kaeleb, who grins back. He sets Walter to the side and pushes the hair off my forehead, peering into my eyes as he states, "I'll help you get lost any time, Sunshine. The deal is you have to promise to come back. I never want to lose you again."

His knuckles brush my cheek and he kisses my mouth, nipping my bottom lip before backing away.

"I'm not going anywhere," I respond, shaking my head.

Familiar words rush through my mind and fear begins to prick my heart.

But looking into Kaeleb's unwavering eyes gives me the strength to push them aside, effectively ignoring the weight of Palmer's earlier implications.

I'm *not* going anywhere.

Chapter 20

Mistakes

"Isn't Josh going with us?" I ask Quinn, who clearly doesn't hear me. I receive no answer other than her yelling "Shit!" from behind the bathroom door.

As we await her arrival, Kaeleb glances at my ballet flats. His lips twitch as he asks, "No Docs tonight?"

I smirk. "No. I got these on sale yesterday when I went shopping with Quinn."

A smile breaks across his face. "And the jeans as well?"

My eyes drift to the jeans Quinn forced me to buy, saying I had "hella ass" and I "needed to show off my goods more."

"Yes, the bra and panties you saw too, but you weren't nearly as inquisitive about those."

"Well, I was . . . distracted. I might need to see them again. You know, so they don't feel left out."

After smoothing my concert tee—because some things never change—I glance at him and grin. "Highly doubtful, but good try."

He cocks his brow in return. "Oh, I do enjoy a challenge."

"Is that so?" I ask, my smile becoming wider.

He says nothing, but saunters over and loops his fingers inside the waistline of my jeans. Pulling me into his chest, he wraps his arms around my shoulders and kisses my forehead.

With his tight, white T-shirt and his worn, dark jeans, he looks delectable. As usual. His tousled hair from our make-out session further enhances his rugged sexiness. I silently applaud my styling skills.

He brushes his mouth against mine. I moan as his taste floods my mouth. Quinn enters the room, clearing her throat, effectively breaking us apart.

Kaeleb winks before turning his attention to Quinn. "Wow, Quinn. You look amazing."

She graciously accepts his compliment and twirls around. Wearing a short black tube dress and killer heels that make her legs look a million miles long, she's absolutely gorgeous. Her hair is up in a tight, sleek ponytail, giving her a sexy-secretary look. She's even donning thick-rimmed, black glasses that, oddly enough, pull the whole ensemble together.

"Thanks, Kaeleb," she responds with a sheepish grin. He drapes his arm around her shoulder and kisses the top of her head, a gesture that I find incredibly endearing. I smile inwardly at their interaction, until my mind changes course.

"Hey, where's Josh?" I ask, *again*.

Her face falls. "He has plans, something with the guys. He just called me."

I fight the urge to shake my head in disgust. Lately, Josh's presence has been virtually nonexistent, and there's only so much hurt I can see on my friend's face before I take action.

Verbally and/or physically.

"Quinn," Kaeleb says softly, "something's off. I don't trust him."

She plasters on a fake smile, shaking her head. "No, he's fine. I think he's just stressed about midterms or something."

"*Or something . . .*" I mutter under my breath. Quinn shoots me a dirty look.

Stopping the argument, I snag my jacket off the couch and shrug it on, segueing to a different topic. "Where are we going, anyway?"

She quickly disengages from Kaeleb and grabs her purse from the kitchen barstool. "We're going to BLUE."

Kaeleb's eyes open wide, and I remark, "Quinn, that's a twenty-one-and-up club. There's no way we can get in there."

She opens her purse and whips out her wallet, presenting a laminated card to both of us. "Surprise," she adds.

Flipping it in my hand, I look it over. I glance to Kaeleb, whose shocked expression is the mirror image of mine. My face pinches when I eye her excitement. "Quinn, these are fake IDs."

She places the wallet back inside her purse. "Don't worry about it. They'll get us in, that's all that matters."

Astonished, I stare at the picture in the corner and recognize it immediately. It was last year's student ID picture.

My hair is black with blue edges, my eyes are completely white with the exception of the black ellipses in the center, and my face is washed-out and grotesquely pale.

This is *Raven*. Not me.

"Quinn, I'm not going to be able to get in with this."

She waves at me dismissively. "Oh my God. Yes, you will. They don't look at that shit anyway, just the date. You'll be fine." She walks toward the front door, grabs her coat, and throws it on.

Kaeleb and I remain standing in place, extremely hesitant to follow her.

The lack of footsteps must have clued her in, because she whips around and crosses her arms over her chest. Tapping her foot anxiously, she looks up and moans to the ceiling.

"Come on, guys."

She folds her hands in a pleading gesture. "Please, I need to get out. I can't study anymore."

My mouth scrunches as I look at Kaeleb. His brows and his shoulders lift as he answers, "I could get out for a while."

I squint, then relax, knowing I really need to get out of here too.

Today was beyond stressful.

Quinn jumps up and down as Kaeleb confidently strides over to me, circling his arm around my waist before we make our way out of the apartment.

Twenty minutes later, we arrive at the club and pass through the entrance with no problem. Kaeleb and I grin excitedly at each other while Quinn makes a beeline to the bar and signals for the bartender.

She turns back to us for our order. "Um," I deliberate, "I'll take a Colorado Bulldog."

Kaeleb jerks his chin to the bartender. "Corona."

Quinn orders herself an appletini and three shots of Patrón, throwing her credit card on the bar. After the drinks arrive, she hands us the shots. We all grin at each other before raising the glasses in our hands.

"To best friends," Quinn shouts.

"To best friends," we cheer back.

Licking the rimmed salt, we slam down the tequila and bite the lime wedges. The soothing liquid courses down my throat and my mouth spreads into a lazy grin.

We find an open table and take seats. "We'll have to open a tab with a waitress," Quinn states, tilting the green concoction to her mouth.

As she downs her sip, No Doubt's "Just a Girl" thumps through the sound system and Quinn's eyes shoot wide open. "OH MY GOD," she screams. "I love this band."

"Me too," I yell back.

And I do. I have their poster on my wall.

Of course.

She swallows her drink in one gulp, slamming the martini glass down when it's gone. Wiping her mouth with the back of one hand, she grabs my arm with the other. "Let's dance."

She launches out of her chair and almost knocks over the table. Our drinks wobble, but thankfully, nothing spills. I glance up to see her press the bridge of her glasses back up on her nose as though nothing happened. She smiles back at me and I cast a sideways look to Kaeleb, who grins and reclines in his seat.

He laughs and says, "Go tear it up, girls."

Before I can say anything, I'm yanked away and pulled to the dance floor. Quinn seductively runs her hands up her dress and sways her hips. I have absolutely no idea what I'm doing. But as the tempo builds and the bass pounds around us, I lose myself in the music. Before I know it, I've kicked my shoes off and found the rhythm with my body.

My movements slow when I see Kaeleb scowling as he stares across the room. I follow his gaze, landing on the source of his anger. My body freezes. I home in on the sight in front of me.

Josh's head rises from Sabrina's neck as her leg unwraps from his waist. She's pressed against the wall behind her; he lowers his face and kisses her deeply.

Once their lips meet, I jump into action. Snagging my shoes from the floor, I march past Kaeleb, who's already standing and falls into step with me.

Quinn's voice comes from behind us, but the only sound I can hear is the roaring in my ears. Still melded together, they don't notice us. With Quinn on my heels, she runs into my back when I stop, a foot from where they stand.

"What the—?"

Quinn gasps, followed by a soft whimper. Her pain slices through the blaring music, muting all sounds around me.

All I hear are her cries. Each one released fuels my anger, pumping her agony into my heart and churning it into a fiery rage inside me.

Kaeleb grabs Josh by the collar, heaving him backward, tossing him to the floor. Sabrina stumbles, but takes in the three of us.

There is no surprise in her features.

No apology.

No remorse.

Just pure malice streaming from her asshole expression as her eyes land on Quinn.

And then she smiles.

"Poor Quinn," she sighs, "I guess Josh is all mine now."

"Josh?" Quinn's broken voice comes from behind me. "Is this true?"

He rises from the floor, avoiding her eyes while straightening his shirt. He stands by Sabrina, giving Quinn no answer other than placing his arm around Sabrina's shoulders.

Fucking asshole.

Sabrina throws her head back in laughter before she eyes Quinn, her whimsical expression settling into contempt.

"It was a long time coming, *sweetie*. And I can't say I blame him." She shrugs her shoulders. "I warned you about that muffin top."

Another heartbreaking sob comes from behind me, and Josh barks out a laugh, setting everything into motion. Kaeleb hauls his fist across Josh's face, snapping his head backward. He crashes into the wall, crumpling to the ground. I throw my shoes to the side and snatch Sabrina by the shoulder. Pulling her face into mine, I shout,

"You fucking jealous bitch." I clench the top of her dress tightly and hold her in place as my open hand flies across her face.

Sabrina gasps and covers the red welts on her cheek. Her face contorts with anger. "Fuck you and your loser friends, freak."

Her hands fly toward my face, but I swipe them away with little effort. I dig my nails into her shoulder and move to strike her again, but I'm stopped when an arm snakes around my waist, and I'm pulled away. A scream releases from my mouth. I claw at the arm and kick my legs, but it's useless. I'm lifted off the ground, still thrashing and screaming at Sabrina, and brought into Kaeleb's side. As he turns us away, I'm face-to-face with Quinn, who's tucked securely underneath Kaeleb's other arm. Her hands cup her glasses as she bawls within the safety of his hold.

My feet drag as he half-carries, half-drags us away in haste, most likely trying to get us out before security arrives. My eyes remain glued to Quinn, and I choke as the reality of what happened drives more tears down my face.

Kaeleb releases Quinn but maintains his hold on me. He collects our belongings and wraps his arm tightly around Quinn's shoulders, whispering in her ear and kissing her on the temple as he leads us to the door.

She clutches his jacket, burying her face. Her shoulders shake, and my heart shatters as her anguish pierces my chest. I wrap my hand around the back of her head, trying to comfort her as we make our way outside.

But it's no use.

The cold air hits my bare feet, but I don't care. I find my footing and pull her tightly into me. Our heads hover together against Kaeleb's chest as he directs us, and I refuse to let go of her until we arrive at the car.

Kaeleb finally releases me, opening the passenger door and shuffling me inside. He shuts me in and releases Quinn. He forces her to face him as he speaks. His gestures are emphatic, even shaking her gently when she looks away. Quinn stares back at him blankly, clearly giving up, but her tears continue to fall freely. Kaeleb swipes them away and eventually stops speaking, pulling her into an embrace.

After holding her for a long while, he kisses her forehead and opens the back door to guide her inside.

As it shuts behind her, I adjust the rearview mirror. She turns from me, avoiding my stare and maintaining her gaze until her face crumples and falls into her hands.

No words are spoken on the way back to the apartment.

Only Quinn's raspy wails sound from the backseat with the intermittent slaps of Kaeleb's palm against the steering wheel as he drives.

Yet to me, the most damaging sound as we make our way home isn't either of those.

It's my complete and utter silence.

I have no idea how to comfort my friend.

Chapter 21 ✳

Regressions

Over the next few months, Quinn dwindles away emotionally and physically. She's almost completely disappeared right before my eyes.

That fateful night broke something in her. Quinn was already cracked and splintered, but now she's completely shattered.

Her eyes no longer sparkle with the fabricated happiness she used to mask her internal struggles. The more she smiled and laughed, the more she was concealing her pain. What happened with Josh and Sabrina would've knocked anyone down, but most people would have recovered by now. Quinn continues fading away into oblivion, each day a fresh nick to the rope of her fraying mind.

And I can't do shit about it.

I tried in the beginning. I would ask if she was okay as I entered her darkened room and plopped down on her bed. She would only turn away and pull up the sheets. After a while, I was relieved she was capable of moving at all.

Then I asked her about classes. Classes she never attended anymore. She managed to drag herself to finals, but that was about it. When she was done, she crawled back into bed and covered her head with her comforter. Nothing was said.

After a while, I quit asking.

I was forced to leave her during winter break, heading to see Linda for a week over Christmas. The trip was a bust because Linda had bronchitis, and I hardly saw her. It was for the best though; I wouldn't have been good company. My thoughts were constantly on Quinn and the state I would find her in when I returned.

I was right to worry. When I arrived back at the apartment, I found her lying in bed in the same pajamas as when I left. It wasn't pretty. I forced her to shower and escorted her back to bed.

The worst happened a couple weeks ago when Kaeleb and I sat her down and attempted an unrehearsed intervention. She slumped on the couch, picking the polish off her usually perfect toenails while Kaeleb shouted at her from the floor. His frustration with her health had become completely unmanageable.

And rightfully so.

Her collarbones jutted from her shoulders as she hugged her knees, unfazed as Kaeleb ranted. The dark shadows under her eyes contrasted with her pallid skin. I was surprised she had enough energy to walk into the living room. I said nothing, but Kaeleb begged her to eat something—*anything*.

My throat swelled shut, listening to his pleading voice, and tears rolled down my cheeks. Eventually, he reached his boiling point at her disinterest, swiping everything off the kitchen island and bursting out the front door. But there was no reaction from her as she remained stagnant on the couch. Her only words were, "We done here?" before heading to her room.

Imagine my surprise when she decided to attend a dinner during parents weekend. We had planned the outing for just Kaeleb, his grandparents, Linda, and me, but when Quinn announced she would attend and had asked her parents to come, my jaw hit the floor.

I couldn't call Kaeleb fast enough to ask him to change the reservation.

He sighed. "Something's not right."

"Kaeleb, *please*," I pleaded. He changed the reservation and informed me he would pick us both up at seven.

And now, as she exits her room dressed in the navy dress I wore on my birthday, I bury my fear from Kaeleb's initial reluctance as hope blossoms in my chest. I disregard the fact that the dress barely manages to stay on her shrunken frame. I ignore the sadness in her expression. All my worry and frustration is replaced by budding optimism as she takes that first step toward being human again.

When she smiles at me, I smile back, looping my arm into hers as we make our way to the front door.

"You ready?" I ask, grabbing my purse.

Walter whines from the kitchen, locked inside a new crate.

Sorry, buddy. No more shoes for you.

Quinn glances at him and then at me. "Yeah. I'm ready."

I eye her closely, pushing away the gnawing notion that her smile is off, one I don't recognize; it's a smile nonetheless, and that's enough for me. We're going to dinner as a family.

All of us.

Together.

That knowledge dulls any nagging feeling I have about her state of mind.

After a quiet car ride, we enter the restaurant. I disregard the fact that Kaeleb has been unusually somber this evening. His only movements were to periodically check on Quinn in the rearview mirror.

Last to arrive, we make introductions around the table. When Linda shakes Kaeleb's hand, she beams her approval and I grin. She's been bugging me to meet him for months, and I can tell she's pleasantly surprised. Her smile widens after he pulls out my chair, and I know he has completely won her over.

"You look beautiful," he whispers as he sits next to me. "I'm sorry. I should have said that before. I'm just . . . I don't know." He glances to the other end of the table. "Something's off with Quinn. I can feel it."

"You think?" I ask. "At least she's making an effort. That counts for something, right?"

He shrugs, unfolding his napkin. "I guess we'll see."

His eyes meet mine and he adds, "Really, Bree. You look gorgeous."

I appraise the off-white layered tunic and black leggings. My nose scrunches.

"Really? I feel kind of underdressed." He's clad in a black, fitted dress shirt, tucked neatly inside his charcoal dress pants. "You look like you're attending a fancy dinner, and I look like I'm going to the movies."

He chuckles lightly. Tucking a strand of hair behind my ear, he whispers, "Breathtaking."

He gives me a wink before picking up his menu, and I grin like a dope. Linda's eyes fill with giddy excitement; her face is practically splitting in two. I shake my head, and she giggles behind her menu. Lifting it to shield us from the others, she says, "I can't get over it, Aubrey. You look so happy."

She takes my hand into hers. "Christmas was a bit rough with me being sick, but I should have said it more. You are so lovely, Aubrey. Just beautiful."

Her eyes glisten, the moisture dancing in the candlelight as she squeezes my hand. She lowers her menu, her eyes still on me. I give her a shy smile as collective laughter from across the table nabs my attention.

Kaeleb's grandparents.

Having met them earlier in the day, it's no surprise he and his grandfather are discussing the latest wave of politics. His grandmother catches my eye and shakes her head and I'm forced to hide my laughter. I fell in love with her the minute we met, and I can't wait to get to know her better over dinner.

Knowing Kaeleb's relationship with his parents is nonexistent, I was happy to see them this year for the parents weekend festivities. Last year we all thought the idea to invite family was lame, so we didn't, but this year the need for family overruled our way-too-cool-for-that-shit mentality.

I think it's nice that they're here. It's something we all find comfort in.

At least I *thought* that was the case, but as I hear raised voices, I find Quinn looking anything but comforted. A couple of servers arrive, placing two heaping plates of fresh calamari at either end of our table, and Quinn's mother loads a plate. She slides it in front of Quinn only to have it stubbornly shoved back in her direction.

Kaeleb and I exchange worried glances before looking back at Quinn and her parents. Quinn's mother is impeccably dressed in her black pencil skirt and matching blazer. But the frantic look on her face contradicts her collected appearance.

She looks from Quinn to her equally immaculate husband. He sternly shakes his head, leaning into Quinn, muttering words that make her chin tremble. He relaxes into his seat and sips his wine after his reprimand. His wife watches Quinn's reaction like a hawk.

Just when I thought Quinn couldn't get any smaller, she folds so deeply into herself that she no longer seems to exist. Worried, I begin to stand, but Kaeleb places his hand on my knee. Watching Quinn, he shakes his head. I relax my leg muscles, but my jaw remains clenched as I stare. Her mother places the plate back in front of Quinn, but when she pushes it away again, I stop watching and turn to Linda, who also eyes their exchange with uneasiness.

With nervous anxiety, my foot taps. Kaeleb squeezes my knee before turning his attention away from the commotion and starting a conversation with his grandparents.

Things simmer down until everyone's main courses arrive.

Then it ignites with a bang.

Quinn's fork clatters as she throws it onto her plate in frustration. It bounces off the china, drawing everyone's attention. Murmurs die down as people drop their conversations and turn to our table. Her mother's face reddens while her father severely glares.

"Quinn, this childish behavior will not be tolerated," he states, the power in his voice vibrating the table until his powerful palm lands flat against it, causing an actual quake. My body jumps, and my heart rate picks up, needing to protect my friend.

I throw my napkin down and place my hands on the table, but Quinn's teared eyes hold mine as she shakes her head. She looks to Kaeleb and dips her head in apology.

Deliberately, she dabs her mouth with her napkin—no idea why—and sets it on the table, rising as she turns her focus solely on her mother.

"I'm extremely surprised, *Mother*, that my appearance seems to bother you. I mean, isn't this what you wanted?" She displays her body. "For me to be skinny and perfect? Yet here I am, skinny and perfect, and it's *still* not good enough for you?"

Her tone crescendos with each question until she's practically screaming. Glaring at her mother, she says nothing else, but throws her napkin onto her full plate, yanks her clutch off the table, and storms off toward the front entrance.

Her mother eyes dart around the table, but not out of anger or embarrassment. It's almost as though she's searching for an explanation.

"Get back here, young lady!" Quinn's father bolts up and follows her, prompting her mother to do the same. My eyes are trained on them as they corner Quinn by the hostess stand. She continues her rant. Her arms flail as she speaks to her parents, her ire evident from clear across the room. When her mother tries to console her by wrapping her arm around Quinn's shoulder, Quinn shrugs it off and bursts through the front door. Her parents scurry after her.

I look at Kaeleb, whose troubled expression mirrors mine.

"Do you think she's okay?" I ask under my breath.

Kaeleb's jaw ticks as he deliberates. "Not sure."

He runs his fingers through his hair. "The weird thing is . . . it's as though she *provoked* that fight. I watched her the entire time. She wanted *something* to go down tonight; I'm just not sure what."

I nod. "Yeah, but maybe she just needed to get angry, you know? We both know that *anything* is better than the complete lack of emotion these past months."

"Maybe . . ."

Kaeleb's uncertain, but as servers arrive to refill our drinks, he masks his concern and smiles at the waitress.

As the drinks are poured, Quinn's parents return to the table. Her mother's eyes are teary and bloodshot, and her father's expression is tightly drawn. Grabbing his jacket off the back of the chair, he looks directly at me. "Quinn has chosen to take a cab back to your apartment. Please have her call us in the morning."

"Yes, sir," I reply.

Tears fall from her mother's chin, and as I watch their descent, I realize her actions were never to intentionally hurt Quinn. I silently hope that whatever damage she's done can be repaired. I know how much unconditional love Quinn has to give, and I find myself saddened that her mother may never be on the receiving end of it.

Quinn's father pays the entire bill, both parents offer their apologies, and they leave the restaurant.

The remainder of dinner is relatively quiet, the awkwardness of the evening dwindling the conversation to nothing. Lost in concern for Quinn, Kaeleb and I eat our meals quickly, practically inhaling our food so we can get back to the apartment.

Everyone grasps our need to hurry as we bid Kaeleb's grandparents a quick good-bye, promising to call them tomorrow.

Kaeleb throws his jacket on as hastily as I do.

"Hey!" Linda's voice calls from behind me. I whirl around, purse in hand. "Mind if I steal her for a bit, Kaeleb? I'll drop her off at home."

Kaeleb shakes his head. "Of course not. I'll head to the apartment and check on Quinn. Meet you there?" he asks, his question directed at me.

I nod and he brushes his lips against mine. I sigh in relief, knowing Quinn will be in good hands with Kaeleb there.

He gives my forehead another tender kiss and embraces Linda. Her face brightens, and for the first time tonight, I notice how tired she looks. She'd mentioned working nights at the hospital, and I immediately feel guilty for asking her to come. The day is gone, and our dinner was a lost cause due to Quinn's outburst. I've hardly had a chance to see her.

She hugs Kaeleb tightly and waggles her eyebrows at me. Kaeleb kisses my cheek tenderly. "I'll walk you ladies out," he offers, which earns another approving grin from Linda.

Arriving at her car, he opens Linda's door, shutting her inside before rounding the front and opening mine. With his hip against the doorframe, he tucks a strand of hair behind my ear and smiles. "See ya at the apartment, Sunshine. You'll know where to find me."

I nod and slide into Linda's car, unaware that in a couple hours Kaeleb McMadden wouldn't be the person I'd be searching for.

It would be Aubrey Miller.

Chapter 22

Hot Fudge Sundaes

"Well, that was interesting," Linda remarks.

"Quinn?"

She nods her head.

Facing forward, my hands find their way to my lap. "Yeah, she's had a rough couple of months."

"Is she okay?"

I ponder Linda's question before answering.

"I hope so. I *really* hope so."

Silence fills the car until Linda sighs.

"So . . . wanna get a hot fudge sundae?"

Her head turns in my direction and anxiety creeps into my chest. My trembling hands grip the seat underneath my legs as a familiar fear, one I haven't felt in a very long time, filters through my body.

"Um, no, I don't want to go anywhere near a hot fudge sundae, actually." I turn away from her, trying to maintain my composure and focus on the view through the window. Anything to stop the terror dictating my rapid heartbeat.

Hot fudge sundaes are always Linda's go-to strategy when she's about to break really bad news. It started with Walter, and consisted of an in-depth introduction to chocolate toxicity as she assured me his death wasn't my fault. The meetings have, unfortunately, continued on throughout the years.

Therefore, the mention of *hot fudge sundaes* means that something is terribly wrong. And whatever it is, it's vibrating the air all around us. I feel it down to the marrow in my bones, the heaviness of unbridled anger and terror coating my lungs.

I can't breathe.

God, I can't breathe.

"Aubrey—"

"NO," I scream, the pressure inside my chest tightening. "Just tell me, Linda. I don't need a fucking *sundae* to make it all better."

She grips the wheel and wrenches it to the right, crossing lanes until we coast to a stop alongside the road. She faces me, her anger evident as her eyes narrow in my direction, and her lips tighten into a thin line. Still panting from my outburst, fury frames my features as we glare at each other.

Shaking my head, I mutter, "Just tell me."

Her face soon falls from that of irritation into one of defeat as she reaches over and pries my hand out from under my leg. Stroking it softly, she says, "I didn't want to do this here, but I don't know when I will see you next, and it needs to be discussed. It's something that affects both of us." Her hand squeezes mine and she exhales deeply. "And I sure as hell didn't want to do it in the car, on the side of the road."

I say nothing in return, but my mind is in such anguish I'm forced to close my eyes.

Tightening her grip, she clears her throat. "I have been diagnosed with stage two lung cancer."

My eyes fly open and I jerk my hand from hers. "No."

"*Yes*, Aubrey." Linda draws her hand back into her lap and continues to nervously watch my reaction. "I knew back in late January actually, but I didn't want to say anything until I found out the prognosis and treatment options. February came and went, and now it's the beginning of March and it's time." She swallows deeply. "I'll be starting radiation next week, and surgery soon after that."

"So . . . Christmas . . . not bronchitis?" I ask, emotionless in my tone as the pieces fall together.

Linda shrugs her shoulders. "Not bronchitis."

"You haven't smoked a cigarette in your life."

"I know. Sometimes it just happens."

You mean, *I* just happen.

The thought lances my brain, pain throbbing inside my head. My throat swells even more, and the pressure beneath my ribcage almost implodes, both suffocating any hope I had for a normal life.

"Are you going to be okay?" I manage to squeeze through my gritted teeth.

Linda's face falls. "I sure hope so, honey."

Moisture lines her eyes, but she nods. She takes my hand and squeezes it gently. "I *will* fight this," she declares, full of determination. The tears slide down her pained expression, and my chest squeezes like a vise, constricting my breathing.

I place my other hand on top of hers. "I know you will."

But because of me, you will lose.

Guilt floods me.

I can't breathe.

I make no further attempt to speak. My heart rate slows; my skin grows cold, my heated anger lessening as I go completely numb.

It hurts too much.

"Linda, would you mind taking me home? I'm not feeling so well."

She sniffles, nods her head, and shifts into drive. Her hand clutches mine the entire way home. Ten minutes later, we pull up to my apartment complex and I say nothing as I open the door, placing my foot on the pavement. Linda opens her own door to join me, but I raise my hand, stopping her.

My voice is soft with my plea. "*Please*, Linda. I need some time. To process . . . all of this."

Her lips curl with a saddened expression, but her head dips in acceptance. She reluctantly slides back into the car. I turn away, sighing with relief as the sound of the gravel crunches under her tires. Her headlights no longer illuminate the stairwell. I make my way, completely encompassed in the darkness trying to consume me.

One final spark of hope ignites in my heart.

Kaeleb.

Knowing he's inside my room, my need for him drives my keys into the lock as I turn the knob in a race to the comfort of his arms. I'm teetering on the edge, trying to keep my head above the black abyss. I pray his strength is enough to keep me safe.

I start to run to my room when Walter barks at me from the floor. His high-pitched whines and needy whimpers pull me from my hurried frenzy. I can hardly make him out in the pitch black room, and as I crouch down, he finds his way into my arms, the warmth from his paws seeping through my leggings. Nuzzling him, I hold him tightly as he licks my face, temporarily soothing my sorrow with his kisses. He stands on my lap, and I notice a familiar metallic scent coming from his coat.

My head jerks back to look at him, but I still can't see much, so I lead him into the kitchen and flip on the light. Bending down and taking his paw into my hand, a surprised gasp escapes me when my eyes land on blood coating his golden fur. I immediately flip his foot over, pressing the pads to see if there's an open wound somewhere. He doesn't whine, just continues licking my face as I look at his other three paws. All coated in blood.

I set him down to grab the first aid kit. For the first time tonight, as the light from the kitchen displays the carpet in the living room, I realize the blood may not be Walter's. My eyes take in the blood-stained prints covering every inch of the floor. I step out of the kitchen and crane my neck, noting the most pronounced prints are located on the other side of the room.

My heart lurches as I follow their trail and end up in front of Quinn's bathroom.

No.

Fresh tears sting my eyes as I push the door open. It creaks, but Walter brushes by me, pushing it fully open as I follow him. The coppery smell of blood saturates the air, the familiarity causing my hand to quake as I flip on the light.

No. No. No. NO! NOO! NOOO! NOOOO!

"QUINN!" I scream as I land on my knees, crawling to where she lies limply, two pools of blood on either side of her body. Glancing at her wrists, I can barely see the huge gashes running up them, blood still pumping through the gaping wounds. "QUINN!" I scream again, grabbing the pair of scissors from the floor, yanking a towel off the bar and ripping it in two. Walter is whining and pawing at her chest so I force him to lie down so I can straddle her body.

Setting her hand between my legs, my entire body trembles as I fumble, trying to tie a piece of towel around her wrist. Sobs wrack through me. I finally manage to tighten a knot, pulling the ends of the towel as hard as I can. Blood seeps through the fibers, leaching through it like a rolling wave. I lift my hand and unsteadily swipe my chin with the heel of my hand before working on her other wrist. Walter whines, his frustration echoing throughout the bathroom, and the sound prompts Quinn to lift her head.

Her voice is weak as she slurs, "I'm so tired, Aubrey."

"Shh. Save your strength." Another cry escapes me when I see the empty look on her pale face. "I'm hurrying, Quinn. Hang on for me."

She sighs, her energy depleting with each pump of her heart. "She came back. That girl from the pictures. Always chanting. Whispering. Telling me things." Her eyes meet mine. "Just let her take me. I'm too tired to fight her anymore . . ."

She slumps over and an agonizing scream escapes me, shredding my throat as it releases.

Somehow through my wails, I hear a loud crash coming from my room.

Kaeleb.

"KAELEB!" My voice breaks midscream, and I put both hands on the floor to lift myself, knowing if I can reach him, everything will be okay. Warmth coats my fingers as I push up, and my hands slide forward in the red pools surrounding them.

I struggle to get my footing underneath me, finding some traction, and stand. I watch the dark-red coating on my hands as it trickles slowly down my forearms, forming fat droplets before striking the floor.

My vision clouds at the sight of the blood, continuing to trail down my skin; the earth splits wide open from underneath me as my Level 5 memory bin explodes from its burial ground, pieces of shrapnel landing everywhere as the titanium door is blown off its hinges.

Pain and agony from the sole memory held within its casing erupts all around me like a geyser shooting from below the ground, blowing my mind into a realm that I never thought I would be forced to visit again.

My legs lose their strength and I hit the floor, barely finding Kaeleb's frantic face before my eyes are forced shut, sealing me inside with no escape from my own tortured mind.

Chapter 23

Losses

I run up the stairs as fast as I can.

Mommy's friend Linda and I were on our way to a movie, but I asked her to turn around because I forgot to give Daddy his birthday card. She said I had ten minutes, so I have to hurry because she's waiting in the car.

I really like Linda. She's been taking me to do a lot of fun things lately. I think it's because Daddy's been really sad.

I like being with her because she makes me smile, even though I'm sad, too.

I miss Adley.

I miss Mommy.

And I miss Daddy, who just isn't the same anymore. He hasn't been since I was six.

He's been visiting with a doctor to make him better, but he only seems to be getting worse. If he's not locked in his office, he's walking around the house, looking at the pictures of all of us together and talking to himself while he cries. Sometimes he talks to Adley and Mommy, but I try not to think about that. It scares me.

But I'm gonna make him smile today. It's his birthday, and I made him a card. It's on purple construction paper, and I drew a picture of me, Adley, Mommy, and him right on the front. We're all holding hands just like we used to. When things were happy.

When you open it up, there's a big heart that I colored in pink marker and then I filled it with glitter and put a lot of my scratch and sniff stickers around the heart. Then right in the middle it says, "I love you, Daddy! Happy Birthday!" with a big smiley face. I worked really hard on it.

I hope it will make him happy. I miss when he's happy. But maybe, just maybe, today will be a good day.

I can barely keep from jumping up and down as I open my bedroom door. I'm so excited.

Out of breath, I run to my desk and grab the card. Glitter falls all over the floor, so I make myself calm down so I don't ruin it.

Turning slowly, I see an envelope sitting on my bed.

For me?

Now I'm even more excited.

I lay the card down and pick up the letter, tearing it open with a smile on my face.

After pulling the paper out, I unfold it and smile even wider.

It's from my daddy.

Aubrey,

Please never doubt my love for you. But the pain . . . it's just too much. I'm doing this to protect you from the absolute agony that is taking over my life. I know I will never be the same. The person who I was will never be again. There is no hope for me. I'm broken, Aubrey. You will be better off this way. I know you will never understand this, and I don't expect you to.

I just hope that someday you will find it in your heart to forgive *me*.

I love you.

I don't understand what he's saying. Maybe he's just having another sad day.

I glance over at my card.

I bet that will make him feel better.

After grabbing it off the bed, I fling my door open and take the stairs two at a time.

Just as I land on the floor, I run toward Daddy's office, knowing that's where he will be.

But when I'm almost to the door, I hear a loud bang. It's so loud, I fall to my knees, barely able to cover my ears because my whole body is shaking so hard.

What was that?

I'm so scared.

I'm so scared.

Crawling toward the door, my fingers shake as I push it open and my eyes fill with frightened tears. I look up and see nothing but smoke in the air and something red dripping from Daddy's desk.

I can do nothing but watch as it falls, forming a dark puddle on the wood floor.

Oh no.

"Daddy," I scream, but there's no answer. Just the sound of the blood trickling as the puddle grows larger.

"Daddy!" I crawl to his desk as fast as I can. I'm crawling so fast I slip in the blood, sliding forward and landing on my elbows.

Blood. It's everywhere. All over my hands. My arms. The front of my favorite blue dress that I wore just for Daddy's birthday.

"NO, DADDY!" I grab onto his pant leg and pull myself up. When I see the sight of his slumped body—his face, his head, the blood—I cry out as loud as I can, but there's no sound. Nothing comes out as I force myself to look away.

The ache in my chest tightens with a pain that I know well. The pain that is always there.

I couldn't save Adley.

I couldn't save Mommy.

Now my daddy's dead, and I can't save him either.

I look at the card still in my hands. Its edges are covered in blood and it trembles within my hand while my tears fall onto its surface, making dark trails across the picture on the front.

My family.

I just want my family back.

I look at Daddy again, and I hold the card tightly as I crawl into his lap. Closing my eyes, I press up on his body with all my strength until I feel him fall backward.

I don't look.

I don't dare look.

I set the card in my lap and feel for his heavy arms with my hands, holding his sleeves tightly and pulling them to me as hard as I can. I wrap them around my body and hold them as I turn to my side and rest my head against his chest. Just like Adley, there's no beating heart inside. Just silence.

I hold onto Daddy's arms, keeping them tight around me, and stare at the picture of my family as I cry.

"I'm so sorry . . . I'm so sorry . . ." I mutter between sobs.

Because as I sit in my daddy's lap, I know.

Every single death is my fault.

It's my fault that Adley drowned.

And because of that, I killed my mother.

Now my daddy died to protect me.

It all makes sense.

"It's my fault, Daddy. I'm so sorry. I love you . . ." are the only things I can say. I repeat them over and over again, hoping that just like in the fairy tale books he reads me, the curse of death can be broken by the power of love.

But I know in my heart that it won't be.

Because I know now.

I am death.

And I bring it to all who love me.

"Bree. Open your eyes for me." A warm touch glides along my cheek.

"I'm here. Right beside you." Kaeleb's voice frees me so I am no longer bound within the memory. But there is no gasping. No need for air. I'm just numb. Hollow on the inside as his voice continues tugging, and I take flight, my body rising in the office where Daddy still lies below me, his face bloody and unrecognizable.

I watch from above as eight-year-old Aubrey Miller stands there, memorizing the gory details to ensure they will never be forgotten again. Once she's done, she looks up at me, and with lifeless eyes she silently reminds me of why she should never exist. Why I buried her in the first place and why she should never again be resurrected. I nod my understanding, casting one last glance at Daddy and the card in his lap, then gradually drift back into the present.

My eyes open slowly, painfully, the fluorescent lighting burning my irises. I focus on the blurry image in front of me until it becomes clear. So does the room as I'm slowly clued into the fact that I've landed myself in the hospital.

"There you are." Kaeleb runs his fingers down my cheek and along my jawline.

Knowing I will be forced to say my good-byes to him soon, the sentiment pierces deeply into my heart, the pain excruciating. I press his palm against my face, leaning into its warmth as tears fill my eyes. The knot in my throat aches along with my heart as my eyes find his, the hazel orbs filling with unshed tears.

I know I have to, but I'm not ready to let go of him just yet.

I need more time.

Fear overwhelms me.

Fear from the memory of my father's death.

Fear from the gory images as they replay in my mind.

Fear in knowing I will be forced to watch it happen over and over, that the memories will never be contained again.

Fear that I won't have Kaeleb by my side to take them away. I will soon be lost, not in him, but inside the recesses of the hell in my mind.

These thoughts send me into sobs, and as I hiccup them back, his arms curl around my shoulders and bring me to his chest. The scent surrounding me brings more tears as I clutch his T-shirt and pull him closer while he murmurs soothing sounds into my ear. His hands rub lightly along my back, and I find the crook of his neck, remaining there until a door opening disrupts the moment.

"Oh my God, Aubrey, you're up." I pull back, surprised as Linda enters the room and shuts the door quietly.

Her heels click on the floor as she makes her way to the side of the bed, holding two coffee cups in her hand. She hands one to Kaeleb before she takes a seat next to him.

"What are you doing here?" I ask her, my voice elevated.

Kaeleb clears his throat. "I called her from your phone earlier. We, uh, brought you here after you passed out."

Oh my God.

Quinn.

The bathroom.

Oh my God.

My eyes dart to Kaeleb, and he smiles. "She's fine. She's going to be fine. They called her parents, and they're with her, right down the hall." He covers my hand with his. "They said you saved her life."

No, I didn't.

I'm 100 percent sure she was lying on that bathroom floor *because* of her association with me. But I don't say that. I just redirect my attention to Linda. Her eyes are still bloodshot from our episode earlier. Her mouth frowns as she says, "I'm so sorry, Aubrey. I know our discussion wasn't easy for you, and then to walk in and find her in that condition . . . it's no wonder you passed out, honey. It was a lot for you to take in."

I make no response. I just shrug my shoulders as I'm reminded that Linda will be dying soon.

I transfer my attention to Kaeleb. "The doctor wanted to see you when you woke up. Just to make sure you didn't have a headache or anything they should be concerned about. But I told him I didn't think you hit your head, so you should be able to be released soon."

I inhale deeply. "Okay."

Kaeleb angles his head, but before he can say anything, the doctor arrives. After a thorough examination, he gives me a clean bill of health and my release papers.

Once I'm on my feet, I shuffle to the bathroom to wash my face. Just as I close the door, I hear Linda and Kaeleb whispering, and they continue until I reemerge. They cautiously watch me grab my purse. "I'm ready to go. Kaeleb, can you take me home, please?"

Kaeleb looks at Linda and then back at me. "Bree, I don't think we need to go back there tonight. Why don't I take you to my apartment?"

I shake my head. "No, we have to go there. What about Walter?" I ask, knowing Walter isn't the reason I need to go home.

Kaeleb eyes me for a second before answering. "I can run up and get him."

"I need clothes."

"I can get some for you while I'm getting Walter."

"I want to sleep in my bed," I remark quickly, looking for any reason.

"Bree—"

"I need to go to MY apartment," I shout at him. Linda's body jars at my raised voice. I avoid her eyes but lower my voice as I plead, "*Please*, Kaeleb."

He glances at Linda, rubbing the back of his neck and looking back at me. His expression is defeated as he responds, "All right, Bree. Whatever you need."

"Thank you," I whisper before turning to Linda. "We'll talk tomorrow?"

Her eyes light up and she heaves a sigh of relief before embracing me. "I'd love that, honey."

I smile at her and step away. Her relieved look breaks my heart. I memorize her face, the light in her green eyes and her beautiful smile, taking in every feature before I turn and open the door. There will be no talking tomorrow.

Good-bye, Linda.

I swallow my tears and leave the room with Kaeleb and Linda not far behind. I hear a familiar cry coming from a room down the way. I slow as I approach it, careful to remain unseen while I watch the interaction.

Quinn is lying in her bed, her face completely hidden by the heads of her mother and father as they both embrace her, their own sobs echoing through the hallway. Her bandaged wrists are wrapped tightly around their necks as they remain huddled together in their grief, their bodies shuddering in unison.

It's comforting they are mending their wounds, and I hope to God her parents will care for her in my absence.

Good-bye, Quinn.

Placing my hand on the doorframe to say my silent, heartfelt farewell, I continue past her room. Heading toward the hospital exit, I'm comforted that there are only two more good-byes to go.

Chapter 24

Burials

I shower and grab my towel, squeezing it through my hair and running it over my body. Once I'm in my flannel pajama pants and T-shirt, I eye the wooden doors beneath my sink and swallow hard. The contents behind them will be in use soon, something that will cause unbearable pain but is necessary to protect the ones I love.

And I do love Kaeleb with absolute certainty. But I also know my love doesn't hold any power over death, an ever-present shadow that hovers all around me, killing anyone who dares to come near its venomous mist.

He needs to be as far away from me as possible. I was selfish to think I could live a normal life. To enjoy simple things like laughter and the love of my family and friends, one lying in the hospital while the other one is being eaten alive by the cancer festering inside of her.

My heart shatters knowing the risk I pose to Kaeleb. My poison has already spread to Linda and Quinn. I can't let anything happen to him. I won't.

Opening the bathroom door, I'm met with a half-smile as Kaeleb sits on the edge of my bed, watching me warily as I stare at his beautiful face. His hazel eyes are filled with apprehension and grief as he reaches for me.

"Wanna talk about it?" he asks, pulling me onto his lap.

"No."

I allow him to cradle me against his body. His soothing scent washes over me. His hand strokes my hair, and I listen to him breathe while watching Walter frolic in his sleep as he lies in the corner.

"Linda told me about your conversation with her while we were at the hospital. I know you're hurting, Bree, and I can't begin to imagine where that beautiful head of yours is with everything that happened tonight. Please, let me be here for you."

I stare into his pleading eyes, and my heart skips, wanting so badly to get lost in him one more time before I lose him forever.

My final good-bye.

Our breaths mingle, the air between us caked with the urgency of the moment. I want to forget the pain. The agony tearing across my chest as I memorize his expression and burn it into my brain.

I brush my lips against his while running my hands over his chest. His heart pounds beneath my fingers as he curls his hand around the nape of my neck and brings me closer, pressing his mouth firmly against mine. Parting my lips, his taste floods my mouth, a taste I never want to forget.

His tongue sweeps along mine, sending goose bumps over my arms. My hands move to his hair, fisting the strands tightly.

"I need you, Kaeleb," I mumble against his mouth. "Please, take me away. Make the pain stop. Please . . . *please* . . . I need you."

I beg him quietly until he wraps his arm around my waist and flips me onto the bed, our mouths working against each other. I pull him close, our movements frenzied and frantic, and I release his hair, digging a path with my nails through his shirt. His groan fills my mouth, and he breaks the kiss, working his way to the hollow of my neck.

Hovering over me, I feel his body heat soothing my pain; his lips brush my skin with gentleness and reverence, his scent overwhelms me, and as I breathe just to find some sort of solace . . . I completely shatter. My chin trembles and tears escape, streaming into my hair as I cover my face with my hands. My shoulders shake as sobs work their way through my throat, the anguish impossible to contain.

Kaeleb's body stills, but his lips press firmly against my neck, trailing to my chin and my cheek, kissing their way through my tears until they land on my temple. He remains there, warming my hair as he mutters, "Let it out, Bree."

He pulls me against his cheek, holding me tightly as I cry. Tears fall as I mourn the loss of Adley, my parents, Quinn, Linda, and

Kaeleb. Sobs wrack my body as I silently apologize to them, the guilt and sorrow filling my throat so I can no longer speak. I allow Kaeleb to hold me tightly, our last moment together; I open myself to him completely. There are no walls. There is only vulnerability as I cry for what I've done to those I love. I allow him to see me stripped bare as I relinquish my heart, fully giving it to him before I say good-bye.

I mourn.

I grieve.

I offer my apologies.

Kaeleb says nothing. He doesn't need to.

With his arms wrapped securely around my body, his presence gives me the strength I need to let go.

And after hours of emotional release, my head lies against Kaeleb's chest. His hold on me is firm as I remain silent, fooling him into thinking I've fallen asleep. I listen to the steady beats of his heart until they begin to slow, and as his breaths deepen, I confirm he's sleeping. Placing a tender kiss on his chest, I take a moment to breathe him in one last time before I carefully move his arms from around me and slide out of bed.

My defenses rebuild, the bitter emptiness mounting within my chest, filling the empty area where my heart no longer remains. All love and light are extinguished. Grief, anger, and fear solidify into the cold blackness forming, its inky tendrils growing and spreading, smothering everything alive until Aubrey Miller no longer exists.

Only death dwells inside of me, and I take comfort as it blankets my pain.

Good-bye, Aubrey.

As I sit in front of my mirror, my eyes land on the scissors. I'd used them to trim my bangs earlier tonight, but the sight immediately reminds me of Quinn's failed attempt. I'd be lying if I said I've never considered that option, that I've never considered taking my own life to be done, but I think somewhere deep inside, my need to punish myself overrides taking the easy way out. I deserve every ounce of it.

The isolation.

The unhappiness.

The constant grief.

The darkness.

It's my penance for simply existing.

So I ignore the metal blades and inhale in preparation.

I open the cabinet doors and pull out a cardboard box, placing it on the counter. One by one, I disperse its contents until it's empty and set it on the floor. I sift through the makeup until I find the beginning of my cloaking ritual. I rub the white powder into my skin, covering my rosy tone with its pallor. Then I take the black eye shadow, caking it on and under my swollen lids, the ease of the ritual numbing my emotions.

Slowly, the dark red stain is applied, and as it sinks into my lips, I grab the black box, flipping it open and digging out my jewelry. One by one, I push them through the tiny remnant holes in my skin, forcing them through openings that no longer exist. I welcome the pain. Tiny blood droplets seep around each one, along my ears and eyebrows, trickling from the piercings in my cheeks. Skull studs shine back at me as I place the final circular barbell through my nose, taking in a calming breath as the process is nearly complete. I take the dye and shake the concoction, allowing the smell to burn my nose, removing Kaeleb's scent as I shake it.

"What the hell are you doing?"

My eyes find Kaeleb in the mirror, his jaw clenched, his body filling the doorframe as I continue shaking the bottle. I give him no response as I look back to my pallid complexion. Lifting my finger off the tip, I lower the bottle to my head and squeeze, but before I can apply the color, it's sailing across the bathroom. A thick black glob spurts from the opening with its strike against the wall, the colorant landing in a puddle next to the bottle as it hits the floor. I glare at Kaeleb. He's towering above me and breathing heavily, but I remain silent as I scoot the seat back, calmly walk over, snag the bottle off the floor, and turn back in his direction.

His hardened expression morphs into pleading as he reaches for me. "Bree, don't do this."

I step back, out of his reach, but he moves forward. His voice trembles, the desperation almost enough to penetrate my steel shell. "I just found you." His chin quivers. "I just got you back, Bree. Please, don't do this. Talk to me."

My emotions remain unaffected as I retake my seat. His face falls as I begin to apply the color, and once my hair is completely saturated, he sucks in a deep breath, anger replacing grief as he slams his hand on the counter.

"I'm right *fucking* here. TALK TO ME!" His face reddens and the veins in his throat bulge as he screams.

I barely have time to face him before he wraps his hands around the arms of the chair on either side of me. Lifting it, he turns me away from the mirror and drops the chair in front of him. I land with a crash but allow no reaction, maintaining my blank stare.

Calmly, I set the bottle down and sigh. "I'm done talking, Kaeleb. I don't expect you to understand, and I'm not asking you to. The only thing I'm asking you to do is go. *Leave.*" My eyes disconnect from his, finding the floor.

Kaeleb releases a growl of frustration, crouching in front of me, forcing his face into my line of sight.

"You think I don't understand? Christ, Bree, I was here tonight too. You think you're the only one who's hurting right now? I checked on Quinn first thing when I came here and she was asleep. I woke up to your screams only to find you *both* on the floor. You think I'm not scared of what could've happened? To either of you?" His chest pumps rapidly as he holds my eyes, the torment in them forcing my swallow.

Maintaining my composure, I reply, emotionless, "It's not about me. It's not even entirely about Quinn. It's about *all* of you."

His head jerks in response. "What? What does that mean? All of us? All of who?"

"All of you, Kaeleb. You. Quinn. Linda. My parents. Adley. All of you."

His jaw tightens with the raise of his head. "So you're playing martyr tonight? Sacrificing yourself for everyone around you? That's your answer to all of this?" He narrows his eyes and shakes his head. "Bullshit."

He pushes himself off the floor, but bends down and leans forward, meeting me eye to eye. "You're not the only one to experience guilt, Aubrey. You think I don't understand that? Feel it? After what I went through?"

Speaking through clenched teeth he adds, "I think about it every single day. How my parents discarded me so easily. The fact that my sister was hospitalized because I couldn't protect her. I deal with that shit every day of my life. But at least I still *live* it."

An aggravated growl passes through his lips. "I'm sick as shit of you using this," he pauses, gesturing at my face, "fucking *aberration* you call *Raven* instead of dealing with it. It's ridiculous. It's time to grow up and face it, Bree."

My jaw clenches, and I tighten my gaze back at him. "You sound like Palmer."

"I'm sure I do," he remarks with a bite. "I've been visiting with him since last year. You want to know why? Because I decided it's time to grow the fuck up. Time to deal with my issues—the anger, the guilt, the women. Things that served no purpose in my life other than making me a shitty human being. It's taking time, but I'm dealing with it. And I'm a better person because I made the decision to do so."

He inches his face closer to mine. Stroking my cheek, his voice is barely above a whisper as he states, "Please, Bree. Don't disappear. I know you can do this. We can do it together. Let me help you."

His eyes search mine and he lowers his hand, defeated. Releasing a long sigh, he shakes his head. "It's no use. You're already gone."

Rising, he looks at me once more before turning away and opening the door. Just as he's about to step out of the bathroom, he twists back slightly. "I wanted to be enough for you. Strong enough. Man enough. Enough for you to find a reason to live again. To give you courage and strength. But now I know *you're* the only one who can do that, Sunshine." The corners of his mouth dip. "As long as you continue to travel through life in this darkness, you will never know how beautiful your light truly shines when you allow yourself to love and be loved. Trust me, it's a breathtaking sight to see. You burn as bright as the sun."

He peers at me with saddened eyes. "You see, I found the strength and courage to fight my demons because of how brightly *you* shined. I hope one day you'll find that source of light and let it heal you, too. Because if you do, it will illuminate your path and eventually lead you home. To me."

With that said, he leaves me in the bathroom, shutting the door behind him.

Releasing a deep breath, I tear my gaze away, leaning forward to perform the final part of the ritual, placing the cat-eye contacts in my eyes. The white covers the bright blue of my irises and coolness washes over me as I seal Aubrey Miller back into her grave.

And as I stare at my reflection, I say a silent thank you to Raven for allowing Kaeleb McMadden to continue his existence, because the world is truly a greater place with him in it.

Good-bye, Kaeleb.

Chapter 25 ✳

Sophomore Firsts

The rest of sophomore year . . . well, I don't remember much. The firsts I experienced were some of the lowest points in my life. I'm not proud of them, but they happened and need to be acknowledged. So here goes:

The first time I cleaned my roommate's blood off her bathroom floor. I refused to cry as the horrific memories resurfaced. There was no sorrow, anguish, or tortuous sobbing, only darkness as I forced myself into oblivion until I felt nothing.

The first time I realized I was no longer a dog owner. Kaeleb must have taken Walter with him the night I said good-bye. I simply put his crate, bowl, toys, and favorite Chuck inside Quinn's room and locked the door.

The first time Linda called after our discussion, hoping to talk as I'd promised. I told her I didn't feel well and promised to call soon. She reluctantly hung up due to an upcoming appointment, and I told myself it didn't hurt when we said good-bye.

The first time Quinn's parents were introduced to Raven. After their initial shock, they told me Quinn would not be returning to school. They stripped her room, leaving it bereft of pink and sparkles, before paying the remainder of her lease. I felt only comfort, watching them leave. Her absence would allow me the room I needed to completely disappear.

The first time I changed the locks and denied Kaeleb entrance to the apartment. He banged on the door and screamed for hours. I never answered though. Not the first time. Not the second. After many unsuccessful attempts, he finally stopped.

The first time I bought alcohol with the fake ID Quinn gave me and brought it home, finishing off a fifth of vodka in record time.

The first time I missed classes due to a weeklong bender.

The first time I accepted the invitation to *party* at my asshole lab partner's place, but it ended up being just the two of us.

The first time I had sex, losing my virginity to said lab partner, remembering only sloppy kisses, rough hands, waking up sore the next morning, and finding a used condom on the bedside table. I threw up as soon as I got home.

The first time I ran into Sabrina, who had the audacity to half-heartedly apologize for what happened at the club. I told myself it had nothing to do with Quinn when I kindly instructed her to fuck off.

The first time I saw Kaeleb on campus, laughing with a group of guys at a cafeteria table. I slunk back into the crowd, but watched him for a while, trying to convince myself I was happy he had seemingly moved on.

The first time I received a D in two of my classes. The professors harped that mandatory attendance was required and explained I could retake the classes next semester.

The first time I stayed on campus during the summer, avoiding Linda who was recuperating after multiple surgeries. She called often, which I avoided, but I would text her back, letting her know I received her messages. I apologized for not being able to be there, and she believed me when I told her the reason was summer school.

I don't remember much other than those specific items as I entered my junior year.

I continued to walk through life unseen, hidden and tucked safely inside my darkness.

Junior Year

Chapter 26 ✴

More Sessions

Session 32:
(Four months ago, the first week of classes)

> *Palmer*: Uh, hello. It's been a while. Please come in.
>
> *Me*: (sits on couch) Yeah.
>
> *Palmer*: (takes seat in front of me) I'm very surprised by your appearance, to say the least. The last time I saw you, you looked . . . different.
>
> *Me*: (pushes the blanket to the edge of the couch) Yeah.
>
> *Palmer*: (narrows eyes) Do you have a problem with the blanket?
>
> *Me*: Oddly enough I do. It used to be comforting to me; now I just want to burn it.
>
> *Palmer*: (raises eyebrows) Hmmm. Well, how is Kaeleb?
>
> *Me*: Haven't seen him.
>
> *Palmer*: Why is that?
>
> *Me*: (inhales deeply) It's for the best.
>
> *Palmer*: (nods) I see. And Linda?
>
> *Me*: She's dying.
>
> *Palmer*: (nods again) Yes, I'm aware. How is she?
>
> *Me*: As well as can be expected, I guess.
>
> *Palmer*: (exhales) And Quinn?
>
> *Me*: She's gone. Surely you know about her suicide attempt.
>
> *Palmer*: I do. Just wondering how she's doing.
>
> *Me*: I have no answers for you there.
>
> *Palmer*: Okay. (shifts in seat) Want to tell my why you've gone back to using Raven as your identity?

Me: (scoffs) Isn't it obvious, Doc? I mean, Linda's dying. Quinn almost died. Aubrey had to be buried. End of story.

Palmer: (nods) Do you think she will ever be brought back to life?

Me: Nope. Never.

Session 34:

(Approximately two months ago)

Palmer: You need to discuss everything that happened last year at some point. It's unhealthy to keep it all inside.

Me: (laughs) My health is the least of my concerns.

Palmer: (glares) Well, you're not giving me anything to go on here. I'm not sure why you insist on visiting. It's obvious you seek no help from me.

Me: True. I'm not sure either. I'll just be going.

Palmer: (exhales as he rises) I'm here if you need me. Like I told you, my door is always open. When and if you decide you want to discuss the true nature of your problems, instead of providing me with evasive answers to my questions, I can help you get through this particularly difficult point in your life. But you have to want to be helped. I can't force that desire upon you.

Me: Yeah. (turns and leaves)

Session 35:

(One day ago, the day before winter break)

Palmer: (eyes wide) You're back.

Me: I'm back.

Palmer: (takes seat) I'm happy to see you. How are classes?

Me: Fine. Not much to do other than study. And drink. (laughs)

Palmer: (leans forward) Are you drunk now?

Me: Why yes. Yes, I am.

Palmer: How did you get here? Surely you didn't drive.

Me: (shakes head) Took a campus shuttle bus. Wouldn't want to unnecessarily endanger people's lives. Give me *some* credit.

Palmer: (clenches jaw and reclines) Why exactly are you here then? After two months?

Me: (laughs again) Because I finally figured it out, Doc. Why I insist on coming back.

Palmer: Why is that?

Me: You see, it's twofold actually. The first reason is I'm pissed.

Palmer: (nods) That's to be expected. What exactly are you pissed about?

Me: (narrows eyes) I'm pissed at you actually.

Palmer: Why is that?

Me: Because you gave me hope. You made me believe I could have something so clearly unattainable. That I could be happy. That I could have things I was never meant to have.

Palmer: Such as.

Me: Love.

Palmer: (leans forward again) Why do you feel you can never experience love?

Me: (shrugs shoulders) Because death annihilates love. I am death. I'm not meant to love. It's a proven fact, Doc.

Palmer: I see. And your second reason for coming here?

Me: Confirmation.

Palmer: What do you need to confirm?

Me: (sighs and rises to leave) That no one can help me now. Not even you.

Chapter 27 ✳

Journeys

Head spinning, I'm sprawled on my living room floor in my pajamas among the trash and vodka bottles. I stare at the fan, even though it's making me sick as it keeps going round and around. My head bobs, identifying with its repeated motions.

Round and around.

Spiraling.

Sinking.

I close my eyes. Round and around in darkness, drifting off to sleep.

"Jesus Christ, Bree." A familiar voice stirs my rest, but I don't open my eyes. I lie there and allow it to take me to another place. I dream of Kaeleb, his soft lips as they mesh with mine, his tongue as he kisses me as only he can. *His* touches aren't sloppy or rough. They're perfect as they blanket the constant ache in my chest.

As my body lifts in my dream, I inhale his scent and wrap my arms around his neck, holding him tightly, reminded of his loss. Being near him soothes my heart, mind, and soul. I'm contented, relaxing and unwinding as his essence carries me away.

I remain there until light penetrates my closed lids, and the rolling road enters my consciousness. My head is pounding, my mouth is parched and pasty, and my body is trembling from the alcohol it processed last night.

Slowly, I try to pry my lids apart, but they slam shut at the bright light surrounding me.

A familiar snicker sounds.

"Some things never change. Once a vampire, always a vampire."

My heart sputters, then races, increasing the throb in my aching head.

Oh. My. God.

Shock morphs into anger and my eyes fly open, only to squint when they're reacquainted with the sun. I shield them protectively before taking in the sight next to me. Kaeleb is in the driver's seat of his car, no smile and hands on the wheel. I find and lift a lever, catapulting me into sitting position.

"What are you doing? How did you get into my apartment?" I shout, immediately wincing.

Another humorless laugh. "It turns out I not only have ninja hands, I also possess ninja charm." His eyes remain forward. "Since you refuse to speak to me, I was forced to keep tabs on you through Palmer. He called me yesterday, worried, and asked me to check on you, so I finagled a key from the apartment manager." He glances at me and shrugs. "*Ninja charm.*"

My eyes roll and break away to look out the window. For the sake of my head, I ask in a much softer tone, "Where are you taking me?"

As the words leave my mouth, I spot a familiar café, which sends another wave of excruciating pain to my brain. It's clear where he's taking me. I pass through this town every time I travel to Linda's.

Dread overrules pain, and I don't give him time to answer before shouting, "NO! I'm not going." Panic floods my chest, and I fiercely shake my head. My nails dig into my seat and I draw my knees to my chest, then hug them tightly as my head continues shaking.

"You're going, Bree. I'm sorry. This has to be done." Kaeleb doesn't bother to look at me. He flicks the turn signal, glides onto the side of the road, and turns the motor off.

"Kaeleb, *please.*" My voice breaks and tears pool in my eyes, chin trembling. "Please, don't make me do this."

"It's not going to work this time, Bree. You aren't going to 'Kaeleb, please' your way out of this. Not today. This is too important."

"Kaeleb—"

"So help me, Bree, if you say *please* again I will lose any self-control I've managed so far." His jaw ticks and he pulls his attention away from the road, glaring at me. "*Please* is what got you into this mess to begin with, landing you in this bullshit martyrdom while drinking yourself to death in the process. And *please* is why I was forced to sit back and do absolutely nothing while I watched it happen." He shakes his head, putting the car back into drive. "Nope. No more *pleases*. Mark my words: This. Shit. Stops. Today."

My mouth flies open, but Kaeleb cuts me off again. "Save it. We can hash this out later, but I need you to remain quiet until we get there. I'm too fucking pissed at you to have any productive conversation. It's better if we don't speak," he adds, his tone clipped.

I grunt my agreement, turn to the window, and watch the terrain fly by. My anxiety grows exponentially with each passing mile. When we finally pull into Linda's driveway, my teeth ache from grinding and my nails have dug into my palm, forming moon impressions tinged with blood.

I turn to Kaeleb. "How do you even know where Linda lives?"

He reaches for the door handle. Opening it, he offers, "In a twist of fate we have become extremely close during your . . . *absence*."

My face falls and I quickly bound out of his car, following him, surprised when he chooses a key and unlocks her house. I straighten my shirt and pajama pants and realize I don't have shoes. "Don't worry what you look like. She's not here. You *do* need to take a shower, however, because I refuse to take you to her in this condition. It would break her heart."

"I can't do anything about my hair, Kaeleb," I respond, his condescending tone not helping my agitated state.

He scoffs. "I'm not talking about your hair. You've got black smeared all over your face, Bree. You look like death warmed over, and if I wasn't so frustrated with you, I'd have a killer joke primed and ready, which pisses me off on its own."

I begin to wipe under my eyes just as he opens the door and waits for me. I pass him by and say nothing, but that doesn't stop him from speaking. Unfortunately.

"I almost forgot." He grins a devious, toothy grin. "When I packed your clothes, I left the contact case. So when you take them out today, your freaky cat eyes will be a lost cause. *Oops*."

I narrow my freaky cat eyes and turn. "What makes you think I'm taking them out?"

He mockingly replicates my expression. "Because I refuse to let you walk into that *hospital*—where that woman has been lying for a solid month now, waiting for you to call her, check on her, give her one single ounce of hope that you give two shits about her, all the while fighting for a life you're so quick to dismiss—and have her see you looking like . . ." he reaches forward and slides his thumb under my eye before bringing it directly into my line of sight, "*this*. She wants *you*. Not *Raven*."

Eyeing the black on his thumb, my throat constricts and I meet his glare. "I can't go, Kaeleb."

He drops his arm, exhaling his irritation before answering. "You owe her this." His features harden. "You've already buried her, Bree, but she's *still* alive." He shakes his head. "Look. I know we're not in a good place right now, but one day when you wake up from this nightmare you're reliving, you're going to realize what you've done. What you've sacrificed." His face relaxes a smidge before he leans forward and whispers, "Regardless of what's transpired between us, I care about you too much to let that happen."

He turns his back on me, and he steps toward the door. "Take a shower. I'll get your clothes. They'll be by the bathroom for when you're ready." He jerks the door open, adding before he steps outside, "And please, for the love of God, take the fucking contacts out."

The door slams shut and I'm completely taken aback not only by his issue with my appearance but by the situation as a whole.

I know Linda has been in and out of the hospital recently, but only because I'm forced to hear the first sentence of her messages before deleting them and texting her back. Kaeleb has a key to the house and knows his way around, which tells me he's been here before. Possibly several times.

"*. . . we have become extremely close during your . . . absence.*"

Having Kaeleb force me to come face-to-face with the situation makes everything real. I've managed to block the pain and detach myself from the reality, but being in this house with the loving memories of Linda everywhere I look, my barricade completely crumbles. I'm no longer secure inside its numbness. I'm thrust into feeling—for the first time in months—every emotion I've been avoiding.

My eyes tear in frustration as I drag myself to the bathroom, my selfishness painfully obvious. I disappeared when she needed me, but in my twisted mind, I figured my presence would only cause more illness, and without me, her chance of survival would increase drastically.

Which, unfortunately, doesn't seem to be the case.

I flick on the light and glance at my reflection, watching the black smudges melt from the tears now being shed. My face is drawn, my skin sallow, and the areas covered in black are puffy. I look like shit on the outside, but I feel even worse on the inside as disappointment seeps through my mind.

Disappointment in my cowardice.

Disappointment in my apathy.

Disappointment in the time I've wasted.

I don't even know who the fuck I am anymore.

"You've already buried her, Bree, but she's still alive."

My hands cover my cheeks and my fingernails dig into them out of pure frustration. My heart aches, knowing she was forced to face this fight without me by her side.

A battle she's waging not for herself, but for me. *For me.*

Overcome with guilt, the pain slices open my chest with the precision of a sharpened blade. Tears roll down my arms, cutting and stripping away layers of decay until only a small sliver of light remains, its flame fueled by unwavering vitality.

I love Linda. She deserves more than I could possibly give her. *Definitely* more than what my nonexistence provided over the last several months.

Shame fills my heart.

I should have been *here*, by her side as she fights this impossible fight.

And with that admission, I grip the shard of light, nestling it closely as I guide it into the voided space in my chest, then release it. As the warmth sparks and spreads, I enjoy the soothing calm of its presence.

It may only be a spark, but I hope it continues to grow.

I open my eyes, the flush in my cheeks returns, and I lean forward and pluck the contacts out of my eyes.

And then, with newfound determination, I flush them and jump in the shower.

Chapter 28

Answers

Kaeleb dropped the bag by the bathroom door, and I'm thankful for the familiar jeans and concert tee he packed, but he must have left my trusty Docs at home with my contact case. I slip on my Chucks and brush my hair, wrapping it into a messy bun. My eyes are less swollen after the shower, and I apply a sheer white shadow to the lids. After brushing mascara through my lashes, I slide gloss over my lips and exit the bathroom.

Kaeleb is in the kitchen bent down, rummaging through the refrigerator.

Sigh.

He's always looked really good in those jeans, hanging low and fitting nicely across his ass. His navy button-up hits perfectly on his back pockets, and I'm mesmerized, watching the way his forearms bulge as he grabs items off the shelves.

God, I miss him.

After carrying practically the whole fridge in his arms, he comes to a standstill when he sees me. My staring is obvious, but I don't feel bad because he reciprocates. His eyes run from my hair, to my eyes, to my chest, and then back to my face before he clears his throat and resumes his steps to the counter.

"You look . . . better. Leaving the piercings in I see."

I reach up and skim my eyebrow with my fingertips before flicking my septum piercing just for spite.

I don't miss his attitude.

"Maybe some other time. Think you can just be happy about the contacts for today?"

His head dips his acceptance and he sets the food down and grabs two paper plates.

Damn, he really does know his way around this place.

"Sandwich?" he asks, opening the bag and throwing two slices of bread on both plates.

"Looks like it doesn't matter what I say," I respond, watching as he places ham on the bread, adding lettuce, pickles, tomatoes, and mustard.

Without breaking eye contact, he flicks his wrist, and sends the plate spinning in front of me. "Nope, it really doesn't."

He adds potato chips to his sandwich, mashing down the bread before taking a bite.

"Eat," he remarks through a full mouth.

"Look," I huff, not taking a bite from the sandwich, "I get that you're pissed at me, okay? But do you think it's possible to not be a *complete* jerk-off today?"

He shakes his head. "No, probably not."

After finishing his sandwich in three bites, he places his palms on the counter and stares at my untouched food. "You need to eat, Bree. But take it slow." Ill humor works its way into his expression. "Your body might go into shock from consuming food instead of the liquid diet you've been drinking nonstop."

He laughs under his breath, but I grab the sandwich anyway and bring it to my mouth. Just before I take a bite, I use the same line he used on me a while ago. "Some things never change, I see. Once an asshole, always an asshole."

Taking my sandwich in one hand, I chuck it as hard as I can, smirking as it lands against his forehead and falls to the counter.

He picks lettuce out of his hair and eyes my pleased grin. His lips quirk at the corners before he straightens his face. "You're lucky you just took a shower."

"Am I?" I maintain a straight face, but the pickle stuck in his hair makes it difficult. The mood lightens when my lips twitch, and for the first time today, his eyes soften. Slowly, he reaches over the counter and places his hand underneath my chin, tilting my head backward. His gaze never breaks, staring deeply as he angles his head.

"Interesting," he murmurs, swiping his thumb under my lip and redirecting his attention to the mess. He opens the pantry door and dumps the sandwich remains into the trash can; my curiosity gets the best of me.

"How do you know your way around so well? How often have you been over here?"

His head falls, and he inhales deeply. Still looking at the floor, he whispers, "Someone had to help her, Bree." His eyes fill with uneasiness. "I'm not gonna bullshit you. It's pretty bad. I've been visiting a lot more over the last month."

A bulge lodges in my throat, and I'm forced to clear it before I speak. "How long have you been talking to her?"

He answers without hesitation. "Since you decided to disappear. She would call, concerned, or I would call to see if she had heard from you. We would speak once or twice a week, but then things started happening. It started with a cough here and there, but over the months, it became uncontrollable. I could hear her over the phone, coughing and gagging. Many times she'd have to go and call me back. I couldn't let her suffer like that, you know? It wasn't right. So a couple months ago, I started coming by on the weekends to help her as much as I could."

I nod my head, trying to fight back the guilt and grief. I amend my previous statement. "Maybe you're not such an asshole then." Rising, I wipe the tears from my eyes. "Thank you." I offer him an apologetic half-smile. "Sorry about the sandwich."

His mouth lifts into his characteristic lopsided grin, as he chuckles. "Don't be. That sandwich was the best thing that's happened to me in a long time, Bree. It's nice to see you smile again. Even if it's at my expense."

My dimple sinks into my pierced cheek. His teeth find his bottom lip as he smiles, clasping his hands together in front of him. "Well, assuming I'm safe from another sandwich-launch to the face, can I make you another one before we hit the road?"

I nod my head, but worry hijacks my heart at the mention of my visit with Linda. Before I know it, I'm full of sandwich and pulling into the parking lot of the hospital. I try to calm my breathing, making no move to get out of the car.

"Ready?" Kaeleb prompts as he pulls the keys from the ignition.

My eyes tear, and I can barely swallow, my throat clogged with apprehension.

What if she hates me?

What if she can't forgive me?

What if she doesn't even want to see me?

Thoughts fly through my head so quickly I barely process them. Gripping the door handle as tightly as I can, I turn to Kaeleb. "I'm scared."

The disclosure propels tears down my cheeks. Kaeleb offers a sad smile, leaning his head against his headrest. "You can do this. I know you can."

My mouth scrunches as I try to convince myself to get out of the car. Kaeleb sits patiently and waits. I eventually release a deep sigh, pulling the door handle and stepping outside. Kaeleb meets me in front of the car, and we make our way to the hospital entrance. I step closer to him and focus on any sound, trying to block the anxiety in my stomach and tightening in my chest. We stop in front of the elevator and Kaeleb presses the up button; my foot taps with nervous energy, my hands tremble.

The door opens and a whimper escapes my throat as fear forces its way out of me. Dread roots me to the floor until a familiar warmth envelops my hand. Kaeleb interlaces our fingers, and I look up to meet his eyes—kind, full of patience and understanding—and in them I find the strength I need. After thanking him with a small smile, we step into the elevator. Together.

Once inside, still joined as he clutches my hand tightly, his steely determination assures me. His resilience continues as we ride up four floors, as the doors slide open, as we walk down the hall, as we knock on room 431 in the oncology wing, and by the time we step inside, his grip is so strong I no longer feel my fingers.

I give a little squeeze to let him know, but as soon as my eyes land on Linda, my light squeeze turns into a vise grip. My feet stop moving, and my whole body goes rigid at the sight.

The person lying in the bed is unrecognizable.

Linda's long blonde hair is gone, her head completely bald. The shadows of her hollowed-out cheeks are almost black. Her skin is no longer glowing, but practically translucent, blue veins appearing amidst bruising along her forearms. Every bone protrudes under her skin, and her facial movements, with each wince she unknowingly makes as she sleeps, show me the pain ripping through her body must be unbearable. Even in her frailty, her strength is undeniable.

I capture my gasp and force it back until it joins the boulder already in my throat, making it impossible to breathe. My entire body quakes uncontrollably as I observe her from afar, every emotion racing through me as my heart slams against my chest. I shake my head and take a step backward, but as I do, Kaeleb's hand cups my cheek and directs my eyes away from her. I lock stares with him and continue to shake my head back and forth.

He brushes away my tears, but says nothing, his expression stern but not uncaring. Clenching his jaw tightly, he releases my hand and curls his around the back of my neck, pulling me into an embrace. I nestle into his chest, allowing his arms to hold me upright as I cry. Tears trail slowly down my cheeks until they eventually fall to the floor. I focus on them, trying to nurture that flickering shard in my chest so it may provide strength to face my fear.

To face Linda.

To face death as it stares me in the face.

Again.

It's long after my cries taper off that I manage to pull away from Kaeleb. His face is drawn tightly, but he places his hands on my neck and gently wipes the remaining tears from my eyes. He glances at his mascara-coated thumbs, before stating, "Now these kind of black smears are acceptable," and throwing me a lighthearted wink.

I can't deny that his humor is exactly what I need.

Of course, I don't tell him. I give him a light shove, causing him to chuckle under his breath.

Drawing in a calming breath, I smile, shrug off my coat, and finally turn to Linda.

Step by step, I make my way to the side of her bed.

I try to maintain my composure while my fingers tenderly brush along the darkened skin of her forearm. My eyes travel over her face, her chest, her hands, her head . . . every part I need to familiarize myself with before waking her.

And when I feel I've absorbed the pain, the guilt, the sorrow, the anger—all those overwhelming emotions I haven't felt for so long—I let them cultivate the light within me, pumping courage into my veins, light I never thought myself capable of having.

Strength drives my voice as I lean over and whisper in her ear, "Linda. It's me. I'm here."

Chapter 29 ✦

Apologies

Linda's eyes drift open, the green color not as vivid as I remember. She turns slowly, painfully, toward me, and my chin trembles. Running my fingers along her hollow cheek, I offer a comforting smile.

Her hand covers mine, and I make sure the IV stays put as she clenches my fingers. Her chest rasps as she finds strength to whisper, "I knew you would come." She looks over my shoulder, tears sliding down her cheeks. "Thank you."

Kaeleb offers her a smile. "You're welcome." He heads toward the door. "I'm going to give you ladies time to catch up. I'll be back soon."

I turn in Linda's direction and take a seat next to her. She sets her hand on my leg, trying to prop herself up higher. She coughs, each one deeper than the last, frantically signaling for something on the other side of the bed. I run to where she's pointing and grab the biohazard trash can, holding it as she continues hacking. She rids her lungs of the blood as it dribbles down the liner. In the bathroom, I grab some paper towels and wipe her mouth. Her eyes are apologetic as she still holds the trash can, clearly exhausted from the episode.

"I'm sorry, Aubrey," she says in a raspy voice. "I hate that you have to see this."

My head shakes furiously. "No, I should have been here all along." Standing beside her, I stroke her face again. "I'm the one who needs to say I'm sorry, not you."

Her lips lift into a weak smile. "I've missed you so much."

I take her cold hand into mine. "Me too."

We remain quiet for some time, both noting the differences in our appearances since the last time we saw each other.

Linda squeezes my hand lightly. "At least you don't have those damn contacts in." She laughs lightly, setting off another coughing episode. Once she's done, I take the trash can from her hand, setting it on the floor before scooting closer to her.

"Linda, do I need to get the swear jar? Your language is borderline offensive."

She grins. "Do you still have that thing?"

"I do." And I know right where it is. It's underneath my bed, the first thing to go when I removed all traces of the people I loved. Even now, the symbolism of that jar is not lost on me. I smile, remembering Kaeleb and Quinn our first night in the dorm room.

Goofballs.

My heart staggers at the memory of Quinn's contagious giggle.

I press thoughts of her aside, hoping we haven't completely severed our friendship.

Turning my focus to Linda, her face falls serious. "Aubrey, I never wanted you to have to go through this, to endure this situation ever again. You've experienced too much. *Seen* too much. The idea of you having to watch this, I just . . ." She sighs, her wheezing becoming more prominent as she speaks.

"Linda—"

"No," she states firmly, "I need to say this."

I nod my head, silencing my objection so she can speak.

"I fought this, I did. There's nothing in this world I wouldn't do, no war I wouldn't wage, no battle I wouldn't withstand to prevent you from experiencing another loss in your life. But my body," she breaks to wipe the moisture from her face, "my body is losing against every single thing. Surgery didn't work. The aggressive cancer had already spread, and chemo and radiation seemed to halt its progress, only for it to come back with a vengeance."

Linda continues to tear, but determination fills her as she states, "I'm looking into other options, though. I want you to know that. I will keep fighting for you."

I swallow deep into my throat, allowing her resolve to wash over me, and as her words fill my heart, I *finally* see it. Right in front of my face as it glares at me, unyielding. The stark contrast between Linda's determined battle and my parents' tragic surrender when faced with hardship and death. The value each placed upon their lives and mine.

Looking at Linda, it's obvious whose footsteps I've been following in . . . and whose I should be.

I look away, and as I replay her words in my head, the shard in my chest converts to a glowing flame, and hope churns throughout my soul, fanning its growth.

Sometimes there are random moments when everything *clicks*. When the fragments of your fractured past fall together, merging to form an image of your future. Each mistake serves whatever purpose necessary to complete the picture, and everything becomes clear.

Sitting with Linda, listening to her, determined to give the gift of *her* life no matter how painful and exhausting that may be . . . well, this is *my* moment. Because sitting next to this brave, ferocious warrior it suddenly becomes clear to me how valuable life really is.

Every being impacts at least one person they encounter during their lifetime. You can change someone's life with a kind word, a hateful one, or by choosing not to say anything at all. Every choice you make creates a ripple effect, trickling into and affecting the lives of others.

Life is a very powerful thing. Truly a gift you can give to others, but by hiding behind my fears, isolating everyone around me, I know my gift has been wasted. There is no mark I've made. No betterment has been achieved. I've experienced nothing I can utilize in teaching others, helping others, or bettering their lives.

As I realize this, the flame within begins to burn so intensely, it illuminates the darkness, lighting the path I must take to become the person I want to be. That I can become. But I know it won't be an easy journey.

There will be heartache.

There will be anger.

There will be fear.

There will be sorrow.

But as with all life, there *must* be balance.

Without heartache, there is no understanding of the true meaning of love. Without anger, passion cannot be comprehended.

Without fear, nothing is gained when overcome. And without sorrow, happiness can never be realized.

My soul glows with the fire inside me. It lifts like a Chinese lantern, brightening the path as it floats, and I watch as eight-year-old Aubrey Miller approaches in the distance. Her features are angelic; her smile is full of radiance and joy. She takes my hand, encouraging me to take my first step.

There is no death.

There is no anguish.

There is no dread or terror.

There is only *us*, standing hand in hand. Two separate entities as they become one.

Her energy seeps through my pores; her presence enters my soul. The darkness around her was only my creation.

Aubrey Miller was *never* death.

Aubrey Miller is just a girl.

A girl who has experienced a lot of loss, losing her way for a long time by choosing to remain buried inside gloom and blackness.

A girl who has finally found her light, trudging through her fears as she is *truly* resurrected.

A girl I am proud to be.

Leaving my dream-like state, I turn to Linda and take my first step down the new path.

"No more fighting, Linda. It's time to go home."

Chapter 30 ✳

Acceptances

It takes a couple days, but when the legal paperwork is finished, she's given the okay to leave, and Kaeleb and I transport Linda home. Taking the staff's advice and renting the best medical bed we can find, we set her up right in the middle of the living room. We hire a hospice service to help with her care and give us direction. They start an IV for pain meds to make the rest of her days as comfortable as possible. They guide us in the little things: helping her to the bathroom, nutrition tips, and how to properly give medication and breathing treatments. Our first trip to the bathroom is surprisingly easy. She puts her weight against me, and I realize how thin and frail she has become.

Over the following weeks, her body slowly withers away, a testament to how hard she was fighting to stay alive. Once Linda allowed her body to give in, there was no turning back.

My time on winter break passes quickly, and I stand here as she sleeps peacefully. Her calm exterior is the opposite of the carnage and destruction inside her body.

Cancer is a merciless pillager.

Kaeleb enters the living room, freshly showered and fully dressed, setting our bags on the floor and standing by my side. He gazes at Linda with concern and offers me a sad, uneven smile.

"You ready?" he asks.

I shrug my shoulders. "I guess. We need to wait for hospice." My heart clenches at the idea of leaving her, even if it's just for the day.

"Of course," he offers and tucks a strand of hair behind my ear. "I see you took your piercings out."

"I did." I tear my eyes away from the bags. "I don't need them anymore."

His smile lifts as he strokes my cheek. "You don't."

Dropping his hand, he adds, "I'm really proud of you, Bree. Not just with the way you've handled all of this with Linda, but also with your decision to stay with her."

My lips form a modest grin. "Thank you, Kaeleb, for bringing me here, to her. You have no idea how much you've done for me."

Kaeleb reaches forward and removes the hair from my face. He inhales a soft breath, whispering, "There you are."

My heart skips, sending my mind to a time I would have jumped into his arms and hugged him for simply being *him*.

He presses his lips to my cheek, cradling my face before releasing me. When he's done, he steps back and gives me a wink. "It's good to have you back."

I remain silent, enjoying the tingle where he caressed me, and watch him grab the bags before heading outside.

Linda stirs. Her eyes are open and she reaches forward. I take her emaciated hand into mine and she gives it a small squeeze, lifting her chin in the direction of the door. "You'd better not lose that boy again or I will personally haunt you for the rest of your life."

A light laugh escapes and I shake my head. "I'm not sure he's mine to have, Linda."

Her eyes close and she inhales lightly. "He's always been yours. And you his . . ." she trails off, nodding back off to sleep.

I lean over to kiss her forehead, muttering, "You're as bad as Quinn, you know." I continue to watch her until hospice arrives.

Once everything is set, I assure them of my return this evening. I've already withdrawn from my classes, explaining the situation here, and telling my professors I need to take some time off but I'll be back as soon as I can. All were understanding, offering condolences and well wishes.

The ride to my apartment is more relaxed and engaging than the trip here. Obviously. We discuss a number of things: classes, food, music, movies, books, and of course, Walter. Who has been a favorite boarder at doggie daycare.

The conversation gives needed relief from the intensity of the past weeks. But soon, I no longer want to make trivial conversation. I want to know what's going on with my friend.

"So . . . since you've been keeping up with Linda, can I assume you've also been speaking to Quinn? How is she?" I ask, my voice hopeful.

Kaeleb gives me an encouraging smile. "She's really good. She's been in intensive therapy since she left school, working out her issues and her relationship with her parents. She had a long discussion with her mother, who was concerned with Quinn's lack of self-confidence when she was younger and made a simple suggestion to start eating healthy and exercising. In Quinn's mind, that turned into things like fat camps, which wasn't the case." He glances at me from the driver's seat.

"The camps were for confidence, and pageants were for self-esteem. But I don't blame her for thinking the way she did. There's only so long something can live in your head before your view gets . . . *distorted.*"

He cocks his eyebrow before turning back to the road.

"Yeah," I answer absently, lost in memories of that horrific night. "I feel so stupid though, you know? I thought she was getting better. I *wanted* her to get better so badly I ignored everything in my gut telling me otherwise. She could've died because I remained oblivious to it all."

Kaeleb takes my hand in his, gingerly stroking it with his thumb. "I think we're both guilty of overlooking certain aspects that shouldn't have been ignored. But you also have to realize some battles aren't yours to fight, no matter how desperately you want that person to get better."

His eyes are full of certainty, wordlessly communicating his statement isn't solely about Quinn. I set my other hand on top of his and give it a light squeeze.

I sigh, grateful to have Kaeleb back in my life, even if it is just as a friend. I refuse to consider the possibility of anything more. Regardless of what my heart wants, my head knows that it's not an option right now.

This time is for Linda and Linda only.

No more is said as we become lost in our thoughts. Kaeleb drops me off at my apartment, leaving me with a kiss on the cheek and a promise to call.

After taking care of everything, I throw my bag into my car and head to campus to hang fliers to sublet my half of the apartment. Quinn's was paid through the rest of the lease, so only mine needs to be taken care of until May.

When all fifty fliers are hung around campus, I have one last stop before going back to Linda.

Entering the psych building, I breathe in the familiar stale air, reminding me of my many sessions in Palmer's office. So much has happened since the first time we spoke, and I'm reminded of every event as I make my way to his office.

I take one more deep breath before knocking on his door.

I'm greeted with surprised eyes and a familiar grin as Palmer takes in my appearance.

"Aubrey, it's good to see you again," he says, gesturing for me to enter.

"You too, Doc," I respond with my typical playful punch to the arm. I take my usual spot on the couch, drawing his ever-present blanket onto my lap while he takes his seat.

His eyes wander over my face, then he reclines in his chair and crosses his ankle over his knee.

"You seem to be feeling better than the last time you visited." He steeples his fingers over his lips, and I smile at the clichéd gesture that he falls into so often.

"I am. I, uh, I guess you could say I had a breakthrough."

He nods. "That's good, Aubrey. That's very good. What, if you don't mind me asking, brought on this breakthrough?"

I run my fingers along the blanket before answering. "Kaeleb basically kidnapped me. That's what started it. Thanks for that, Doc." I give him a disapproving look in jest, and Palmer chuckles. "He took me to see Linda. When I walked into her hospital room and witnessed how hard she was fighting, everything just kind of made sense. My own issues seemed trivial in the grand scheme of things." I shrug my shoulders. "I don't know. It's hard to describe."

Palmer leans forward, placing his foot on the ground and his elbows on his knees. "There's no need. I understand what you mean."

"Anyway, I'm here to say *thank you*. For everything. Your patience, your guidance, your willingness to just listen. Without you, I wouldn't be here as the person I am today. So, thank you."

I break into a smile, and his cheeks begin to redden. "You're very welcome, Aubrey. Like I said, I'm always here, even when you don't need me anymore."

"Well, that's the thing, Doc. I might need your guidance over the next couple of months . . . if you don't mind."

He tilts his head, curious.

I clear my throat.

"Linda . . . well . . . she's not doing well. I've withdrawn from classes this semester to stay with her." He nods slowly in understanding as I continue to speak. "I wanted to ask if it would be okay to call you, you know, if I need to talk?" My voice sounds timid with the question.

"Of course, Aubrey. Feel free to call anytime." He heads to his desk and offers his business card. "Day or night."

I take it from him and slip it into my back pocket, glancing back to the couch. "Um, I know this is a weird request, but can I take this?" I gesture to the blanket.

His face breaks into a grin. "I take it you don't have a problem with the blanket anymore?"

"No, the opposite actually. It's given me comfort when I needed it most, and I would like to take it to Linda's if that's all right. I'll bring it back."

Palmer steps forward, picks it up, and hands it to me. "No need to return it. It's yours."

I cradle it to my chest as we walk to the door and step outside his office.

"I mean it Aubrey, anytime."

"Thanks, Doc." As I turn away from him, he clears his throat, halting my footsteps. Pivoting around, my eyes meet his.

"I'm really proud of you, Aubrey. Facing your fears isn't easy. It seems you've done that and more since I've seen you last." He pauses and peers at me, emphasizing his next statement. "You did all of that on your own. You thank *me*, but don't forget it was *your* strength that got you here. If you feel that strength wavering, focus on that, okay?" His eyes are caring with his offered advice.

I nod and exit his office as my mind considers the inevitable.

I know the road ahead isn't going to be easy. I know there will be times I'll be unsure and afraid. But it's those moments that will define my future and mold me into the adult I will become.

But I also know I'll get through it.

I have no other choice.

I want no other choice.

Because such is life, and I'm finally ready to fully embrace it.

Chapter 31

Stages

I called Quinn when I arrived at Linda's and was welcomed back into her life with a complete rundown on what had been happening since I'd seen her last. I already knew a lot from Kaeleb, but I let her talk anyway. We skated over what happened to me, but before we hung up, we said what needed to be said.

"Aubrey, I'm so sorry for doing that to you. It was really selfish of me. I know that played a part in what happened with you, and I don't think I will ever be able to apologize enough."

"Quinn, you needed help, plain and simple, and I chose not to see that. It's as much my fault as yours. So let's agree to leave it in the past and move forward, okay?"

And that's what we've been doing ever since. We text multiple times a day and talk at least once a week.

This is our third text today.

QUINN: Dude, this guy sitting across the coffee shop from me is H-A-W-T!

ME: What? Your parents let you out unsupervised today?

ME: You're taking too long to answer. Your mom is right next to you, isn't she?

Q: Maybe. But that's beside the point. Let's get back to the guy.

ME: Description, please.

Q: Blond hair, clear blue eyes, shaggy hair. Surferish.

ME: Nice. Body?

Q: Drool worthy.

Q: OH SHIT!

ME: WHAT?!

Q: He just looked at me and smiled. OMG! He has DIMPLES!

ME: Nice! Go say hi!

Q: Hell no. Not with Mom here.

Q: DOUBLE SHIT!!!

Q: He's coming over.

ME: WHAT?!

Q: Hold on.

Five minutes later . . .

Q: OMG! He introduced himself as Tommy and totally asked
   if he could buy me a coffee. I said yes. So he did. And HE
   LEFT HIS NUMBER ON THE COFFEE CUP!! How cute is that?

ME: He did this with your mother there?

Q: He totally did!

ME: I like him already. ;)

ME: Linda's waking up. Gotta go. Talk to you soon.

ME: And call his ass.

ME: Love you.

Q: *giggles* Love you too.

I smile and turn to Linda. Quinn's excitement is just as contagious via text.

But my grin immediately fades.

Something's wrong. I can tell by the expression on Linda's face.

"Linda?" I move to the side of her bed, sitting beside her fragile body. I'm no longer surprised by her gaunt frame, the pallor of
her skin, the blood on her nightgown, or the sight of the few thin
strands of hair poking out from the top of her head. None of these
horrendous manifestations to her body faze me.

I've cleaned up vomit, blood, and excrement. I've nursed food
into her mouth and wiped it off her face and neck when she refused
to eat. I've dressed wounds that mysteriously appeared on her body.
I'm now a pro at catheterization and can even put in an IV if necessary. There's not much I haven't been exposed to while caring for
Linda. The majority hasn't been pretty.

The past five months have not been easy for either of us. In talking to Palmer, I learned about the five stages of grief, and could spot each one as Linda went through the phases. I went through them as well; witnessing her impending death forced me to experience not only the grief of losing her but also the loss of my family.

Denial and Isolation:
I'd been in denial for years. And I guess I went through the isolation phase. Kaeleb called, I avoided him. Quinn called, I sent her to voice mail. I would text them to let them know I was okay but didn't feel like talking, which they respected and understood.

Linda's denial manifested along with her isolation. Once she became frustrated and tried to get to the bathroom on her own, causing one of the worst coughing attacks she'd ever had. It left her weak and completely bedridden for days. Then she refused her pain medication—when I knew she needed it. One night, she tried to convince Kaeleb and me she would be fine on her own; she didn't need our help, and we could leave her alone. Needless to say, it didn't work.

Anger:
This was the worst stage for both of us. Kaeleb had come for the weekend to relieve me. I drove about ten miles into the middle of nowhere, stopped the car, and screamed until I had no voice. I beat the steering wheel, opened the glove compartment, and ripped up every piece of paper I could find. I held the torn bits in my hands, squeezing the shredded material so tightly, my arms were shaking and my palms were bleeding. I screamed for every single loss I'd experienced—Adley, Mom, Dad, and the one imminent loss to come. My face was flushed and covered in tears when I returned, and Kaeleb held me until I composed myself and headed back beside Linda's bed. It happened every weekend for a month.

And Linda? She handled it by being an asshole. She was an asshole to me—yelling when the temperature of her food wasn't right, or when her bathwater wasn't warm enough, or when I would accidentally knock the bed when I passed by. She was an asshole to the nurse—tearing the IVs out and chucking them clear across the room, arguing about the medication levels, and telling her she was a pitiful excuse for a caregiver. The nurse took it all in stride as if Linda's yelling was normal, which I suppose it was. The only person lucky enough to escape her wrath was Kaeleb because he was "a guest." At least that was her answer when I asked. I shook my head and rolled my eyes, which pissed her off again. It's a real shame I didn't bring the swear jar. Linda's swearing alone would have guaranteed my retirement.

Bargaining:
Asshole Linda transformed into Prayer Warrior Linda. She prayed all the time. All. The. Time. When she woke up in the morning, at breakfast, lunch, and dinner, after each nap, and before bed. "God, please" is how they would begin, and each would last at least twenty minutes. I could hear her pleading, and I found myself silently begging along with her.

Offering to be a better person, a better friend, to go to church . . . I pulled out all the stops. But when I began bargaining for my family, that took an immense amount of strength to pull myself out of. Guilt consumed me as I thought about Adley, wishing I had pulled her from the tub and not left her alone. Grief swallowed me as I thought about my mother, wasting away by choice. Maybe if I had told her I loved her, instead of staying away as instructed, she would be alive today.

But my father's death? I needed Palmer's help for that one. I recounted the story to him and howled my anger, asking him the same questions I was asking myself. Why didn't I come home sooner? Why the hell did I leave him alone in the first place? I was there. Why couldn't I stop him?

Palmer's response? *"It wasn't your fault, Aubrey. None of those things would have made a difference. That was his choice."* I felt as feeble-minded as a child as he repeated those words while I sobbed. I refused to believe him and finally hung up the phone, still lost in my grief.

It took weeks of working through the blame until I was physically and emotionally exhausted and decided I couldn't keep doing this to myself. Only when I hit *rock bottom* could I accept Palmer's mantra into my heart with no lingering doubts. Then I knew it was time to let go. To finally let them all go. And with them went the guilt and anguish I had harbored in my heart.

Depression:

But with that release came depression. Mourning resulted in weeks of constant tears being shed. I had never truly grieved their deaths, I suppose, so I was making up for lost time. Facing Linda, another loss to be had, compounded my emotions. A lot of time was spent in Kaeleb's arms during this phase as he whispered words of encouragement, telling me how proud he was and how strong I was for going through all of this. I didn't feel strong; I felt incredibly weak, but I relied on his presence to keep me sane.

Linda just stopped. Not in a bitter way, she flat out had no desire to eat anything or to speak. She stared vacantly out the window, making no notice of my presence. After a week or so, she broke down. Together we cried, we wailed, and we sobbed, me on her chest with her arms circling my shoulders. That was one month ago.

Acceptance:

Linda has completely withdrawn into herself again over the last week, and I'm sure this is what Palmer labeled as her acceptance phase. She's been quiet and reserved, maybe reflecting on her time and things she wishes she'd done differently. Or maybe she's in a calm state, ready to accept death as it looms closer. I don't know. All I know is I miss her. I even miss Asshole Linda and the fighting. But she's exhausted and tired from the long battle. I don't blame her.

I've been a bit reserved lately too, lost in memories of when she was healthy and happy. When guilt comes into play over how I wasted our time isolating myself as Raven, I balance it with a good memory as Palmer suggested. I focus on her beauty, her love, and her laughter. The random moments she would burst into my room, scaring the bejeezus out of me to perform some weird dance in an attempt to make me laugh. All the nights she would lovingly brush my hair and tell me bedtime stories. The hugs and kisses she gave me over the years, no matter how much I refused them. Many memories have been running through my mind lately, and I try to replace all the bad with good.

Like when Adley and I built a fort in the middle of my bedroom after Mom and Dad went to bed, staying up all night telling scary stories, and the time my parents threw the only surprise birthday party I ever had. All of us together, laughing and loving each other. And as

I focus on the happy memories stored in my bins, the images begin to evolve. I let them flow freely, abolishing each bin after the memories are finally released. I've accepted I won't be needing them any longer.

My mother's beautiful face replaces the sunken one. My father's eyes are no longer lifeless but the shade of blue that matches mine, full of life with crinkles of happiness outlining them when he laughs. And Adley is no longer the cold, naked body I cradled on the bathroom floor. She's the angelic creature I remember—laughing and skipping through the house, giggling as I chase her down the hall.

So between both of us being lost in whatever phase of acceptance we may be in, it's been quiet around here to say the least.

But I see the expression on Linda's face, and I know what's coming. Suddenly our silence seems like wasted time. I want to tell her about every memory that's crossed my mind this week. I want to talk about the stupid romantic movies she would make me watch, and the dumb plotlines for the romance novels she used to read. Things I secretly found funny but never told her. I want to shout from the rooftops so many memories that I hold close to my heart as her mouth works strenuously to form her own words.

But my wants are not the priority here. It's her time, and she needs to have this moment.

Taking a long, calming breath in preparation, the bed dips with my weight as I perch on the edge. I grip her hand tightly and lean forward, watching her lips barely move as she says on a light breath, "I'm ready."

She squeezes my hand and a tear trails down her cheek. Full of clarity and the life that I've missed, she says her final words. "I love you, Aubrey . . . best thing to ever happen to me."

A downpour streams down my face in this final good-bye. "I love you too, Linda." Trying to swallow the sorrow, I crawl into her bed and pull Palmer's blanket over the two of us, allowing its comfort over the last months to work its way through me as I wrap my arms around her shrunken frame.

Mumbling soothing words with my embrace, I hold onto her and don't let go until she passes.

Chapter 32

Parting Words

"God, Bree . . ."

Kaeleb rakes over my new appearance. My hair is above my shoulders, back to its original color and cut into a slant bob. I'm dressed in one of Linda's vintage dresses: a simple black number with lace overlay that fits snuggly from the square neckline and Juliet cap sleeve, clear down to the hem, ending just below my knees. My Mary Janes are four inches high, complete with straps. I'm also donning Linda's favorite pearl earring and necklace set, off-white in color as they shimmer from my ears and neck.

"You look absolutely gorgeous. Dare I say, *breathtaking?*" he finishes.

I accept his compliment, trying to ignore the flutter in my stomach at the sight of him. His hair is freshly cut, shaved along the back and sides, but longer at the top, styled away from his forehead, forming his signature off-center peak. A black button-up covers his upper body, snug across his chest, tapered at his waist, and his sleeves are rolled up over his muscular forearms. Charcoal pants complete the look, hanging low on his waist, accenting his toned derrière and long legs, forming a crease across the top of his shiny, black slip-on dress shoes.

I know my thoughts are inopportune, as we're heading to the church for Linda's service, but something tells me she wouldn't have it any other way.

"You too, Kaeleb. Really, you look amazing," I respond, a warm flush racing across my cheeks.

With a sexy smile, he enters the house. But as I shut the door, he grips its edge and stops the movement. Giving him an inquisitive look, he merely chuckles. "I've got a surprise for you. Close your eyes."

My expression tightens, not really sure if a surprise is what I need today. I'm already nervous and a bit flustered.

He angles his head, and I know his stubbornness will outlast mine, so I close my eyes and wait. I hear some shuffling, then a familiar giggle fills the air. My eyes shoot open, and my hands fly to my mouth.

"Quinn?"

She bounces up and down, excitement overwhelming her, and runs into my arms, crushing me with her embrace.

I stumble back, catching her midmotion, righting our bodies and squeezing her as tightly as my arms will allow. Then—I kid you not—we bounce in a complete circle, squealing and giggling. Once through, we each take a step back, maintaining our hold as we survey our changes in appearance.

Quinn's hair is impeccable, wrapped tightly into a bun at the top of her head. Her body is healthy, and her skin is glowing. The weight she's gained has filled out her beautiful face, making her more gorgeous as her green eyes shine with pure happiness. They're no longer tinged with hidden pain. They're bright, joyful, and full of life. Her black maxi dress is simple. The top is layered with a beaded, long-sleeve cardigan, and the bottom composed of sheer black layers that flow gracefully, lightly sweeping the floor with her movement.

"Quinn, you look . . ."

"Wow, Aubrey, you look . . ."

We break out into laughter, my heart filling to the brim with joy. I look away from Quinn and see Kaeleb, who's smiling as he watches our interaction. The fact that we're all here, together, makes my chest feel like it's going to explode.

I mouth the words *thank you*, and he simply dips his chin in return.

Redirecting my attention to Quinn, I ask, "How did you get here? I mean, I know your parents have been pretty overbearing lately."

She throws her head back in laughter. "Yeah, you could say that, but Mr. McMadden here charmed the pants off my mother."

I slowly turn in his direction, his hands flying up in his defense. "That was purely metaphorical." Throwing a wink at me, he adds, "*Ninja charm.*"

"Oh. My. God. Get over yourself," I say. Kaeleb laughs outright and Quinn makes a pitiful attempt to shield her giggle.

God, I've missed my friends.

Our reunion is short-lived, cut off by our need to get to the church. Once in Kaeleb's car, my body twists, practically hanging on Quinn's every word as we catch up.

"What's going on with that surfer dude? *Tommy?*" I ask, grinning with Quinn's love-struck smile. I notice the difference between the one I saw with Josh and her newfound love. The previous one never reached her eyes and was wrought with insecurity, but this one is full and beaming, as her eyes light up with the confidence she's gained since I last saw her.

"He's definitely *not* a surfer," she responds with laughter. "He's just, gah! You know?"

I giggle at her lack of explanation because as I look to Kaeleb, with his smile spreading across his face while he drives, I know exactly what she means. Sometimes it's impossible for mere words to encompass how you feel about someone. There's nothing you could possibly say to emulate that person's presence in your life. It's an overwhelming, indescribable feeling that consumes your heart and captivates your soul.

It simply just *is*.

Kaeleb tears his eyes off the road. He strokes my cheek, offering me a simple, knowing smile. Our eyes catch, and although no words are spoken, so much is being said.

Five minutes later, we pull into the church parking lot only for my nerves to begin racing when I see people gathering by the entrance.

Quinn hops out of the car, but I remain firmly planted in my seat. My foot is tapping nervously on the floorboard; I wring my hands in my lap. Kaeleb covers them with his own, forcing me to look at him as I nibble my bottom lip.

"You're going to do fine."

I inhale deeply. "You think?"

"I know," he responds with a wink.

"Okay. Let's get this over with."

Quinn knocks on my window and opens the door. I reluctantly slide out of my seat, linking my hand with hers and the other through Kaeleb's arm. Their presence fortifies me, and we enter the church together.

Through the entire service, I focus on the framed portrait beside Linda's casket, remembering her beauty and the life she willingly gave me. The definition of unconditional love can be found in her smile. A few tears course down my cheeks amid the sniffles, but I find comfort knowing she's no longer suffering. Wherever she may be now, she's happy and no longer in pain, and that knowledge soothes the ache in my chest.

As silence falls around me, my time to speak has arrived. Releasing Kaeleb's and Quinn's hands, I walk to the podium. With trembling fingers, I pull out my speech, gathering the courage to look at the crowd. My eyes drift over their faces. Some people I don't know, some I do, but one person catches my eye and gives me the needed push to speak.

Nervously smiling at Palmer, I give him my thanks with a nod of my head, then clear my throat to begin.

"Um . . . I know the majority of you are surprised to see me up here. I'm sure some of you didn't know I could speak." A collective laugh fills the air, spurring my confidence. "My name is Aubrey Miller." I glance to Kaeleb, then look down at the paper in front of me. "For those of you who don't know, Linda Walker was my legal guardian. She took me in when I was eight years old, after my parents passed away, and has been the one prominent figure in my life ever since. She was my mother, my sister, my friend, and my teacher. Her love was unconditional, and her strength was admirable. Accepting me into her world, taking sole responsibility for me . . . well, she sacrificed a lot. I was her life from that point on, plain and simple. There was never a moment I didn't know how much I was loved and cherished, as she often conveyed the endless depths of her caring, no matter how difficult I made it for her to express those emotions."

Tears roll from my eyes, and I pause before continuing to speak. "To say I was stubborn is an understatement. But Linda . . . well, she was tenacious. And she was until the day she left us. Her battle with cancer was incredibly difficult to watch, but as I witnessed it, I gained a newfound respect and admiration for this thing we call life. You see, Linda Walker not only gave me a home, a family, and unconditional love and patience. On top of those things, she gave me the greatest gift of all: in her death she showed me the importance of learning how to fully *live*. Finding wonder and amazement with each passing day. Realizing certain things should never be taken for granted."

I look at Kaeleb, and as his eyes glisten back at me, I know he will understand the meaning of my next statement. "The absolute necessity of letting yourself love and be loved."

A shy smile forms on his lips, and Quinn literally claps beside him. A slight laugh bubbles into my throat, but I force myself to stifle it as I end the eulogy.

"And for her many, many gifts she so lovingly bestowed upon me, I will be eternally grateful. I love you, Linda. You are missed more than you will ever know."

After wiping my cheeks, I fold the paper and exit off the chancel. My eyes are trained on Kaeleb as I head back to my seat, knowing there will be no need for her to waste her time haunting me from the beyond.

There's no way I'm *ever* letting this man go.

Chapter 33 ✳

Old/New Acquaintances

"GO!" Quinn pushes me out the door, her face attempting to look fierce. It's not working. I can't take someone seriously when they're in pink flannel pajama pants and big bunny slippers, with ears flopping.

"Quinn, let me in! I want to change!" I yell back, trying to get back through the front door.

"No changing! GO!" she adds, with another shove. I cross my arms over my chest.

"Quinn, Kaeleb left half an hour ago. I would look like an idiot if I went over there now."

She shakes her head and closes the door behind her. "No, you wouldn't. You would look like you're going to get the man you love." She sets her hand on my shoulder. "You told me you were finally *living*. I can't imagine a better way to start than with that man by your side." She laughs when I give her a conceding shrug, then pushes my body away. "Go."

"What about you?" I ask.

"I'll be fine. You showed me the bedroom. That's all I need to know. Lord knows I'm stuffed with all the casseroles tonight. I'm going to call Tommy, then head to bed."

I tighten my gaze. "You sure?"

"Positive," she responds. "Now get that hot ass of yours into that car and GO!"

I finally relent. "Fine."

She claps as she follows me to the car. Once inside, I roll my window down, uncertainty settling into my stomach. "What if—?"

"Nope. Not gonna happen." She heads to the door, gesturing excitedly for me to call her afterward. I watch her disappear into Linda's house.

We had a lot of people for the repast. There were tears, hugs, laughs, and A LOT of casseroles. Quinn wasn't exaggerating about that. Palmer gave me his condolences and surprised me with a tender embrace before he left. As the visitors began to dwindle, Kaeleb also left, explaining he was getting a hotel room so Quinn and I could catch up, which I had planned on doing until she forced me out the door.

I'm still unsure as I leave. She could have let me change into something more comfortable.

As I drive down the highway, I glance down, feeling a little overdressed and underprepared to deliver my speech of a lifetime. My nerves are at an all-time high, and my brain is in overdrive, listing every reason that Kaeleb might not take me back. Doubt replaces confidence with each thought.

I left him when he needed me.

I hurt him on purpose.

I lost my virginity to someone else. And I don't even remember it.

That last one almost convinces me to turn around. I'm not looking forward to that conversation.

But I know what I want. And I want him.

I'm hoping he still feels the same way.

Once I arrive, I bypass the front desk and head to his room. Quinn repeated his room number at least fifty times. I take a deep breath and press the elevator button. My heart is bouncing, ricocheting like a speeding bullet. I can only think that my life will soon be drastically changed.

For better or for worse.

I smooth my hair when the doors finally part. My mind fills with apprehension and anxiety as I take my first cautious step out of the elevator.

After two rights and a long hallway, my tortuous journey ends: 256 stares back at my face for about thirty seconds before finally I knock on the door. Heavy footsteps approach, and I close my eyes and take another deep breath. When I open them, I'm met with a sexy smile and beautiful hazel eyes. Eyes that don't look stunned to see me. They actually look . . . *relieved.*

"Come on in."

Slowly I step inside. Candlelight flames flicker, dancing over every inch of the room. Kaeleb is behind me, and I turn to face him. I finally take notice of his appearance. An undershirt clings snugly to his chest and biceps, and he's wearing the pants and shoes from the funeral. His silver belt buckle catches my attention before I work up to his face.

And then it dawns on me.

They had this planned the whole time.

No wonder Quinn threw me out of the house.

I smile when the revelation hits, prompting Kaeleb's grin to broaden.

"Damn it. I had a really good speech planned too," I remark with feigned disappointment.

He gestures for me to sit on the bed. My eyebrows lift at his presumptuousness, sending laughter through him. "Don't let my wooing, as you like to call it, stop you. I'm very interested to hear this speech you prepared."

He sits on the bed and leans back against the pillows, locking his arms behind his head. He kicks off his shoes, stretches out his legs, and crosses his ankles. His face is amused as he signals for me to begin. "Come on, Sunshine. Don't get all shy on me. Let's hear it."

My face pinches and my eyes narrow. "Really?"

"Really."

We stare in some sort of stand-off for a couple minutes before a conceding sigh passes my lips. "Fine. I need water though."

Nothing like preemptive stalling.

On my way to the sink, I run through my speech one more time in my head. Once I've downed the water, I kick off my shoes, stride to the bed, and take a seat beside him.

Clearing my throat, I begin. "I've been thinking about this," I gesture between us, "about *us.*"

Kaeleb gives an encouraging nod but remains silent. "While we were apart, I changed. I mourned. I lost. I accepted. I grew. But the most important thing I did was survive. I survived everything that frightened me the most. And do you want to know how I did that? What I focused on?"

His eyes hold mine as he reaches for my hand. "Of course."

Interlacing our fingers, I answer, "Balance."

"Balance?"

"Yes, balance." I tighten my grip on his hand. "You call me your *sun*; you're my *moon*, Kaeleb. I know it's not the most romantic thing I could say, but it's true. You're *my* balance. You're the ebb to my flow. You're the day to my night. The light to my dark. With all the bad I've experienced, you are the *good* that balances my life."

Happy tears rise in my eyes. "This new, beautiful life I'm now living doesn't work without you in it. I need you, Kaeleb, like the sun needs the moon."

A smart-aleck grin breaks across Kaeleb's face. "You know, technically the sun doesn't need the moon." A chuckle escapes and his shoulders bob. I pull my hand from his and narrow my gaze.

"*Really?* You're dissing my extraordinary speech with your know-it-all tendencies?"

His face falls serious. "Will you let me finish before you get all huffy?"

I cross my arms and . . . huff.

"But I *do* understand what you're saying," he continues. "I think some people are inexplicably bonded. Drawn by forces beyond their comprehension, they have no choice but to gravitate toward each other. Destined to cross paths until they *finally* get it right."

He strokes my cheek. "So, yeah. I understand completely. Because the way I see it, we're two people, so intertwined, that without one, the other ceases to fully exist. You call me your moon; I call you my *soul mate*."

My breathing stalls, and my heart hammers. Before I can say anything, he reaches forward, and draws me into him, brushing his lips against mine. The taste of him . . . the scent of him . . . the feel of him . . . flare all my senses, bringing forth my need to absorb him, for our bodies to become one, to immerse so deeply in one another there is no recognition of where one begins and the other ends.

I kneel onto the bed as he rises onto his knees, our mouths insatiable. My fingers grab his nape, pulling him close to savor his taste.

Our tongues tangling, he trails his fingers along the curve of my hips . . . the tops of my arms . . . the elastic of my cap sleeves. He follows the crest of my shoulders and finds my jawline. I moan when he forces my head back, exposes my neck, and nips the hollow of my throat.

I need to tell him about my indiscretion. The one mistake that could end all this before it starts.

"Kaeleb." My voice shakes as my fingers splay along his cheeks, trying to force him away from my neck. "Kaeleb, I need to tell you something."

His body stiffens as his head rises, bringing his face in line with mine. As he peers into my eyes, realization flashes across his face. He leans and whispers in my ear, "I don't want to know. I just need to know if you were safe."

A relieved sob escapes and I nod my head, his scruff grating against my cheek.

"I'm sorry, Kaeleb." The words become lodged. "I was so lost. Searching for . . . something. *Anything* to take away the pain."

He shakes his head, then looks directly into my eyes. "I've made mistakes too, Bree. You know that better than anyone. If you think I have a right to judge what you've done, you're mistaken. Right now. *This* is what matters. Not the fucked-up shit we've done in the past."

He swipes another tear. "This is *our* moment. A beginning and an end. Are you with me?"

My lips lift into a comforted smile. "I never want to be *without* you. I love you, Kaeleb."

"I love you too, Bree. Always have. Always will." He fastens his fingers around my nape and crushes his lips to mine.

My moan escapes into his mouth, and I swallow his resulting growl. Our bodies mesh together, his hands finding the zipper on my dress. He unzips it slowly, sending shivers down my body as he slides the dress down my arms and over my hips. My knees lift, the dress is whisked away and my panties soon follow. His eyes roam over my naked skin, free of clothing and inhibition.

I lift his undershirt just as deliberately along his arms and over his head. My virginity may be lost, but I know this isn't about sex. This is about two people who are about to give the ultimate gift to one another. Sex is one thing, but the act of making love, of joining together giving your heart, your mind, your soul to another person, that's something I never want to forget.

When my hands reach his belt, I glance upward at his beautiful face. Our stares latch. They remain locked as I unbuckle his belt, slide his pants over his hips, and pull them off. My body hums with desire, causing the air to spark between us. Full of anticipation, need, longing, passion.

He flips me onto my back, settling between my legs. His elbows dip the bed as he places his hardness where I need it the most. Pressing up, I grind against him, euphoric as he lowers his head to my neck. Our sweat-covered chests glide with our movements. My nipples pebble as my legs wrap around his waist, lock around his back, and pull him closer. A hiss escapes his mouth, silenced as it seals over my breast. His warm lips and teasing tongue send my back arching off the bed. My hands tug and pull his hair, and I allow him to work my other breast.

"Kaeleb, please."

With one long stroke, his tongue trails between my breasts, along my neck, over my jaw, ending with his teeth grazing my chin. I gasp and Kaeleb takes full advantage, dipping his tongue into my mouth, sweeping over mine, sending my body into a heated frenzy. I release his hair and pull his boxers past his waist, letting my feet finish the task. My fingers dig into him as he presses against my core. He positions himself at my entrance but pulls back, sending my body into panic.

"Bree, I need to—"

"No, you don't," I cut him off. "I've been on the pill since I was twelve."

A laugh fills the room. I open my eyes to see a cocky grin on his lips. "Eager are we?"

I don't smile.

I don't laugh.

I don't respond.

I reach up, grab his neck, and devour his mouth with mine. He kisses me back, our lips working with equal fervor. As he positions himself, my entire body quakes, and he whispers in my ear, "If the sun and the moon were to actually collide, it would set off a cataclysmic reaction of epic proportions. Are you ready to have your world completely obliterated?"

Laughter bubbles before I press my lips to his, mumbling, "Oh my God. Please, stop talking."

He chuckles and slowly presses forward, filling my body with his length. All humor is lost as our bodies become one. I take all of him as he settles in, claiming me, what's always belonged to him.

He withdraws and reenters slowly, as though memorizing me. I clench tightly around him when he hits a place I never knew existed. "Damn. Don't stop."

"I won't, Sunshine. Not until you see stars." His pelvis grinds against my core, heavy and aching for release.

I tighten.

I clench.

I build.

Until my body explodes, and I do, in fact, see stars.

"Bree, God, that feels so . . ."

Kaeleb forms no more words as he becomes lost in me, driven by his own need. He pumps without reserve, and I absorb each thrust, screaming for more. His body goes rigid as he explodes and he continues thrusting until I come once more, draining his release.

His chest falls onto mine, and his forehead nestles into the crook of my neck.

"Jesus. I think *I* saw stars," Kaeleb mumbles, sending tingles all over my body.

I laugh, sweeping my hand through his hair. "Definitely a life-altering experience."

He lifts onto his elbows and pushes the hair out of my eyes.

"*You* are a life-altering experience." Leaning forward, he presses his lips against mine.

I giggle against his mouth. "Well, I *am* the sun."

He inclines his head, surveying my face as his mouth stretches into a beaming smile.

"And oh, how brightly you shine."

Chapter 34 ✳

Junior Firsts

After Linda passed, I registered for summer classes at Titan, hoping I could get back on track. Junior year was huge for me personally, emotionally, and spiritually. Most of it has been covered, but there were a few new firsts I managed to squeeze in over the summer:

The first time I *actually* attended summer school, taking eight hours both summer semesters and aced all of them. 4.0 in all my classes. Biochemistry, Genetics, Anatomy and Physiology, and Zoology, all with labs. Two of those were retakes from the previous semester. I attended every class—mandatory requirement and all.

The first time I welcomed Quinn back to Titan. Both she and her therapist pleaded with her parents, explaining her need to be in the real world. Quinn came back to school at the end by the summer, ready to start anew. I recognized her determination and self-assurance, giving me no doubt that Quinn would be *just* fine. We rented a new apartment, signing a six-month lease.

The first time I met *Tommy Larkin*. If I thought Quinn's eyes lit up when she spoke of him, seeing her with him, she positively glowed. He was a perfect gentleman, opening her doors, giving her kisses all the time, touching her constantly. I never thought it was possible to see *love*, but I can now add that to this list of firsts. There was a radiance that beamed all around them when they were together.

The first time I was tackled to the floor by Walter. After I got over my initial shock of how much he'd grown, we played for hours,

Kaeleb leaving us alone for much of the reunion. After hours of tug-of-war, we both passed out on the floor.

And when I thought there were no more firsts to experience, Kaeleb gave me a big one. But it didn't happen until the middle of my senior year.

Senior Year

Chapter 35 ✳

Engagements

Quinn and I attempt to eat in the cafeteria courtyard. The sky is gray as the winter wind whips around us, leaving us shivering in our coats. I don't think the sun has shined once during the last week.

"Quinn, it's fucking cold. Why are we eating out here again?" I try to spread the warmth of my soup through my freezing body.

"Because I haven't seen daylight in weeks. I'm sick of being cooped up in my room, or the apartment, or the library. Finals are finally over, and I intend to enjoy the outside air for the next twenty minutes. Deal with it," she ends and takes a bite of her sandwich.

My head jerks at her snarkiness. "Damn, Quinn. You *do* need to get out," I remark.

She nods and continues to chew.

Swallowing, she asks, "Speaking of finals, how were yours? You're done, right?"

"Yeah, Pharmacology was surprisingly easy."

Quinn smiles. "It's like it was meant to be. Have you heard anything back yet?"

"No, not yet. I forwarded all my mail to Kaeleb's address though. Who knows the last time he checked."

Quinn's grin spreads and her eyes sparkle with excitement. "Oh my God, I can't believe you're moving in with him and Tommy will be here next semester. We will both *officially* be living in sin."

I crinkle my nose and shake my head. "I know. Weird, right?"

Quinn sighs. "Not really. You just know when it's right, you know?"

"Yeah." I see Kaeleb heading toward the table with a grin on his face. The sight of him makes my heart race. "You do."

Quinn notices my distracted gaze and turns over her shoulder, then twists back to face me. She waggles her eyebrows and I shake my head. "You're ridiculous."

Her familiar giggle sounds. "I'm not. I'm romantic. And I like to see you happy."

She winks at me while Kaeleb takes his seat. He smiles as we fall silent. "Interrupting something?"

"Not really," I respond.

"We were talking about mail," Quinn interjects, obviously impatient for my letter. "Have you checked yours lately?"

Kaeleb laughs and bends toward his backpack, unzipping the front pocket. "I have, in fact." An envelope flies across the table and lands beside my soup, *Midwestern University College of Medicine* stamped on the corner.

My eyes grow wide as I stare at it. Raising my head, a pair of green eyes brim with glee and a set of hazel-brown ones fill me with reassurance. "You've got this, Bree. Open it." Kaeleb dips his head to the letter.

My hands tremble as I pick it up. Slipping my finger beneath the flap, I slide it slowly until it pops open, the typed contents on the inside screaming for me to remove it. I glance at Quinn and Kaeleb, before extracting the letter. I open it and read the first two lines:

"Dear Ms. Miller,
Thank you for your submission. We have reviewed your application and are pleased to inform you of your acceptance . . ."

"Oh my God!" My head jerks up.

I bound off my seat and shout, "OH MY GOD!"

Kaeleb laughs and stands, and I scoot down the bench until I'm free, jumping into his arms and wrapping my legs around his waist. He squeezes me. "I told you there was nothing to worry about."

I tighten my hold around his neck. "Kaeleb, I'm going to med school!"

He chuckles. "I know, babe, you are. And I'm going with you."

I gasp and push away from him. "What? Did you get yours today too?"

He nods, lifting his own letter. "Midwestern University Physical Therapy Program, baby."

"AH!" Quinn shouts and jumps from the table, running and circling us with her arms. "I'm so happy, I'm about to cry."

Kaeleb kisses both of us on the top of our heads.

Quinn looks at Kaeleb and me with pride. "Well, I guess this is as good a time as any to tell you I've finally picked a major."

"Really?" Excitement courses through my voice. With her extended absence, she's technically a junior next semester. She's been debating a few options, and I can't wait to hear what she's chosen.

"I know it's no acceptance letter, but I've made *the* decision." She looks at both of us. "I want to major in sociology so I can become a social worker. I want to help whoever I can." She appears shy. "So much of my life has been wasted on things that don't matter, you know? I think I can atone for that by making a difference in other people's lives."

I place my hand on her shoulder and give her a knowing smile. "I completely understand, Quinn. More than you realize."

She grins at me as Kaeleb adds, "Quinn, you're going to make a difference no matter what you do. It's your most innate quality." Her cheeks redden as he pulls her into his waist. "You'll make a terrific social worker."

As she embraces him, I watch the exchange. The two most important people in my life are standing in front of me on what is probably the biggest day of my life. I wouldn't have it any other way. It feels . . . complete.

We all take our original seats, the bitter cold no longer noticeable.

"Wow. It's a big day," I remark.

Kaeleb glances at me with mischief in his eyes. "Indeed it is."

He leans forward. "I've got something else for you."

My brows furrow in question as he speaks to Quinn. "I figured *you* of all people would want to be present for this."

Quinn's eyes triple in size, and I meet her stunned expression with one of my own. We're speechless, as the zipper on Kaeleb's backpack breaks the silence around us.

He makes his way to me while Quinn jerks her head, indicating I should be looking at Kaeleb instead of her.

Yeah, she's probably right.

I shift my body, facing him as he kneels on one knee in front of me. A crowd has formed around us, but I couldn't care less about them as Kaeleb presents me with a black velvet box.

He swallows deeply and clears his throat.

"Bree. I lost you once when we were eight years old. I never realized my heart had been searching for yours until that day I walked into my boarding buddy's room." He breaks his speech to grin at Quinn before looking back to me. "And even though *you* didn't know it at the time, I knew I had finally found you. My soul breathed for the first time in ten years. That's how I knew it was you. It was always you."

A lump forms in my throat and tears roll down my cheeks.

"I lost you again soon after. I allowed you to return to your darkness. But I knew you were still there, somewhere. You see, we're intertwined. Tethered. Bound. And even when you thought you were alone, you weren't. I held strong to that cord connecting us, and there was no way I was letting you go. I will always be your anchor, Bree."

His eyes shine. "These ties can't be broken. Our bond is secure."

Quinn sniffles beside me, but I remain fixated on Kaeleb.

"But I couldn't tell you that, because this time, it wasn't about my search for you. It was about you finding yourself. Your courage. Your strength. Your love. All the amazing things that make you, *you*. And you managed to do it. You worked your way back, until you rose up and found your way back to me."

He pauses before finishing his proposal. "And what I'm asking is, now that you've found your way *home*," he gives me a sexy smile, "will you continue your life journey with me, as my wife?"

He flips open the box, and I cover my mouth.

Inside is a perfect, round, canary diamond. It's outlined with a single crescent shape filled with tiny white diamonds. I smile, and my heart leaps at the thought of wearing a constant reminder of Kaeleb's love.

I'm mesmerized as he says, "You have always been, and will always be, my sunshine."

"The sun and the moon," I whisper in response, my eyes still trained on the ring.

"Naturally," he responds, as murmurs and gasps sound around us.

My eyes look up just as someone yells, "ANSWER HIM!"

A smile breaks across my face and I nod vigorously. "Yes!"

Rising off his knee, Kaeleb whisks the ring out of the box. He takes my hand into his, brushing his lips against mine. "I love you, Bree."

"I love you too, Kaeleb." He holds the ring directly in front of me, tilting it so I can read the inscription inside the band.

Shine bright. Shine always.

I sob and face Kaeleb. Nodding, I whisper back, "Always."

He slides the ring onto my finger, placing another kiss on my lips. The crowd hoots and hollers around us. I hurriedly take my seat across from Quinn. Kaeleb, however, bows to the crowd, eliciting an eruption of more cheers.

Quinn bounds from her seat, clapping. "You guys are getting married. I told you. I *knew* it!"

I roll my eyes, shake my head, then grin.

Yep.

That boy is all mine.

For the rest of our lives.

Thirty minutes later, after lunch, we grab our backpacks and head to the parking lot. Quinn leads the way as Kaeleb and I walk hand in hand behind her. I glance at him, smiling widely. He hugs me, brushing his lips against my forehead.

We're so lost in our bubble of love that we run into Quinn, who has stopped unexpectedly. "Quinn, what's wrong with you?"

Pulling Kaeleb behind me, a nasty, evil, malicious snicker rises above the murmurs of the crowd.

Sabrina is standing with a contorted leer on her face, eyeing us like she just stepped in dog shit. I can feel Kaeleb's seething anger beating against the back of my neck.

"Oh. My. Gawd," she begins, thrusting her huge purse over her shoulder while smacking her gum. "Look. It's the *freak* and the *freak* lover, getting married." Her eyes land on my hand. "I can't wait to see the monstrosities you spit out of your body, *Raven*. I'm sure you'll have a household of freaks at your disposal."

"It's Aubrey," I reply calmly. Kaeleb's body tenses against mine, so I reach behind me to keep him still.

"Whatever, *Aubrey*. A tiger can't change its stripes, no matter how much dye it uses to cover them. Once a freak, always a freak."

And for the second time today, we find ourselves surrounded by a mass of curious people, drawn by Sabrina's threatening words.

Quinn steps directly in front of us, placing her tiny body protectively in front of mine and Kaeleb's. I try not to smile, but I find it damn near impossible. Kaeleb doesn't bother as his laughter hits my ear.

"Get the fuck out of here, Sabrina. No one wants to hear the hateful shit that comes out of your mouth," Quinn spits. And just as Sabrina opens said mouth, Quinn's voice strengthens and she yells, "Do you?" She gestures to the people around us. "Does ANYONE want to hear ANYTHING she has to say?"

There's a collective "no" among the herd. Someone adds, "You're a bitch," while another person throws in, "Go away, Sabrina," just before a squeaky, timid voice from the back shouts, "You're an awful person."

That one makes me smile.

Quinn looks around and a grin crosses her face in appreciation of the comments. Sabrina, however, winces as her face blushes beet-red.

But Quinn's not done yet.

"Where's Josh? Oh, that's right. He's with Candace now. They're engaged, yes?" Quinn asks, her face serious. "Sucks, doesn't it? That explains why you no longer have friends." She glances at me and Kaeleb. "Well, I *do*. I've been waiting *four* long years for this day, and I refuse to let you ruin it for me." She pauses. "Or for *them*. Sorry guys."

"It's okay," I yell-whisper back to her.

She looks at Sabrina. "So go. No one wants you here," Quinn adds, shooing her away with her hands. The crowd erupts with clapping and cheering when Sabrina turns away, clearly embarrassed as she trudges down the sidewalk.

I relax my body into Kaeleb's. He wraps his arms around my shoulders, his body shaking with laughter. "Damn. Just when I thought this day couldn't get any better."

"Right?" I respond as his lips find my ear.

Quinn turns around with a beaming smile, clapping as she bounces up and down. "That was so *awesome*."

I laugh. "Hell yeah, it was."

I extend my arms, and she rushes into them. Kaeleb steps to my side, ruffling her hair. "Damn, girl. Remind me not to piss you off."

She giggles and I tighten my gaze in confusion. "How did you know all that stuff about Josh and Candace?"

She shrugs her shoulders. "My therapist told me I needed to work on letting go of what happened. So one day I called Josh, and he apologized. Like, a *sincere* apology. I could tell." She lifts her eyebrows, trying to convince me, but I have no doubt it was.

Sabrina is a virus, feeding off people and infecting them with her evil while manipulating their minds. Not that I condone what happened with Josh, but if his apology was enough for Quinn, it's enough for me.

"It only took a week after what happened for her to turn that maliciousness on him and Candace. I guess with me out of the picture, she had to find someone else to attack." She sighs. "He broke it off with her shortly after and tried to get in contact with me to tell me how sorry he was. He's not a bad person, and neither is Candace."

She releases another long breath. "It's no surprise Sabrina bullied them into doing things that weren't indicative of who they are. Because a bully is all she is. All she ever will be. It's sad, when you think about it," Quinn states, a sad smile on her face.

Leave it to Quinn to forgive like that. Another reason she is an amazing person.

"I let go a long time ago. But there's no way I was going to let her ruin today. For *any* of us," she adds with a giggle, glancing down at my hand. "Speaking of which . . . let me see that ring again."

I lift my hand and she *oohs* and *aahs* appropriately. My eyes land on Kaeleb, and his sexy, confident smile makes my chest flutter.

My heart takes flight, and the first appearance of the sun in over a week brightens the day.

Coincidence? I think not.

I shield my eyes, looking at the single beam, poking through the clouds. Absorbing its warmth, I feel the love of Linda as she sends her message of approval. Her essence floods me, knowing she's happy and she will always remain present as she guides me through life.

Kaeleb credits me for finding my way out of the darkness, but as I feel Linda permeate my being, I know she was always right beside me, in both life and death, tugging with all her might until I found my way.

Until I navigated my way right to this moment.

And dropping my hand, I give her a silent *thank you* before facing Kaeleb. With his eyes full of adoration and caring, I know she's helped steer me right where I need to be.

Home.

Chapter 36

Last Session

Palmer: So, you gearing up for graduation?

Me: (nods) I'm on track for May.

Palmer: Only a month left then?

Me: (smiles) Yeah.

Palmer: And Kaeleb? He's ready as well?

Me: Yep.

Palmer: (grins) I hear you two are getting married. Congratulations, Aubrey. I'm very happy for both of you.

Me: (laughs) And to think it all started with the Elements of Trust. Who knew you had mad matchmaking skills?

Palmer: (chuckles and strokes his beard) I'm multitalented, what can I say?

Me: You're more than that, Doc. You're a miracle worker.

Me: (furrows brows) Why did you quit? Practicing, I mean.

Palmer: (laughs) It would seem I never really did, wouldn't you say? (sighs) I do enjoy the teaching aspect, helping people learn to break through whatever issues they have with trusting others. But sometimes there are certain individuals who silently call to me for my guidance, such as you and Kaeleb. I don't need to get paid for it. I do it because that's what I feel I've been put on Earth to do.

Me: (nods) I understand completely. That's why I'm going to med school, I think. To use my experiences to benefit others.

Palmer: That's very admirable, Aubrey. I have no doubt you will find yourself very satisfied with your chosen profession. That passion is unyielding, and when you witness a complete transformation, such as I did with you, there is truly no greater reward.

Me: (leans forward) I don't think I can ever convey how much you did for me, Doc. If it hadn't been for you, I'm not sure I would be sitting here.

Palmer: You would be. I have no doubt. The strength you possess can't be taught. It's inherent. As I've said before, you did all the work. With or without me, you would have found your way eventually.

Me: Well, I'm not so sure about that. (laughs) But thank you. (rises from couch) I guess that's it, Doc. I just wanted to stop by and say thank you again, for everything. See you at graduation?

Palmer: Of course. (stands) It's been my utmost privilege to watch you grow over the last four years. Thank *you* for allowing me to be a part of it. I hope you will keep in touch in the future. I will . . . miss our chats.

Me: (swallows back tears and punches him in the arm) Oh, Doc. You can't get rid of me that easy. I've got your number, remember?

Palmer: (laughs and opens door) Well then, I look forward to hearing from you. (face falls serious) I'm very proud of you, Aubrey. You have overcome so much over our time together, and I have no doubt you will make a profound impact on your patients, no matter what area you choose to specialize in.

Me: (jerks head back) Did I not tell you?

Palmer: I don't think you mentioned it, no. I would have remembered.

Me: Oh. (exhales) Well, since I had such an *excellent* mentor, I will obviously be pursuing psychiatry. Working with children and adolescents specifically.

Palmer: (grins widely) I think that is an excellent choice.

Me: I thought you would. (laughs) So you will most definitely be chatting with me a great deal in the future.

Palmer: (dips his head) I can't imagine a greater honor. Thank you, Aubrey.

Me: (steps out of his office and turns with smile on face) No. Thank *you*, Doc.

Chapter 37
Senior Firsts

Today is officially my last day at Titan. The year passed by in the blink of an eye, but it wasn't without some new firsts that should be mentioned:

The first night Kaeleb and I spent together in our house. Rental house of course, but it's our home . . . *for the meantime*. After christening it multiple times, I stared at the swear jar on our bedside table, reminding me of the meaning of unconditional love. Linda's. Quinn's. And of course, Kaeleb's. Although he reminded me often. Hence the reason we didn't leave the house for an entire week.

The first (and only) time Quinn became engaged. Tommy Larkin proposed at a candlelight dinner via serenade and she happily accepted, giggling the entire time. They'll be getting married this summer, right after us.

The first time we managed to have a successful family dinner. Quinn's and Tommy's parents, Kaeleb's grandparents, and I celebrated the new engagements. It was bittersweet without Linda, but as I looked at the people around me, I knew I would never be without family. They surrounded me as we retold the details of the proposals to everyone and even gave encouraging hoots when we went into Quinn's stand-off with Sabrina. The pride on her mother's face told me she finally grasped that there was no need to worry about her baby girl.

The first time Kaeleb caved to his grandparent's insistence and spoke to his parents. It wasn't easy, but he's finally worked through what he needs to find closure. They speak once a week as they work on mending their relationship. They're here today, along with his sister.

And as I sit here, waiting my turn to cross the stage, I reflect on my years at Titan University.

I came here a terrified girl, completely hidden inside my darkness and ruled by my fears.

Yet somehow, even while consumed by darkness, I found my way.

I found the courage to make new friends. Lifelong friends.

Friends that provided strength when I had none.

Friends that forced me to face my greatest fears, no matter how much I protested.

Friends that gave me a reason to wake up each day.

Friends that made me laugh for the first time in years, held me when I cried, and rooted themselves in my heart, refusing to cut the ties that bound us together when I pushed them away.

They taught me the meaning of true friendship, and for that I will forever be grateful.

I found love. True, absolute, everlasting love.

Love that was so readily given even when I refused it.

Love that when finally accepted, spread throughout my heart and soul, giving me the strength to look deep within myself and face my past.

Love that doesn't end with death, but conquers it. Because in death, I found the true meaning of love and laid to rest my fears, emerging the person I was meant to be.

And most importantly, I found myself. I found the light that had been yearning to burn inside me all along. And once I found it, I held on tightly and nurtured it until it infused my heart and my soul, washing away the darkness. Cleansing me. Preparing me. Healing me.

I died when I was eight years old.

I existed inside death for many years until I discovered the true meaning of life—a gift to be utilized and never be taken for granted.

And I will leave campus today alive and breathing, ready to make my mark on this world . . . Fully resurrected.

Epilogue   ✳

"So there it is folks. The story of my resurrection, my journey as I finally found the light. *My* light.

"I hope you find something to take from my story. The next four years of your life journey will be some of the greatest and possibly most difficult years. There will be so many of your own firsts to experience. Take time to learn from each one.

"In the audience, you will see the people who made a difference in my life during my time at Titan. Well, most of them. There's Kaeleb McMadden, with his patented crooked smile, right there in the front row holding our six-month-old baby girl, Adley Walker McMadden in his arms. Next to him is Quinn Larkin, formerly known as Quinn Matthews. Yes, the one bouncing up and down in the chair. And next to her is her husband, Tommy Larkin, along with their very handsome young man, Ethan.

"Behind me in that chair right there, is Professor Martin Palmer. He invited me here and gave me the opportunity to share my story with you. So thank you for that, Doc. You know how I love speaking in front of crowds. I'm pretty sure this is some sort of therapeutic exercise in which I'm unknowingly participating. That being said, if you have a chance to take his Elements of Trust course, I highly recommend it.

"All kidding aside, I wanted you to see all these people because without their help, I wouldn't have become Dr. Aubrey Miller, and I wouldn't be standing here in front of you today. You see, whether it's the assignment of a roommate, the pairing of your boarding buddy, a certain class you take, or even a particular relationship you form with one of your professors . . . no matter how trivial it may seem, every situation you will find yourself in over these next four years has the potential to change your life.

"I was lucky. I was given a second chance. And I'm using that gift to counsel patients who need help dealing with their darkness. To help them navigate through the particularly hard times in their lives. That's my purpose. What's yours?

"You may not know now, but during these next few years, I hope you discover what *your* true passion is. College is a time for learning and growth. So here's my advice:

"Face your fears and overcome them. Become the best person you can be as you grow into your impending adulthood. Find what drives you and hone those skills. Practice and perfect them, so that you can leave this world in a better state than you found it.

"Be thankful for each day you're granted on this earth. Form friendships. Find love. Feel passion. Embrace destiny. *Your* destiny. Because, at the end of these four years, you will most likely not be the same person you are right now. It's up to you to decide who you will be. What you will do. And how you will do it. Choose wisely.

"Thank you so much for allowing me to speak at this year's freshman orientation. I'm extremely honored to be the first to introduce you to this campus. I look forward to witnessing the indelible marks that you will most certainly leave upon this world as each and every one of you complete your own separate journeys here. So, with that being said . . . Congratulations, Graduating Class of 2018. Good luck to all of you, and of course, welcome to Titan University."

THE END

Chosen Paths continues with…

Under the Influence
Out of Focus

Turn the page for a sneak peek of *Under the Influence*!

PROLOGUE

Dalton

I am not a good person.

And I don't pretend to be.

There may have been hope for me at one point, but now, as I stare back at the hardened face and vacant eyes in front of me, there's no denying the truth. All hope for me was lost years ago, stripped clean from my mind as they broke me. The life I'm indebted to now is one packed with corruption and polluted with lies.

I try to breathe in deeply as I rinse the freshly spilled blood from my hands, but I begin to feel the bitter pang of disappointment in my chest. It seeps along the previously etched grooves that line it, burning the hollow channels created with each punch to my stomach and blow to my ribs.

I rarely have these moments of weakness, when I wish I hadn't allowed myself to be drawn into the darkened path that is this life. But right now, I wish I had been strong enough to brave my childhood on my own. That I had been able to fend off the monsters that lurked in dark rooms and reeked of alcohol, able to protect myself from the multitude of broken bones and black eyes inflicted by the hands of those who were supposed to fucking *protect me.*

But I wasn't. And now I'm stuck, hopelessly adhered to a life in which I have chosen to forgo conscience for security.

Little did I know that the day I met Silas Kincaid, I'd be making a deal with the devil. That I would be forever bound to a life from which there is no escape.

Although I started out as his lackey, I grew quickly—both physically and within the hierarchy of his organization—to become his weapon. Not only his muscle, but a tool that has many uses. His most-prized possession.

And now here I am at eighteen years of age, long since graduated from errand boy. I watch the familiar streaks of someone else's blood swirling around yet another porcelain sink. Someone who also made a deal with the devil but didn't deliver on his end.

I always deliver.

After drying my hands, I curl my fingers over the lip of the sink and place my palms flat on the cool surface, silently watching the reflection in the mirror. Cold, dead eyes stare back at me. Not a spark of life left in them.

Not anymore.

In fact, Spencer Locke is the only bit of humanity I permit myself to indulge in. She's the one thing, the one person whose mere presence provides some sense of relief from the constant sense of asphyxiation I feel.

She is my reprieve.

My air.

Spencer Locke is the *one* slice of happy I have in this shit pie I call life. Silas Kincaid is a ruthless motherfucker.

The two will never cross paths.

I would, with absolutely no hesitation, lay down my life to make sure that never happens. Spencer's safety has been and will always be my concern—no, my priority. And in order to ensure that safety remains, she must never know the real me. The cold, calculated, hardened criminal that I am. She will only know the Dalton Greer I permit her to know.

Just like everyone else I come into contact with.

To Rat, I'm the entertaining best pal. To Spencer, I'm the overprotective friend. And to Silas, I'm the lethal weapon.

None of them truly know *me*.

Because the truth is, there's nothing more frightening in my world than those who know you—who *really* know you. The ones who know your deepest, darkest secrets. The ones who know what you're going to do before you do it. The ones who know not only what buttons to push when they seek your attention but also the ones that can be used to completely incapacitate you.

They can be your strength.

But they can also be your weakness.

And just as a chameleon changes color to blend for protection, I've learned to evolve into the person I need to be in order to survive the situation at hand, all while keeping people at arm's length. Yet sometimes I can't help wonder what my *true* colors would have been had I not been subjected to this life. I question what it would be like to just let someone in, to tell them my unforgivable truths and discover they still love me in return. *Something so unattainable.*

I find myself utterly fascinated, awestruck even, that there are people actually capable of truly loving someone without wondering when and how they'll be betrayed. However, the knowledge of their existence also saddens me because the cold reality is, I will never know that type of love. I will never know the freedom to just *be* with someone—without pretense or fabrication, without the endless lies and untruths.

Maybe that's why I keep holding onto Spencer when I know I shouldn't. When all my instincts scream for me to let her go, to cut those ties and just let her be.

I can't.

I'm too selfish.

Therefore, I will plaster on my overprotective big-brother face so I can see her again, just to get my fix of relief she provides. And in turn, I will continue the lies.

I will continue telling myself the *only* reason I insist on my frequent visits is because I want to see to her protection.

I will continue convincing myself the things I say to her are merely *pretenses* that accompany my facade.

But in this rare moment, I will also concede that like a moth to a flame, I'm *drawn* to her.

To her innocence.

To her kindness.

To her ability to love.

To all the things I wish I was capable of but have sacrificed in order to survive.

Because just seeing her willingly share those traits with me and with others, the knowledge that the ability to do so actually exists in a world outside of mine, somehow frees me—no matter how temporarily—from the chains that bind me here in this suffocating place.

Yes, Spencer Locke is indeed my air.

I desperately hope the immorality I've chosen to bury deep within my soul doesn't one day pollute her very essence.

Chapter 1 ✳

Spencer

"Soooo . . ." Cassie says as we make the trek from track practice to Londonderry Street.

I glance to the right and warily eye my friend. Her long brown hair is pulled tight in a low ponytail that whips in the wind as we walk, and her face is flushed from our recent five-mile run. And, of course, in typical Cassie style, her track shorts are about three inches too short and barely cover the cheeks of her ass. She grins slyly as she swings her gaze to meet mine.

The skin on my shoulder objects to my heavy backpack, so I sling it over the other one before the nylon strap saws off my arm.

"Soooo?" I can only imagine what is going to come out of her mouth next.

"So," she begins subtly, then screams, "Jonathon Hawkins asked me to prom!" Her pitch increases as she begins to rattle off the details and my face falls with lack of interest before totally zoning her out.

I tend to zone out a lot when it comes to Cassie. It's not that I'm uninterested or don't want to hear what she has to say, but there are so many needless details she insists on including. She's one of those people who begins a story only to become sidetracked by another one, then another, and before long there are so many subplots going on I have no idea what she's talking about.

It's easier to listen for key words when she speaks and then piece them together on my own. That way she thinks I'm listening and I avoid losing my ever-loving mind. Plus, I tend to have a lot of inner monologue going on, so there's not a lot of extra room to store her stories in their entirety.

For example, with this conversation, it would go something like this:

Locker. (Meaning it happened at school)

Roses. (Pretty standard)

Serenade. (Nice touch)

Sex. (Time to pay attention)

Gah. She gets me every time with that one.

"Wait, hold on. Back up." I cease walking and turn to face her, dumbfounded. "You had sex with him? Outside the school? Before homeroom?"

She giggles and eagerly nods. I just shake my head back and forth to clear it because her recent revelation is just so ass-backward. "Aren't you supposed to wait until *after* prom to have sex with your date?"

Cassie shrugs her shoulders. "I guess, but what would be the fun in that?"

"Cass—"

"I mean, prom is like *two* months away. There's no way I'm going two months without sex. Absolutely not happening."

My eyebrows rise in question. "Okaaaay, so are you and Jonathon exclusive then? Like, sexually exclusive?"

She scoffs and looks at me like I've sprouted another head. "Um, I'm not sure what *he's* doing, but I plan on living it up for the remainder of this year. And that means *muy* drunken sexual encounters in my near future."

She places her hand on my shoulder and squeezes. I'm dumbstruck. "We should work on getting you laid too. Being a virgin in college would be *no bueno*, my friend. Trust me on this."

I close my jaw and, in hopes of a much-needed topic change, I say, "Excellent use of the Spanish language there, Cass. Your Spanish teacher was a fool for failing you."

She grins. "Right?" She looks toward the sky and exhales loudly. "Coach is an asshole. He was just pissed I wouldn't sleep with him. My Spanish is just fine."

Instead of sheer horror, I'm strangely relieved by this statement.

She takes another deep breath, then looks back at me. "Ready?"

I nod and shift the backpack yet again as we begin walking. Soon after, we turn onto Londonderry and make our way toward my house. A very familiar 1969 Camaro Z28 is parked in my driveway and the driver sitting on my porch, patiently awaiting my arrival.

I lift my hand to shield my eyes from the sun. Taking in his appearance, I'm whisked away from the present and deposited in my past. Five years ago to be exact.

"Hi."

My voice is small and unsure as I attempt to speak to the boy sitting alone on my front porch. The crackle of the gravel under my feet, however, is the only answer I receive. As I hesitantly approach, I mentally peg him as being only a year, maybe two, older than me.

The tips of his sandy-blond hair gleam brightly as the setting sun strikes, highlighting both the top of his head and the strands that peek at me from behind his ears.

Receiving no response to my presence, I watch silently as dust takes flight when he drags his foot through the dirt. My eyes fall to the tops of his shoes, the shredded holes displaying his gray socks underneath. Slowly I notice the frayed patches of his faded blue jeans, the brown stains on his white tank top, and finally the yellowing bruises lining the right side of his jaw.

Internally I cringe, but my voice remains steady as I offer gently, "My name's Spencer. What's yours?"

His body stiffens before he lifts his piercing blue eyes to meet mine. My breath stills at the sight of them. They're the most fascinating color I've ever seen.

So light blue they're almost gray.

So clear that I immediately recognize the pain he's trying to mask.

He watches me cautiously for a moment, taking in my appearance before his face pinches into a scowl. "Spencer? That's a boy's name."

I nod. "Yeah, not the first time I've heard that one."

His expression tightens before he finally breaks eye contact to focus on the much more interesting soil below him.

This isn't the first time we've had a foster kid show up at our house. I might be twelve years old, but I know a lot about this kind of stuff. I know his life has been difficult. His annoyed and hardened response isn't something I haven't dealt with before. Therefore, instead of being insulted

*like most girls my age, I simply take a deep breath and sit next to him,
saying nothing else while we watch the sun set in front of us. Both in
complete silence.*

*Once it has disappeared below the horizon, the boy blows out a long,
deep puff of air, as though accepting his current situation, then drags
his fingers through his messy hair before turning to face me. The side of his
mouth barely curves upward into a subtle, yet playful, version of a grin.*

"So . . . Spencer, was it?"

*I finger the strands of long, blonde hair that have blown across my
face and pull them away while offering him a tiny nod. He gives me a
slight nod back and then jerks his chin in my direction before he speaks.*

"Well, Spencer. Wanna get high?"

And that's the day I met Dalton Greer.

A wide, goofy grin crosses my face at the memory.

Right after he asked his question, I punched him in the arm.
*Who in their right mind would offer weed to a twelve-year-old girl they
just met?* Then I proceeded to take him up on his offer, catching him
completely off guard. He busted out laughing, I took the first puff of
many, and we've been friends ever since.

My heart springs to life as he rises, donning his typical playful
smile and his ever-present Yankees cap, pulled low to hide his
eyes. Although he still strongly resembles the kid I met that day,
he's about a foot taller and definitely more man than boy now.
Once standing, Dalton stretches broadly and the white V-neck
T-shirt clinging to his chest lifts a couple of inches, exposing a
small sliver of his muscled stomach. His frayed jeans hang low
on his waist, so I also catch a glimpse of the glorious *V* marking
his hips as he passes his hands through his longish, shaggy blond
hair.

I sigh out loud.

I know we'll never be more than friends, but my heart is relentless. And a traitor. It abandoned me that day on the porch, leaving
me to suffer in silence with my unrequited crush.

"Girl, you are in so much trouble with that one," Cassie mutters
under her breath as we pass my mailbox.

I shoot her a sideways glare. "Shh . . ."

As usual, my attempt to shush her delivers the exact opposite effect.

"Dalton is so gorgeous, Spence. You know, you should totally cash in your V-card with him. I'm willing to bet he would take very, *very* good care of you." She sighs. "I hate that he graduated last year. I used to watch him walk down the halls. That ass in those jeans . . ." She actually moans after the last word and I elbow her in the ribs.

Clearly insulted, she stops and gasps. "Ouch, bitch!"

"Shut. Up. You know it's not like that with us," I snap. My tone is harsh, but when I catch a glimpse of her wide-eyed expression, I struggle to hide my amusement.

Narrowing her gaze, she leans into me and whispers, "You and I"—she gestures between us—"are going to figure this out. I'm going to go home and come up with a plan, like now. And then I'm going to come back over tonight and we are setting this brilliant plan I haven't even thought of into motion." She giggles and wraps her arms around my neck, pulling me into a tight embrace.

I hug her back, laughing in her ear. "You know, you make absolutely no sense, but I love you anyway."

A giggle sounds before she responds, "Love *you*, times two."

Releasing me, she turns to cross the street to her house, evidently to concoct the plan of the century. I smile as I watch her cross safely, then turn toward Dalton, who is making his approach. He grins crookedly at me and reaches to take my backpack. I hand it over willingly.

"Thanks," I state, rubbing my shoulder. Dalton switches the backpack to the other hand, then curls his fingers over my shoulder and begins to knead my aching muscles.

"Anytime," he answers, still smiling. With his hand still massaging, he urges me forward.

I glance up at him and squint. "Why do you always wear your hats so low?" I reach up and tug the bill of his cap. "It hides your eyes."

He frowns. "That's exactly why I wear them that way. If you can't see my eyes, you can't see me watching. And I watch everyone. All the time."

I snicker. "Okay, because *that's* not creepy."

He shrugs as we continue to walk. "What's Daisy Mae up to these days?"

I laugh. "You know that's not her name. And you know she hates it when you call her that."

The previous tension of his face fades as he grins and angles his head. The cap on his head fulfills its purpose and shields his bright-blue eyes. "I also know you hate it when I call you *Pencil*, but that doesn't stop me either."

"It's only cute when it comes out of the mouth of a five-year-old little girl who can't pronounce Spencer," I remark, straight-faced, as memories of little Anna Grace from the shelter fill my mind. She wasn't there long, but during the short time, she lovingly gave me the nickname *Pencil*. Although, Dalton is the only one who uses it, so I guess she gave it to *him*.

His laughter echoes around me as we make our way to my porch. "Stop lying to yourself, Pencil. You think it's cute when I say it too."

I do, but that shall remain unsaid.

"Plus, if Cassie doesn't want to be called Daisy Mae, she needs to wear longer shorts."

I nod in agreement. "To answer your question, she's up to no good," I answer truthfully.

His features draw taut and he turns to look at me with his face now hardened. Protective. "You know she's not a good influence."

I bark out a laugh and shake my head at his blatant audacity. "That's rich coming from you."

Dalton narrows his eyes. "What's that supposed to mean?"

"You, my friend, have introduced me to pretty much everything my mom has warned me to stay away from. You're not the best influence yourself."

Finally at my porch, Dalton shakes my backpack off his shoulder and onto the front step as we take our usual seats. His on the left and mine on the right.

I inhale deeply and turn to face him, and as I do, I watch his expression morph from that of protection to one of internal argument. I can see it so clearly in his blue-gray eyes when he's warring within himself. I've seen this struggle frequently over the past five years, and I've yet to figure out a way to help him through it.

My eyebrows draw together, and without hesitation, I lift my hand and tug on the bill of his cap. "Hey, what's going on with you?" I ask softly.

My hand falls to his shoulder while he continues to stare off into the distance. I remain silent, allowing him the time he needs. We've danced this dance many times before.

The day he showed up on our porch, something happened while we watched that first sunset together. I don't know how or why or if I can even put it into words, but we became forever connected. My hidden pain cried out for his, and his fiery rage searched for mine. It was as though the most deprived parts within each of us sensed the other's, then reached out and grabbed hold, essentially melding us together and making us whole.

I know it because I felt it.

I felt *him*.

And soon after, the number of sunsets watched became too many to count, the amount of easy laughter shared immeasurable, and the quantity of weed and alcohol consumed between the two of us . . . *copious*.

Yet with all this time between us, amid the sunsets and laughter, not once did we dare discuss our pasts.

As far as Dalton knows, I'm the only daughter of Deborah Locke, and my father is deceased. I'm a habitual visitor of domestic violence centers, alcohol/drug rehab clinics, and homeless shelters because my mother volunteers nonstop. With no one else around, since I was a little girl, I've had to traipse wherever she went and sometimes still do. I have seen horrors that no one should ever have to witness during these visits, which obviously had the intended effect because I'm actually very thankful for my life. Thankful for the chance I've been given, and thankful I have a loving mother.

While Dalton is aware of all of this, there's also a lot he doesn't know. But he has his skeletons too.

Dalton is very secretive about his former life—or *lives*. I know nothing more than I did the day he showed up on our porch. My mom, however, was provided in-depth knowledge of the various reasons he was removed, because as his emergency foster parent, she *needed* to be privy to the information upon his arrival. She has never shared that information with me out of respect for him, and I would never ask her to do so, for the same reason.

Every single child that lands themselves in our spare bedroom is given that same respect. But I know enough to understand that if they have found their way to our house in need of emergency foster care, the situation is never a good one, as it's typically needed for the child's protection.

We only housed Dalton for a matter of weeks before he was placed with the Housemans. My mother worked closely with Dalton's social worker to have him placed within their care. Through the relationship built while volunteering at the local abuse shelter, she knew from experience that they were very kind people with vast experience when it came to fostering abused children.

The bond Dalton and I formed that very first sunset strengthened over his four-week stay into our friendship today. Even after he left for the Houseman's home, he was still near enough to stop by whenever he wanted. His visits never ceased, and even though he "aged out" of foster care last year, they still continue.

In the time we've spent together, I've vowed to try to help him. To teach him the lessons I've learned. To find a way for him to let go of the past that so clearly haunts him, which means I must have patience during times like this.

And I will wait as long as he needs.

The corner of my mouth lifts into an encouraging smile. Breaking his eye contact from the ground to meet my patient gaze, he hesitantly reaches up and removes my hand from his shoulder to encase it in his own.

"I just worry about you, Spence." He shakes his head in frustration. "I mean, you said it yourself, I'm not the best influence. I've never pretended to be. But what you need to understand is people like me, like Cassie, we find ourselves unintentionally drawn to you because deep down, we want *you* to influence *us*. Not the other way around."

Familiar storms brew in his eyes. "You're such a *good* person, Spence. I just worry that one day, being surrounded by people like us, well . . . I worry that what makes us who we are will eventually destroy the person you are meant to become."

I hold his gaze, assessing him, then smile. "Dalton, I'm not a freaking piece of china. I'm not some delicate, fragile *child*." I laugh boldly at his assumption. "*You* are not going to destroy me. *Cassie* is not going to destroy me. *No one* is going to destroy me."

I shake my head. "We're all just *people*, Dalton. People make mistakes. Some more than others, but every person deserves to be judged on how they learn and adjust from mistakes made. Not defined by tragedy or happenstance. I know who you are *now*, Dalton, and that is a good person who just happened to make some crappy decisions along the way. That's all. Same with Cassie."

He remains expressionless, but when his jaw clenches, I sense his objection. Shrugging my shoulders nonchalantly, I add, "You know, I'm always here if you want to talk about *before*. You never do, but I just wanted to let you know while we're having the 'no discriminatory judgment' conversation."

I watch as his eyes soften and the storms within them calm, before Dalton, in typical Dalton style, completely disregards my offer by deflecting. "I also worry about you alone in that goddamn high school. St. Louis Parochial High School is full of nothing other than rich, pansy-ass douchebags whose brains are capable of processing exactly two things: spending their daddy's money and satisfying their dicks. I'm one hundred percent sure Cassie's no help in the latter department, either."

Laughter bursts from my chest. "Um, I go to that school, so that blows both your theories, since I'm clearly lacking in those areas. I'm only able to attend that school because Mom works there and well"—I look at my lap and shrug—"I'm clearly lacking."

He fights a smile. "*You* aren't like anyone else in that school."

"Cassie isn't either, and neither were you."

"I don't even want to know what Cassie had to do to get in that school. And I only got in because your mom pulled strings to get me some obligatory we-care-about-poor-people-too scholarship."

"That's not true and you know it, Dalton." And it's not. He had to be tested before he was accepted, and his scores put him right at the top 10 percent of his class. Mom did relay that information to me.

Dalton returns his gaze to the ground in front of us and mumbles, "Yeah, well, I hate that I'm not there anymore to watch over you."

I grin. "You are aware that it's March, right? I've already made it through the majority of the year unscathed. I think I'll be okay for two more months."

He nods stiffly as I continue, still smiling, because I kind of find this whole thing adorable. "Is that why you come by? To make sure I'm surviving without your *protection*?"

His face becomes solemn as he releases my hand, relaxing back onto his elbows and stretching out his long legs. Facing forward, he stares at the horizon.

"Not the only reason," he answers softly. "I miss our sunsets."

Without a word, I lean back and mirror his position, stretching my legs to match his. We watch together in shared silence.

Just as the sun begins to set, I whisper, "Yeah. I miss you too, Dalton."

He continues to look forward, face blank, no words spoken. They never are. But I know he heard me when he finally releases a long, contented sigh, because my own heart warms in response.

I know because of the bond we share . . . That's what it feels like when Dalton's heart smiles.

LOOK FOR *UNDER THE INFLUENCE* AT YOUR
LOCAL BOOKSTORE OR BUY ONLINE!

Other Books by
L.B. SIMMONS

Chosen Paths Series

Into the Light
Under the Influence
Out of Focus

Mending Hearts Series

Running on Empty
Recovery
Running in Place

Author's Note

There are several subject matters in this book that sadly affect millions of people all around the world. If you or someone you know is battling depression, dealing with being bullied, plagued with thoughts of suicide, or in need of help accepting the loss of a loved one, please go to the appropriate site below to access information about mental illness and finding ways to get help.

No one is alone.

DEPRESSION: The National Institute of Mental Health—
    http://www.nimh.nih.gov/health/publications/
    depression/index.shtml
BULLYING: Stopbullying.gov—http://www.stopbullying.gov/
    what-is-bullying/
SUICIDE: Prevention, Awareness, and Support, Suicide.org—
    http://suicide.org/
GRIEF COUNSELING: Medline Plus, A service of the U.S.
    National Library of Medicine and the National Institutes of Health—http://www.nlm.nih.gov/medlineplus/
    ency/article/001530.htm

Acknowledgments

There are so many people to thank in this section. So many people who worked with me, listened to me, and helped me when trying to get Aubrey's story where I wanted it to be. I hope I get everyone . . . First, and foremost, my husband, who painstakingly dealt with our three children as I wrote this book. Taking them to dinners, to movies, feeding them ice cream—whatever I needed so I could write undistracted. Your faith in my writing and your strength when I had none will never go unnoticed. But they do, sometimes, go unmentioned. So thank you, honey, for everything. You are *my* anchor.

To my girls—I love you and thank you from the bottom of my heart for your patience. I know it's not easy, but you never complain. And I love you so much for that. You are truly the loves of my life. I. LOVE. YOU.

Jena Eilers—GAH! Our fourth book. Yikes. Thank you so much for just being there. Building me up when I feel nervous, listening to me go on and on about the storyline, giving me ideas, and helping me when trying to figure out where to go next—with all of my books. You are the definition of true friendship, unconditional love, and unyielding support. I love you so much. THANK YOU!

Karen Lawson—Woman. You are a miracle worker. Thank you so much for whipping Aubrey's story into shape. I proudly reread this book as a stunning achievement because of your hard work. Your support means the world.

Stephanie Johnson—Thank you for being there from the VERY beginning. You were there when this was supposed to be another story entirely. You helped me work out the details, listened to me ramble on, and on, and on—forever! You never complained and cheered me on as I wrote. I love you so much. Thank you for being my friend and one awesome beta reader.

Lisa Paul—My sister. Thank you for taking calls every five seconds, reading my random excerpts, bouncing ideas with me, and giving me excellent advice when coming up with the plot clear until I typed "The End." And even long after. I have been SO incredibly blessed to have you in my life. You are such an amazing friend and I love you clear to the depths of my heart.

For all the bloggers who continuously share my teasers and generate excitement for my upcoming books. I would be absolutely nothing without you. My works would remain unread if it wasn't for your reading, reviewing, and pimping. You do so much for the indie community, and please believe me when I say, you make a WORLD of difference for every indie author you promote. And you do it all because of your love of books and for no other reason. Completely. Amazing. Thank you.

And finally, to the readers, thank you so much for reading Aubrey's story. I truly hope that you took something away when you were through. That her journey made a difference in your life, in some way, shape, or form. I can never truly express my gratitude for taking a chance on this book. Thank you.

About the Author

Two Sons Photography

After graduating from Texas A&M University, L.B. Simmons did what any biomedical science major would do: she entered the workforce as a full-time chemist. Never in her wildest dreams would she have imagined herself becoming a *USA Today* bestselling contemporary romance author years later.

What began as a memoir for her children ended up being her first self-published book, *Running on Empty*. Soon after, her girls were given reoccurring roles in the remainder of what became the Mending Hearts series.

L.B. Simmons doesn't just write books. With each new work, she attempts to compose journeys of love and self-discovery so she may impart life lessons to readers. She's tackled suicide, depression, bullying, eating disorders, as well as physical and sexual abuse, all while weaving elements of humor into the storylines in an effort to balance the difficult topics. Often described as roller coaster rides, her novels are known for eliciting a wide range of emotions.

Connect with the author

L.B.'s Website:
  http://www.lbsimmons.com/

L.B.'s Facebook Page:
  https://www.facebook.com/lbsimmonsauthor

L.B.'s Twitter Page:
  https://twitter.com/lbsimmons33

L.B.'s Instagram:
  https://www.instagram.com/Lbsimmons33/

Contact L.B.:
  http://www.lbsimmons.com/contact-me

CPSIA information can be obtained
at www.ICGtesting.com
Printed in the USA
LVOW08s0205240317
528305LV00003B/4/P